Within the Attic

by
Marian
Parisher-Nichols

E-BookTime, LLC
Montgomery, Alabama

Within the Attic

Library of Congress Control Number: 2011917819

ISBN: 978-1-60862-334-1

First Edition
Published October 2011
E-BookTime, LLC
6598 Pumpkin Road
Montgomery, AL 36108
www.e-booktime.com

Dedication

Just a fond thank you to everyone who aided me in getting this book to print.

To a couple who helps with the editing and cover design, thanks. You will never know just how much your help is appreciated.

To my family who always encouraged me.

And thankfully to God, whose Spirit sustains me.

Contents

Chapter One

Shadows and Scents

Forgetting that it was the middle of the night and that lightning was dancing around the darkened bedroom, Nathan sat up in his bed with the sensation that someone was in the room with him! Nathan was five; he and his widowed mother had just moved this very morning into the Victorian style house, on an old farm left to her by her grandparents.

The two-story house was nearly two hundred years old! The three bedrooms plus a bathroom were upstairs. The rooms were on the same side of a long narrow corridor, which had three tall windows facing towards the front of the house. The stairwell emerged on the second floor from the entry hall downstairs, between the master bedroom and the two smaller bedrooms, with a banister forming a fence around the landing. At the opposite end of the hall was access to the attic, which was closed off from the rest of the house by a small grey door.

The front porch had a white railing encircling it and a red front door set between two large picture windows with faded red shutters. The door opened into the receiving hall. The living room was on the right and the den on the left as you entered. The rear of the hall opened into the dining area through a wide arch. The stairwell, on the left of the hall, housed the downstairs bathroom beneath it. At the very back of the house, the elongated kitchen was entered by way of a swinging two-way door and exited on to a small screened-in porch. Behind the house, about a hundred feet or so, stood a battered red barn. The house, a weathered grey color in need of painting, appeared for the most part to be in good condition.

Nathan's mother, now twenty-eight years old, had been raised by her maternal grandparents after the untimely death of both her parents in an automobile accident, when she was only three years old. She didn't remember them, as Nathan didn't remember his own father who had died as a soldier in the Iraq War, when Nathan was just a few weeks old.

Fearfully, Nathan stared at the shadow, unsure of what it could be. It looked like a man but it didn't appear solid, often changing in size and shape but always returning to that of a human. At one point, it disappeared and then re-appeared. Nathan strained his eyes, peering into the darkness; he sank beneath the covers, bringing them up over his head. He could feel his heart pounding against his ribs. He wanted his mother; he wasn't accustomed to being so far away from her. In their old apartment, he had slept in a child's bed next to hers, in the one bedroom apartment. However, she was now down the hall and he would have to pass by the shadow to reach her.

So, in his sanctuary beneath the covers, Nathan squeezed his eyes shut and whispered his bedtime prayer, "Now I lay me down to sleep, I pray to God my soul to keep, But should I die before I wake, I pray my soul You will take. In Jesus' name, amen!"

A long moment passed, then realizing that the air underneath the covers was getting stale, he lowered them ever so slowly beneath his nose, inhaled deeply, then raised them again. With just his eyes peeking from beneath the sheet, he peered hard into the darkness. Lightning then flashed through the window illuminating the room, followed closely by the shocking clap of thunder!

Nothing! No, not a thing stood in the corner beside of the door. The shadow was gone! But now the room was filled with a nasty smell, which made him feel sick, but one he did not recognize. Maybe he should call his mother. After a brief hesitation, he called her. At first, his voice was nothing more than a loud whisper; he swallowed and tried again, "Mama!"

A flash of lightning, followed closely by a thunderclap, answered him. Then finally, the rain arrived, pelting the roof violently. He called again, this time a little louder. Now he heard the unmistakable sound of her soft footsteps coming quickly down the hall. His bedroom door swung open with a squeak and he saw his mother outlined in the dim light.

"Nathan, what's wrong?" she asked, as she came to his bed and sat down. "It's only an thunder storm, baby, nothing to be afraid of," she said, as she took him by the shoulders and pulled him close to her warmth and sweet fragrance, which always comforted Nathan.

"I saw a man standing there in the corner," he whispered.

His mother, startled at this prospect, reached over and switched on the bedside light; bringing a welcome warm glow to the room. Kristyn looked around the room, reassured nothing was amiss; she smiled at Nathan. To Nathan, she was the most beautiful woman ever; she was his whole life as any single parent would be to an only child. She had dark blond hair that she kept trimmed just above her collar, with the same sage green eyes as her son. Her complexion was fair and mother and son favored a great deal. If there was any resemblance to his dead father, it was weak.

"Mama?"

"Yes sweetie?"

"What's that smell?" Nathan asked looking up at her.

Kristyn took a moment, sniffed, waited and then replied, "What odor are you talking about? All I smell is the fish we had for supper. It does tend to linger a long time after cooking," she said.

This was their first day here and Kristyn hadn't had time to get the house in order; only the two smaller bedrooms and the kitchen, just enough so that she had been able to prepare a hurried meal of fried flounder, pork & beans and slaw with cornbread.

"No, no, it isn't fish. I've never smelt it before." He too sniffed the air. "It's gone now, anyway."

"That's good. You know the house has been closed up for a long time and should be aired out. Tomorrow, we will open the windows to let in the fresh air and sunshine."

"Will you stay with me," asked Nathan.

"Sure, but only for a while. You are a big boy now and you must learn to be on your own. Now lie back and I will sing to you."

Nathan drifted off to the soft lullaby sung by Kristyn.

****

Seeing her son deep asleep, Kristyn stroked his blond curls away from his baby face, "I think you are in need of a hair-cut, young man," she whispered. Having just turned five a few weeks ago, he was still very much a baby, with his pink round cheeks, rosy puckered lips and long eyelashes that most women yearned to have. There were a few freckles scattered across the bridge of his nose, the only feature that reminded her of his father, Corporal Nathan Lance Spencer.

Her heart wrenched at the thought of her departed husband and how much she missed him, although they had had only a few months together before he went off to war, leaving her having just learned of her pregnancy. Nathan Ayden was born June 5, but Nathan Lance had never met his son; he was killed instantly several weeks later by a roadside bomb as his Hummer rolled over it. One other man had also died and another was badly injured, losing a leg and an arm in the ambush.

She felt her eyes burn as they filled with tears, which overflowed, running down her cheeks. She had managed to keep her independence after Nathan's death and continued working as a dental assistant. She received two checks from the government, a widow's pension, and a support check for Nathan. Not long afterwards, her grandparents had moved into a nursing and retirement center for the elderly. The old farmhouse had been padlocked and boarded up.

Grandfather had died at the age of eighty-five, only four years ago and her grandmother died also at eighty-five the following year. Kristyn and Nathan had been left the farm. It took another year to settle debts and that meant selling off the land, everything except the land the house and barn stood upon. This did leave them with a sizable amount in a savings account but Kristyn would still need to work. For now, they were fine and she had taken time off from her job to relocate here and to get settled into the house.

Mentally shaking herself, she came out of her reverie. Now the storm had lessened up in intensity; she kissed her son's forehead and retreated to her own room.

****

The next morning Kristyn awakened to the crow of a rooster. She hadn't heard this sound since leaving the farm, after graduating from high school and moving out on her own to begin her two-year studies as a dental assistant. Now, the bright Carolina sun peeked in through the tattered shade at the window, casting sunbeams across the covers of her bed. The bedroom windows faced the back yard, which was the eastern direction; the front of the house faced west, being rewarded with the most beautiful of sunsets.

Kristyn already could tell that this was going to be a typical July day with sweltering heat, and a long day of sorting through their belongings. The house was furnished with her grandparents' furniture, which was great because she had lived in a furnished apartment in the city of Rock Haven. So there were just small things she had brought, like her HD television, CD-player, her cell phone and her laptop and personal items such as clothing and jewelry.

After awakening Nathan and getting him fed and dressed for the day, she began the task of exploring the house and opening it up to ventilate. Nathan went outside and she warned him to stay close so that she could keep an eye on him.

****

Kristyn began on the second floor with the bed-rooms. She had already removed the white throw cloths covering furniture from the bedrooms she and Nathan had used and now she opened the windows and knocked down cobwebs that were between the screen and the glass. The windows certainly needed washing but they wouldn't get it this day.

Using the broom, she removed any cobwebs that she had missed the night before, and gave the floor a quick sweep before doing the same thing in her bedroom.

Next was the master bedroom, the room that had been her grandparents'. This room had been closed up longer than the rest of the house by at least two years. When she had lived here, her bedroom had been the center bedroom where she had slept last night and, at the far end of the hall and just before the bathroom, was the guest bedroom where Nathan had slept. Faced with the disquieting chore of cleaning her beloved grandparents' bedroom, she took a deep breath and pushed open the old worn door. It protested weakly as it allowed entry and stale air rushed out to greet her.

The door frame was blocked by a thin veil of web, which she tore down with the broom. For whatever reason, throw cloths had not been applied to this room's furniture and everything was covered in a layer of fine, grey dust. Immediately she felt a sneeze and soon expelled it violently; she sneezed a few more times before the seizure ended and she stepped inside. There were just way too many webs dangling from the ceiling and decorating the bed, the chair, the dresser, the lamp, everything! She tiptoed across the room to the window, where she pushed back the heavy drapes, which cause the dust to swirl, triggering her sneezes again. Enduring the torture a little longer, she pushed up the window and then hurried from the room.

"I'm going to need a cleaning crew," she spoke aloud, as she took her cell phone from its holster at her waist and began placing a call, all the while heading downstairs to check on Nathan.

She found him sitting on the bottom step at the back door. His little chin rested on both of his fists as he stared at the barn. She sat down beside of him.

"What are you thinking so hard on, Nate?" she asked gently.

Nathan shrugged his small shoulders and mumbled, "That old building."

"That 'old building' is called a barn," she smiled, as she placed her arm around his shoulders.

"What's it good for?" he asked turning sage green eyes her way.

"Well, when I was a little girl, I used to play in there on hot summer days like today."

Still looking at his mother, Nathan's expression changed to one of puzzlement, "Why? Couldn't you go to the park?"

"No, not back then," she smiled.

'Back then!' she thought to herself, as if it were the last century. Still, it was, when she thought about it. But even so, it wasn't more than fifteen to eighteen years ago that she ran around this farm with no worries and played until exhausted and 'Grandma' called her inside.

The older she became, the more adventurous she had been and often hiked down to the creek to swim in its clear shallow depths. She could walk across the stream and the water only came up to her knees, even though she was a child at the time. For a short moment, memories of those hot summer days returned and she smiled.

"What're you smiling for, Mama?"

"Oh, I was just thinking. Would you like for me to go with you into the barn and look around?"

Not replying but standing and taking her hand, he led her across the dirt and graveled back yard to the closed barn door. Kristyn chuckled to herself and knew that her 'brave little man' wasn't always so brave.

Kristyn looked around the yard. It was unkempt and this saddened her as she remembered her grandmother's loving care of her flower beds and the vegetable garden, in which she grew all varieties, as well as herbs. Many a day she had aided her grandmother in weeding those flowerbeds and harvesting the garden. In the hot July heat, without extra watering, the beds were overgrown and brown. A few stubborn bulbs like the gladioli and day lilies still bloomed, even though surrounded by grass as tall as they were.

The same held true of the entire yard surrounding the house. There was plenty of work to be done and, as proficient as she was, it was still too much for her. She would need to engage a landscaper as well. Looking up, she saw a blue white sky with a lone cloud drifting by. The heavy purple clouds of the storm last night were gone, leaving only a hint that they had even been here. Water droplets glistened here and there in the mid-morning sun but were rapidly succumbing to the unmerciful heat.

"What's ya looking for, Mama?" asked Nathan, as he too took in his surroundings. It was all new to him. Kristyn had brought her infant son to the farm to help her grandparents make the transition to the retirement villa; by this time, she was a widow.

"Nothing special," she replied looking nonchalantly towards the upper floors of the house. There were the three windows to the bedrooms and the much smaller window of the bathroom, situated above the roof of the back porch. The window on the right belonged to the master bedroom, which was the only bedroom with two windows; one faced the backyard, and the other faced the right side of the house. All had dark red shutters.

Unseen from the outside but Kristyn knew were there, were the enclosed stairs to the attic. Protruding out from the sharply sloped roof, with that very Victorian style, were the two small gables of the attic. These were the dormer windows, dark and foreboding in their appearance. Kristyn knew that there were two matching gables at the front of the house. "I wonder what is up there," she whispered.

Having stopped in their tracks as this surveillance continued, Nathan asked, "Up where, Mama."

"The attic," she smiled down at his upturned face, with his squinty eyes, as he fought to see her through the glare of the sun.

As though on cue, as she and Nathan watched, he suddenly said, "Who's that?" pointing at the attic windows. Startled for a moment, Kristyn was sure that the bright light must be playing tricks on her eyes, for it certainly looked as if a white glowing shape just passed by the window on the left.

"Oh that isn't anybody," she laughed, although without humor, "It's just the sun and clouds reflecting off of the window glass."

"You sure?" he asked with inquisitive eyes, like that wasn't what he saw.

Drawing a deep breath and then smiling at him, she replied, "I'm sure. Who would want to be in a dusty hot attic on a day like today? Why, they would roast up there. It would be as hot as an oven."

Cocking his head to one side, he took her at her word but still he wasn't fully convinced, "Okay," he agreed. Turning his attention back to their goal of investigating the barn, he placed a small grubby hand on the wooden door and pushed. "It won't open," he declared with his bottom lip poked out.

"I'll help," said Kristyn and taking the wooden handle, she pulled rather than pushed. The heavy barn door slowly swung outwards, releasing a dust cloud that had the same nauseating putrid smell that Nathan remembered from the night before.

Covering their noses and mouths with their hands, the pair backed away from the door as fits of coughing overtook them. "I guess the barn needs airing as well," said Kristyn as tears welled up in her eyes from the dust. Looking down at Nathan, she could see that he too was having trouble, so she took his hand and began to lead him back towards the house.

Stopping abruptly, he shouted excitedly, "That's it!"

Stopping also, she peered at him, "That's what, Nate?"

"That stinky smell that I smelt last night!"

"I think an animal must have died in the barn," she said by way of explanation to him as well as to herself. "I'm getting some people to come and help us clean the house, the yard, and now... the barn."

Chapter Two

The Visitors

Over the next few days, Kristyn worked hard cleaning out the house and overseeing the landscapers. She told them not to worry about planting anything new but just to weed the beds and revive what was there.

It was late in the growing season, too late for a garden but she could have the soil prepared for next year's growing season. She looked forward to fresh garden vegetables and sweet smelling flowers and that thought alone spurred her forward with the renovation the house and grounds needed.

She had contracted *Efficient Maids* to tackle the inside of the house and *Jordan's Landscapers* to take care of the grounds. But the landscapers had said that the barn did not fall under their work description and thus they declined that part of the job. So the barn remained shut fast.

****

Nathan was curious of all the labor going on about him and often found that he was underfoot and was asked to 'please stay out of the way.' But what was a five-year-old supposed to do when everyone around him was too busy to take up time with him?

After lunch that Friday, his mother took him upstairs for a nap. The bedrooms had been the first to be thoroughly cleaned and Kristyn had had AC window units installed in the windows of each bedroom, all but the master bedroom. Since no one slept there, she felt it unnecessary for the moment.

Mother and son sat down on the bed. "Now, you take your nap and we will have ice cream a little later," Kristyn said, as she helped to settle him.

Nathan grinned and nodded his head. Kissing his forehead, Kristyn left, partially shutting his door. The window unit hummed as cold air infiltrated his room. He watched as the curtains fluttered in the air current. Lying back on his pillow he only paused a second before closing his eyes and then quickly drifting off to sleep; after all, he was only five and sometimes a nap was all too necessary.

How long he slept, he did not know but a buzzing in his left ear dragged him from his slumber. It was a whisper invading his dream and startled Nathan to wakefulness. Still groggy, he lay still and listened. He watched as light rays moved smoothly across the wall. He had never seen this before. There were no shapes except the outlines of furniture silhouetted within light. These recognizable shapes were what moved as the light source moved. Then the whisper came again, this time in his other ear, "Come," resonated many voices.

Then the shapes moved back across the wall and stopped. "Nathan!" the words now seemed to be inside of Nathan's mind as well as from the other side of the room from within the light.

"What do you want?" he answered, sitting up.

"Much," the voices again came from within, as well as without. "Come."

"I am afraid!"

"No need. Come! Come!" they continued, with each word spoken louder, more urgently.

"Don't shout at me," Nathan whispered back.

"Come now, come, come now, come," they whispered. Then Nathan's bedroom door opened wider. The light came to a pinpoint at the door, hovering just above the wooden planks of the floor and pulsating. Nathan swung his legs over the edge of the bed, stood and then tip-toped towards the pinpoint of light.

Just as he reached it, the light moved ahead of him, then waited, as Nathan caught up with it. Then the sphere of light moved further into the hall. Nathan stooped over to better keep his eyes focused on the light and followed it. Now it floated smoothly, without jerks towards the opposite end of the hall; Nathan kept a vigilant eye on the sphere of light, all the while moving with it.

Now it halted, flickered a few times, then slid beneath the door... the attic door. Nathan straightened up, and looked up at the small grey door with flecks of paint peeling off of its surface. With his finger, he pointed at the door and said, "I think I'm 'posed to go in that door."

The door had an old fashion crystal knob, which had a black placket with a keyhole just beneath the knob. Nathan was at the right height to see into the keyhole and so he peeked. But only darkness greeted him. Backing away, he contemplated his next move. He remembered staring up at the attic window and seeing a white glow move by it. Was that glow the same light as this light? It must be.

He placed his right hand on the knob and turned – nothing! He turned it the other way and pulled on the door, still nothing. Dropping his hand to his side, he studied the knob. He tried again, this time he pushed on the door and, without warning, it opened, slamming hard against the interior wall with a loud thud. This revealed narrow steps, going up into the attic.

He peered inside and up; there were cobwebs dangling from the ceiling and heavy dust on the steps. The stairs were completely encased, with a single handrail on the left. He tried to see what was at the top, but what light projected into this darkened stairwell ended abruptly halfway.

He lifted his right foot and placed it on the first step when he heard, "Nathan! What are you doing?" It was his mother.

She hurried towards him and took him by the shoulder, "You cannot go into the attic," she said rather sternly.

"But the light..." Nathan began.

"I know there is no light, that's why it's dark in there. I wondered what that loud bang was. It startled us. We will discuss this later, right now come downstairs with me, we have company."

Immediately Nathan forgot the light and the attic and taking Kristyn's hand, gleefully followed his mother. Unseen by the pair of them was the self-closing of the attic door and an audible click as the door locked.

****

Kristyn thought to herself as she guided her wayward son downstairs, what if she hadn't heard the bang and checked on Nathan, he could have been locked in the attic. He could certainly die from the heat that collected in attics on hot summer days. The first thing she would do after the pastor left would be to lock *that* attic door.

Kristyn and Nathan entered the living room downstairs. It was clean, with sparkling windows veiled by light airy sheers. She had had the heavy dusty drapes removed and immediately the room had lightened up. This old house had never had modern carpeting of any sort and her grandmother's old oval braided brown rug was all that covered the wooden planks of the floor.

Her new high-definition television certainly looked out of place sitting on her grandmother's sideboard. There was the curved-back sofa, which looked in remarkably good condition seeing how it was nearly two hundred years old. There was the old rocking chair where she had often sat on her grandmother's lap and had stories read to her from the *Tales of Uncle Remus*. She had also learned her nursery rhymes there and later, her ABCs and 123s. She had also learned of the *birds and the bees* while sitting on the floor at her grandmother's knee.

There was a huge fireplace in this room, made of stone and standing six feet high. On hot summer days, she would sit inside of that big fireplace where it was so much cooler than the rest of the house. Her grandmother would call her '*Cinderella*' whenever she would find her there.

Not far from the fireplace was the old armchair that her grandfather claimed, with an ottoman in front. She could see him sitting in it even now, with his farmer's hat laying on the floor, his shoes on the back porch, where he removed them before entering Julia's cleaned house. He would sit there with the *Farmer's Almanac* and his pipe dangling from one corner of his mouth, as the smoke rose lazily in circles above his head and with his stocking feet propped up on the ottoman. She could still smell his pipe tobacco. The chair was looking rather worn now and she was considering replacing it with a recliner.

Centered in the room was the big round coffee table, where she had done many a homework assignment, right up to the time she had graduated from high school. There were two end tables on either side of the *Queen Anne* sofa and sitting on one was the ivy she had purchased. Her grandmother had always had houseplants around and the house looked so unhappy until she had added a few.

She sighed; there were only happy memories for her here and she so loved being back home. She felt happy and sad at the same time. She had her beloved son with her and that made her complete but there was still a void in her heart for Nathan Lance. Would it ever be filled again?

Sitting now in her grandfather's chair was the pastor. He was in his early sixties with short graying hair. He was a nice looking man, with a ready smile when he saw them. He stood and spoke, "Aaahh, I see you found him. How are you Nathan?" He held out his hand and Nathan politely shook it.

"Fine," was the child's short reply.

Winking at Nathan, the pastor asked, "Was it you making that noise upstairs?"

Kristyn guided Nathan towards the sofa and sat down, as did the pastor.

"Yes, it was the attic door. I caught him just before he entered," she explained, paused and then, "How kind of you to visit and invite us to services," said Kristyn resuming their conversation where it had left off when she had gone in search of Nathan.

"Well, you are certainly welcome," he replied. "I know you don't know me as I replaced Pastor Jamison who was here when you attended the *Church* with your grandparents. As I said, I am Thaddeus Doyle and I have been at the *Church* for ten years now. I did get to meet your grandparents, Clyde and Julia, but shortly afterwards, they moved to the retirement villa in Redfield. I paid them visits and the congregation kept in touch with them. They had many friends and were devoted followers of Christ. Their going-away services were beautiful and the church overflowed with mourners; what a beautiful way to leave this Earth and begin a life with Christ."

Kristyn smiled as Nathan looked up at her. Yes, *'going-away party'* as funerals were sometimes known; she had attended too many in her twenty-seven years. "Yes, Nathan and I would love to attend services, and thank you for coming by and inviting us."

Pastor Doyle got up to go, with his hat in hand; he was dressed casually. He walked towards the door. "Were the trespassers ever caught?" He asked, as an afterthought.

"Trespassers?" asked Kristyn with a lowering of her brows in a look of puzzlement.

"Oh, didn't you know of it?"

"No.... not a word. When?"

"Well, it was after your grandparents left the farm, and the house had been boarded up, but they were camping out in the barn. Vagrants, I am sure, but they were a rough bunch. The county Sheriff is the one that spotted them, but they took off into the fields and the woods and as far as I know, were never caught. The barn was in some disorder but no permanent damage was done that they could tell. But you haven't heard anything about it?"

"That I haven't," said Kristyn shaking her head. "That's unusual too because Nathan and I opened the barn door and there was the worst stench I have ever smelt! I'm certain an animal has died in there."

"Have you gone inside and checked?"

"No, there've been more pressing things and that just fell low on my list. I asked the landscapers to check it out but they declined, so nothing has been done about it."

"I see. Well, I know of someone I can get to help out, if that's okay with you. But for now, my advice is to stay clear of the barn. It could be real nasty if something dead is in there. Well, God bless you both. Shall we have a moment of prayer before I leave?"

Kristyn assured him she would be grateful and so, while standing at the opened front door in the entrance hall, the three of them lowered their heads in prayer.

"In Christ's name, we do pray. Amen," said Pastor Doyle, at the prayer's end. At that precise second, a loud crashing sound was heard from upstairs.

"Not again!" Kristyn exclaimed. "What on earth is going on...?"

The three of them looked towards the stairwell.

"Shouldn't we check," offered the pastor.

"Yes, let's. But for the life of me, I can't fathom what could have caused that noise!"

Upstairs and standing on the landing, it was obvious from whence the noise came. One of the ivies, which Kristyn had hung from the ceiling in front of the middle windows, was now on the floor with its basket broken and plant and dirt splattered.

"Well, I see we have our answer but another question is how. I'm certain I secured the hook firmly into a stud in the ceiling," said Kristyn.

"I'll help you clean it up," offered Pastor Doyle.

"Thank you, but no. I'll get one of the landscapers outside to help. I guess I didn't have it as secure as I thought."

"Well, okay, then if you are sure."

They went back downstairs and Pastor Doyle said, "Goodbye, we look forward to seeing you both at church."

"We'll be there," Kristyn assured the pastor.

****

As soon as the pastor had left, Kristyn, with Nathan tagging along, retrieved a dustpan, a broom and a trash pail and headed back upstairs to clean the disaster. Kristyn had another shocking surprise; the window was also broken, blown outwards, having received a blow from within the house! There were no glass shards lying on the floor, they were all within the window frame and the outside screen; the screen was torn but nothing had penetrated it.

Stifling a gasp, Kristyn, suddenly, was freezing. She looked at Nathan and saw his breath! "Are you cold too," she asked.

He nodded his head and shivered. "Let's go back down stairs," said Kristyn, and she picked up her son and went downstairs to the living room where she settled him next to her on the sofa. She would clean the mess up later. She saw that Nathan wasn't feeling well and he was her primary concern just now. Pondering the frigid temperatures upstairs, she did not know what to make of it. After all, they were at the end of July and today was as hot as any for this time of year, with the outside thermometer reading 95°F.

Holding Nathan close to her side and without speaking, she looked at him and saw that his eyes were shut. He no longer shivered and his rhythmic breathing told her he had fallen asleep.

"Well, little guy, I guess you didn't finish your nap." Kristyn lowered his head onto her lap and stroked his forehead while he slept. Many a time since his birth, she often held him as he slept. Neighbors would criticize her for it, claiming she was spoiling him and that he would never learn to sleep on his own. But Nathan was all she had and if there was another life for her in the future, with husband and more children, that would be grand but that was the future and the future was uncertain.

****

Later, she decided that she really needed to clean up the mess upstairs before it got any darker. So, while Nathan snoozed on the sofa, she headed back up the stairs to complete her task. "I'll lock the attic door too," she thought, making a mental note.

Finally, the dirt and broken planter were in the bucket, the ivy she decided could be saved and for now, she would place it in a vase of water to be re-potted later.

"Now, to lock *that* door." But going over to the small grey door of the attic, she saw that it was closed. "Well, I guess I must have closed it when we were here earlier. But it still needs to be locked, so that Nathan won't be tempted to go in there again." As she spoke, she tried the doorknob; it would not turn. Nothing she did would open the attic door. Exasperated, she decided if she couldn't open it, neither could Nathan and she would attend to it tomorrow.

****

Sunday morning dawn overcast, with the prospect of more rain. Tomorrow would make a whole week that they had been back in her childhood home. She roused early, right at dawn, with the lone rooster performing his duty, announcing the new day. She checked in on Nathan and saw that he still slept. He had not completely awakened from his late evening nap yesterday and she had carried him upstairs and undressed him and put him to bed. He hadn't gotten his bath so she would need to get him up for that, but first they would have breakfast.

Kristyn loved the early morning hours; for her it was the best time of the day. Often she would have her morning chores completed before waking anyone else, but for the last five years, it had been only Nathan. Since it was Sunday, she did not jump into any mundane chores, just allowed herself time for a morning cup of coffee while catching up on the news. Not too much new going on, the *War on Terror* still trudged along with no end in sight.

The war that Nathan Lance had died fighting. She didn't know how much she supported the war, only that it seemed a necessary evil for survival. That had been ongoing since 2002, after the Events of September 11, 2001, almost nine years ago this September 2010. She hadn't met her husband by that time; she was eighteen years old, and in her last year of training as a dental assistant when the events of 9/11 happened. By the autumn of the following year, she had met Nathan Lance during her final year of study and his final year of a four-year graduate degree. They dated and he asked her to marry him in the spring of 2004. They married that May.

As the economy was getting bad, although nothing like the crash it experienced several years later in the fall of 2008, the young couple considered Nathan joining the military. They knew that it was very possible that he would see combat, but thought the risk was one they would take. As they made their plans for this separation, Kristyn learned of her pregnancy in October, with the deployment of Nathan Lance just before Thanksgiving of 2004.

They spent their first Thanksgiving and Christmas apart. Her husband was still away when she gave birth to Nathan Ayden on June 6 of 2005. She and her husband had decided not to make him a junior; Nathan Lance was sure he would be called 'Junior' rather than Nathan. So, Nathan Ayden it was.

Corporal Nathan L. Spencer was killed in action that July, exactly five years ago this month. Nathan Ayden turned five in June 2010. Father and son never met! A lone tear formed and then ran down her left cheek. She wiped it away and was determined not to let sad memories bring her down into depression.

****

After finishing her morning cup of coffee, she showered in the downstairs bathroom, which was off from the entrance hall beneath the stairwell. It was originally a closet but modern improvements by her grandparents had changed its usage. Then she dressed in fresh jeans and t-shirt and went to the kitchen to prepare breakfast. It was early yet, but Nathan needed his bath and Sunday School started at 9:45.

Chapter Three

Shocking Revelations

A few hours later, Kristyn pulled her seven-year-old Mazda into the church's parking lot. She had changed her jeans for a light blue suit with sling-back white heels. Nathan wore dress trousers, a vest and a white shirt with a bow tie.

"Is this the church, Mama?" asked Nathan from the back seat.

"Yes, Nate, this is it. This is where I went to church when I was a little girl." Before getting out of the car, she surveyed the church grounds. Not too much had changed since she had attended. This church was located out on old 446, just off of the four-lane highway that replaced it. The church dated back to 1848; there had been renovations over the years but the church retained its conservative façade. It had been modernized as much as possible, with electricity and insulation plus central air and heating.

When the church was first constructed, it had only been a large one-room sanctuary, which received its warmth by way of wood burning stoves situated at both ends of the room. Two large rest rooms had been added and the outhouse at the back was long gone.

Also added were several sections that were now the Sunday school classrooms and a Fellowship Hall. She had wanted to be married here but it just didn't happen that way. There had been no time or funds for a large ceremony and so she and Nathan Lance had eloped to South Carolina.

The church retained its historical veneer. But now the structure sported white aluminum siding, which had been added as an upgrade from the clapboard originally used, although the appearance was unchanged. On both sides of the double doors were two stained glass windows and Kristyn recalled that five more stained glass windows lined each side of the church's outside walls, making a total of twelve; a symbolic number. They also had been part of the renovations of the church, replacing the older glass panes.

Concrete steps replaced the original wooden ones; Kristyn knew there were twenty-four of them because she had counted them as part of a game she had played with the other children. Solid white double doors opened into the narrow receiving hall while another aperture, without doors, just a graceful arch, opened into the sanctuary. The one wide aisle had pews on either side, twenty each.

The steeple had the bell tower located within it and now the bell tolled the call to worship.

Kristyn had given her life to God when she was twelve and had been baptized in the church's new baptismal vat a few weeks later.

For a long moment, she felt grief at the fact that she had not attended church on a regular basis since leaving home at eighteen. But she had placed Nathan in a Christian daycare where he had learned his Bible stories and how to pray. This they did every night. It was the simple child's prayer of *Now I Lay Me Down to Sleep* and it ended with special blessings and small requests. There was always a request for a pet but he had only been allowed stuffed animals in their apartment - the apartment she had shared with her husband and continued to inhabit after he had left for duty.

Even after Nathan's birth, she had remained in the one bedroom apartment, her last link with Nathan Lance.

Kristyn knew, but was unable to see from her present location, that there was a cemetery located behind the church. It was actually older than the church by several years and at one time had been a private cemetery. It was considered an historical landmark and funded for upkeep by the *United Daughters of the Confederacy,* because many a young rebel soldier was laid to rest there, as were her parents, her beloved grandparents and her only love, Nathan L. She hadn't visited the graves as often as she would have liked, but living in Rock Haven made her a good hour away from this part of the state, which was east and south from her apartment.

The cemetery had been modernized with a tall white picket fence and a white swinging gate. It had a schedule for viewing by tourists that were interested in the history of the people that were entombed there. There were varieties of burial methods, from graves with head stones to mausoleums. It was unlocked on the weekends, on Wednesdays and by appointment for schools and other organizations. The caretaker lived in the grounds of the church, and he pretty well knew all there was to know about the cemetery, often acting as a tour guide for visitors who requested his services.

More and more vehicles were pulling into the parking lot, with the parishioners headed for the church. Kristyn glanced at her watch and saw that it was nine thirty eight; they needed to head inside too. As they made their way across the parking lot, she was greeted and welcomed to the church. Some were old friends from her childhood and they were glad that she had returned.

She followed the crowd, which she saw was heading for the back of the church, for Sunday school. With help, she found her class but declined taking

Nathan to his class; since this was his first time here, she did not want to leave him alone. The class more than made her feel welcome and before the study of God's word began, she was told of all the local gossip about people she had known, where they were and what they were doing.

After the Sunday school class, she followed them to the primary Sanctuary; she could hear the organ pumping the deep tones of an unknown hymn long before reaching it. She wondered if Miss Applegate still furnished the music, and, as she entered, she saw that she indeed did.

She and Nathan took a seat on the fourth pew on the left side of the church. Most parishioners left their children in the nursery or children's church if they were nine and older. Looking around, she saw that the church was integrated with African-Americans and Hispanic members. She liked this idea a great deal, for what did the color of one's skin have to do with anything. Nothing, and all were children of God.

There was singing of hymns, one was known to her and two not, then a prayer and then Pastor Doyle made his way to the podium. Before getting into his sermon, he took a moment to introduce Kristyn and Nathan to the congregation. The pair stood as requested and waved as the parishioners acknowledged their presence.

"Turn your Bibles to Revelations, chapter two ..." instructed Pastor Doyle and the sermon began. At the end of the sermon came the altar call. Kristyn decided she needed to renew her relationship with God and the church and, during the song, *'Just As I Am'*, she took Nathan's hand and they made the short journey down the aisle, up to Pastor Doyle.

She said a prayer of repentance and made a request to renew her membership. After the song ended, Pastor Doyle asked the congregation if they accepted the pair into the church and there was a resounding applause as the motion carried.

Now the parishioners lined up and each one personally welcomed her into the church, with many inviting them to their homes for a meal. Nathan was a little overwhelmed by all these strangers and stayed close to his mother's side with one arm about her knee. Kristyn felt his apprehension and was reassured by the warmth of his young body next to her, as she knew he was near and safe.

Long minutes later, on the outside, as she was heading for her car, Pastor Doyle called to her and she waited for him to catch up, "Mrs. Spencer I want you to meet someone. Wait a moment, he will be right here." Straining to see through the crowd, he saw the one he wanted and called to him, "Tyler, can you come over here?"

A young man of about thirty-two or three approached them. Tyler was nicely dressed in a dark blue suit, with a pinkish shirt and a striped pink, blue and grey tie. It was his eyes that drew Kristyn's attention however, and she felt her heart skip a beat. They were a cobalt blue, insightful and compassionate.

"Hello," he said, with a deep baritone voice and met her eyes with a piercing look that sent tingles down Kristyn's spine. He was deeply tanned, with a strong jaw, a straight nose, narrow mouth and heavy brows.

'*Stop it!*' she silently scolded herself. "Hello, Mr. ..." she hesitated.

"Doyle," he smiled, extending his hand to take hers in a warm and firm grip. He looked deeply into her eyes and smiled, sending new chills through her, then glancing at the Pastor, said, "This is my father. Dad told me something about the situation with the barn when he returned home the other day, I would be glad to get my crew to check it out and even clean it up for you."

"That would be nice," she replied still mesmerized by his gaze. "But I wouldn't want to impose upon your time. I am sure I will get to it myself in the next few days, as soon as I find someone suitable."

"I think you have found someone," said Pastor Doyle, giving her a knowing wink.

Kristyn smiled shyly and turning back to Tyler, said, "Thank you then. Any time is fine with me. I am home all day right now. But I do admit I must be making plans to return to work."

"Did you get the broken pot cleared away, okay?" asked Pastor Doyle.

"I just went ahead and did it myself," replied Kristyn.

"Now, I would have done it if I had known you weren't getting help," smiled Pastor Doyle.

"It was rather strange when I went to clean up the mess."

To which the pastor raised his eyebrows, and asked, "Strange? How so?"

"Well, the window was broken. It was broken from the inside, but how could the pot have broken it just by dropping from the ceiling?"

"That is odd," said Tyler after silently listening to the conversation for a bit. "Was the pot hanging within the window frame?"

"No, I made a point of hanging it from the ceiling; I didn't want water or dirt to splatter onto the glass when I watered the plants, so it was at least a foot and a half from the window. Also, it was like a freezer when I went back upstairs, right after Pastor Doyle left. Now that is just wrong, I mean, it was ninety-five degrees outside. I have an AC window unit in two of the bedrooms but they aren't powerful enough to bring a chill such as that out into the hall."

"Cold?" inquired Pastor Doyle. "Cold like cooler or freezing like winter?"

"Like winter," she emphasized. "You could see our breath, that's how cold it was."

"That's not so unusual if it's cold enough but the question is, what made it that cold?"

"It wasn't the AC," declared Kristyn. "It felt like thirty-two degrees or colder, cold enough that Nathan was shivering!"

"That's odd for this time of year!" said Tyler. "I have a thought on that but we'll wait for now."

For a moment, Kristyn considered this remark and wondered what 'that' could be. Deciding not to pursue it, she remembered the attic door being jammed and said, "And while you are there, maybe you can help me open the attic door. It's stuck!"

At that, Nathan joined into the conversation, "That's where the light lives."

"Light?" asked Kristyn looking down at her son. "Whatever do you mean, Nathan?"

"The light!" he replied excitedly. "'member, I told you, Mama."

"I do not remember anything about a light. Yes, it was dark in the stairwell because there isn't a light in there."

"That's where the light lives," Nathan insisted.

By now, Pastor Doyle and Tyler had both squatted down to Nathan's level. "What makes you think a *light* lives in the attic?" asked Pastor Doyle.

"I know! 'Cos I saw it go under the door," stated Nathan firmly, as if a little irritated that no one believed him. He poked out his bottom lip and crossed his arms in front of his chest. "It wanted me to go in there too."

"Is he given to flights of fantasy," asked Pastor Doyle glancing up at Kristyn who stood close to her son with her arm about his shoulders.

"No more than any other five year old," she replied. "Nate," she said squatting down next to him too, "darling, now is not the time for make-believe, what makes you think that the *light* wanted you to go into the attic?"

"It said so," he replied.

Tyler took up the questions now, "What did the light say?"

"It woke me. 'Member, Mama, I was taking my nap? It was a bi-i-i-g light," now Nathan unfolded his arms and stretched them wide as he dragged out the word 'big'. "It covered the whole wall. It said, 'Come.'"

"Are you sure you heard the word 'come'?"

Nathan nodded his head vigorously. "'Come, come, come, come', is what it said. Then it got *real* tiny," said Nathan drawing out his last word while bringing his hands together in a cup. "That little."

By now, the adults were looking at each other and wondering how much Nathan was making up and if any of this was true. Not wanting to make Nathan think they didn't believe him, Kristyn said, "What did the light do then, Nate?"

"It went out into the hall and wanted me to go too. It was sooo little that I had to bend over to see it. It went down the hall! It stopped at that door."

"The attic door?" asked Tyler.

Nathan nodded.

"Then what," continued Tyler.

"It went under the door," said Nathan. "It's *real* little, so it could do that but I'm too big. I cain't go under any door. So I opened it. It was real hard too. But I pushed and I pulled and it opened really fast and made a loud bang when it hit the wall. That's what y'all heard, Mama. It was real dark in there and I was scared! But I was going to go up those steps until Mama stopped me."

The adults stood up and looked at each other with questioning expressions. Kristyn spoke, "When I checked the door later, it was shut but I don't remember closing it. I tried to open it but it would not open. I wanted to lock it but then it came to me that I had no key. I don't know where the key is."

"Can you and Nathan sleep downstairs?" asked Tyler.

"Well, I guess. There's a hide-a-bed in the den. Why? Is there something wrong upstairs? Something you aren't telling me!"

Father and son looked at each other and then Pastor Doyle said, "I am going to be honest with you, but first, do you mind if I call you Kristyn?"

"No, please do. But you were about to say..."

"Something strange *is* going on there. Not to frighten you but the church does believe in spiritual visitations."

"Spiritual visitations? What is that supposed to mean?"

"Visits from the spirit realm," he said.

"You're joking, right? You don't mean ghosts?"

"No, not ghosts, especially. Not the way most people think of ghosts. No, there are other members of the spirit realm. God and Jesus are part of the spirit realm as are angels and demons."

"Okay..." Kristyn paused as this thought sank in. Here was a man of God telling her that spirits might be haunting their home. "My house could be haunted?"

Nathan had listened to this dialog intently and he began jumping gleefully, "Oh boy, Casper!"

Now all of the adults looked at each other and burst out laughing. Kristyn just shook her head in a way of apologizing and said, "Cartoons."

A flash of lightning, followed by a thunderclap, alerted everyone that the storm which had been anticipated, was upon them.

Tyler quickly escorted Kristyn and Nathan to her car and aided in getting Nathan secured in the backseat, after which he told Kristyn, while leaning his hands against her door, "Don't sleep upstairs tonight and I will see you tomorrow evening after I get off from work."

Then the rain broke hard and furious, Tyler exclaimed, "Well, gotta run, see you tomorrow!" He then made a mad dash to his truck.

Chapter Four

The Skeleton Key

Kristyn and Nathan, later that evening, made up the hide-a-bed in the den. Nathan would sleep with her for now, until they learned what was going on upstairs. Kristyn had never considered the paranormal or the supernatural; life itself was paranormal enough for her! She had been so unhappy for such a long time, that having to deal with another aspect of existence was just too overwhelming.

She moved her TV from the living room into the den. They could watch TV while in bed; Nathan would love that. The den's comfy furniture was newer than that in the living room or the bedrooms, about ten years old or so. Kristyn had already moved out when her grandparents bought it. The hide-a-bed was a sofa that when you tilted the seat upwards and pulled forwards, it came out of the frame into a double bed. There was one recliner and another armchair in there. A small rectangular coffee table sat in front of the sofa and now was the stand for the television. On one end of the sofa was a freestanding floor lamp. There was a small fireplace into which a coal/wood burning stove had been fitted, with a chimney pipe, but the mantel remained.

On the floor was a room-size throw rug, also purchased new for the den. The den had one of the two picture windows of the house but Kristyn had left up the heavier drapes after sending them out to be thoroughly cleaned, for they were new as well. They did a great job of keeping out the late afternoon sun. There were no overhead lights anywhere in the house. That would have required major overhauling to hide the wiring in the ceiling. Kristyn's Grandfather hadn't thought the expense worth it.

"I thought you said I was getting too old to sleep in your bed, Mama," Nathan grinned as she settled him on one side of the hide-a-bed.

"You are. But this is a special occasion, so don't get used to it. We will be back in our rooms upstairs in no time."

"That's because of Casper, I know."

"Now, there'll be no talk of Casper. There are no such things as ghosts, not even a *friendly* ghost. Now, let me hear your prayers."

Dutifully, Nathan got on his knees at the bedside, folded his hands and said his child's prayer ending with, "Dear Jesus, can I please have a kitten? We don't live in that 'partment any more. Mama always said that is why I cain't have a pet. Thank you. Amen."

Kristyn smiled, "Last time, it was a puppy, Nate. Are you sure about a kitten?" Each time he had asked for a different pet.

"I'll take a puppy too," he grinned.

"I just bet you would," she smiled at him. Thinking for a long moment, Kristyn said, "We will ask Mr. Doyle if he knows anyone who might have a puppy or a kitten, but for free."

Nathan sat up, wrapped his arms around his mother's neck and said, "Thank you Mama! See, Jesus does answer prayers! But it did take him a lonnnggg time."

"That's because He knows the best time to answer prayers and even whether those prayers should be answered. Not everything we ask of Jesus is for our good. If we are unselfish in what we ask, then there is a better chance of our prayers being answered."

****

Next day, she got Nathan settled in the den with his Lego and with cartoons on the television, but Kristyn couldn't stand the suspense any longer and when Nathan wasn't paying attention to her, she crept upstairs. For a long moment, she stood at the head of the landing and just looked down the hall. It was hot up here, almost stifling, and everything was so still. The doors to the bedrooms were shut; the bathroom door was open.

Inhaling deeply, she went into her bedroom, turned on the AC, and then did the same in Nathan's room, leaving the doors open to help cool the hallway. She went to the attic door; there was nothing strange about it. She attempted to open it again but it was still stuck. "There's got to be a key, but I can't remember where the keys to the house were kept or even if there was a key for the attic."

In all her years of living in this house, she had only been in the attic a few times and then with her grandfather. She had never ventured in there on her own, had never wanted to. It was hot and stuffy in summer and freezing in winter.

Any Christmas decorations that were stored up there were placed into and taken out of the attic by Grandpa. "I wonder if the key might be in their room," she thought aloud and recalled that she had not entered her grandparents' bedroom since that first day, leaving its cleaning to *Efficient Maids*.

Now, she faced in that direction, inhaled again and, like a solider, marched determinedly to the opposite end of the hall. As she passed the two bedrooms, she felt the cooler air rushing out into the hall, already bringing its temperature down to a more bearable level. Stopping at the bedroom door, again she drew a deep breath, summoning her courage to enter. She turned the knob and pushed open the door. With the door open, Kristyn was shocked; this bedroom had not been touched! Not by her and certainly not by *Efficient Maids*!

"What's up with this," she said, beginning to feel annoyance at this room being deliberately ignored, after her instructions to clean the upstairs bedrooms! Taking her cell phone from its holster, she quickly dialed the company, as she stepped back out into the hall and ambled down to her bedroom door to catch the cool draft emerging from it.

Listening briefly, she said, "It was locked?" Sighing after another exchange, she said, "No, that's okay, I'll take care of it myself."

She looked towards the master bedroom and wondered how the door had been locked. She hadn't locked it and it wasn't locked now, so what was going on? Turning back downstairs, she checked on Nathan and asked if he needed anything, telling him to call if he did and she would be right there. She retrieved the necessary cleaning items and headed back upstairs with both hands full.

"This is going to take all day," she said. "Maybe I can get it done before Mr. Doyle comes this evening." That one little thought of him made her heart skip a beat and for a second she thought of him. A thought that was too personal invaded her mind's eye and she mentally shook herself. "Back to the task at hand," she said aloud.

Back upstairs, she immediately noticed how much cooler it was; that was good because she knew that her next chore was going to be a sweaty one. But no matter, it was a dirty job, someone had to do it and she was going to be that someone! First things first, and that was to sweep down all those cobwebs! That was a job she hated the most. She tied a kerchief over her nose and mouth and another around her hair and set to work.

Soon she had the ones dangling from the ceiling gone, now for the walls and furniture. Kristyn, swept, dusted, vacuumed and washed windows until noon. She was hot, sweaty, thirsty and hungry. Glancing at her watch, she realized she hadn't heard a peep out of Nathan. What a horrid mother was she and she hurried downstairs to check on him. She breathed a sigh of relief when she saw he was still busy with his Lego.

"Want some lunch, Nate?" she asked.

After a lunch of *Lunchables* and milk for Nathan and a *Lean Cuisine* and soda for her, she decided to settle Nathan for an afternoon nap in the den, while she finished up upstairs.

Kristyn stayed with him and read him a story from *Dr. Seuss', Green Eggs and Ham*. Seeing him nod off, she headed back to the job at hand, and said, "I guess I need to pull the furniture out from the wall and clean behind each piece."

She started with the bureau or as it is called today, chest of drawers. It was no easy task, for these were large heavy pieces by the makers of *Thomasville*. Kristyn's grandmother had inherited this farm from her grandparents. The house retained the very same furnishings that they had used. Kristyn was unsure of the age of this furniture but she did know that it was from around the thirties. The main thing she knew was it was in excellent condition, heavy and dusty. Why the dust covers had not been applied over the furniture in here was a mystery when the rest of the house had been so protected. With the webs and dust cleared away, she shoved the bureau back into place. She did the same with the dresser and then came the roll top desk.

It was at this desk that Grandpa had kept care of the farm's business and Grandma had addressed cards and letters. While most times a desk would have been in the den downstairs, for whatever reasons her grandfather had kept it here. It was a piece of furniture that was much older than the rest. It came to Kristyn's grandfather from his grandfather, and was not a part of the household furniture that Kristyn's grandmother had inherited from her grandmother. Kristyn knew this because her grandfather often spoke of his grandfather and the close relationship they had had, and that it was the one thing that he had inherited from him.

The desk was huge, stood four feet tall and about three feet deep. Its top had cubbyholes and a large flat writing surface, which was easily hidden by a roll top cover. Its front had a long single drawer and beneath that drawer, was a divided section with two large drawers on the left and four smaller drawers on the right. It was a heavy piece of furniture!

"I just bet that keys were kept in this desk. I don't know if it's been searched since their deaths. I would think that Grandpa would have taken any documents concerning the farm with him."

Kristyn began her search but was disappointed. No keys of any kind were found, nor were any documents, or papers, not even a paper clip, the desk was as clean as a whistle! But the desk was the last piece of furniture to be moved and she began the arduous task of inching it out into the middle of the floor away from the wall.

"Want some help?" a deep voice came from the bedroom door. Jumping at the sound, Kristyn looked up to see Tyler Doyle standing in the doorway with Nathan holding his hand. "I'm sorry if I startled you. I knocked and this little guy opened the door. He said he would take me to you. I called your name but I guess you didn't hear. I was worried when I didn't see you downstairs and Nathan seemed to be alone. I thought that perhaps you were up here."

Standing, and inhaling, Kristyn brushed wayward hair from her face, "That's perfectly alright. I guess I was so engrossed in moving this desk, that I didn't hear anything."

"Didn't my father tell me that you had had help cleaning out the house? I know it has been boarded up for five years now and it must have been a huge chore. So, why are you cleaning by yourself?"

"Well," she began, "It seems that this room was missed. *Efficient Maids* said the door was locked but it wasn't locked for me. I think that maybe the rain the night before might have caused it to swell. I think that's what's wrong with the attic door, too. I know that it was opened because I saw it when Nathan was about to enter, but it is stuck fast now. If it's locked, it locked itself! I am glad Nathan let you in, but Nate," she continued, looking at her son, "you should not answer the door when you do not know who is there. You should have called me."

"I'm sorry. But Mama, I do know him. 'Member we saw him at church. I looked out the window and saw him and his truck."

Feeling a little sheepish at being harsh with him, Kristyn said, "It's okay but let's lay a few ground rules. You do not answer the door alone. Understood?"

Nathan nodded, "Okay, but why?"

Now Tyler spoke up, "Yes, you do know me but still your mother is the grown-up and should be the one to answer doors and phones unless she tells you to do it."

Since Nathan's birth, Kristyn had been the sole disciplinarian of her son, allowing for the staff of the day-care he attended, of course, and she found it a good feeling to have this support. "You got that Nate?" she asked him now.

Again, he nodded.

Addressing Tyler, Kristyn expressed her thoughts on his unexpected arrival. "I wasn't expecting you till much later, after work you said."

"Mrs. Spencer, it is after work, four-thirty, I get off at four. I came straight here because of the situation you described to us."

"My goodness, how did it get so late? I have been cleaning this bedroom since nine this morning. I knew it would take awhile but that's six or seven hours. I should be able to clean the whole house in that time."

"Shall we finish moving this desk?" he asked with a wink, which made Kristyn's heart race.

"Yes, it's the last thing to do and the heaviest. I had hoped the attic key was in it somewhere but the desk is cleaner inside than out and there's not a paper clip to be found."

When Kristyn placed her hand on the desk to begin its eviction from the spot it had occupied for probably seventy-five year or so, Tyler waved her to the side and, bracing his hands on either side of the desk, hauled it forward. Away it came out into the middle of the floor, and just as Kristyn suspected, it was covered with cobwebs and dust, both the wall and the desk.

Smiling at Tyler's shocked expression, she said, "I know, it is horrible." She took the broom and started sweeping away the webs and dust.

"Wait, Mama!" shouted Nathan.

Stopping quickly, Kristyn thought that she had accidently struck Nathan with the broom, "Are you all right, Nate?"

"See," he said, pointing at the back of the desk.

"See what?" both Tyler and Kristyn spoke simultaneously.

"That!" he answered, still pointing his index finger at the back of the desk.

"Nathan, I do *not* see a thing," declared Kristyn.

At that, Nathan bent low to the floor, and reaching towards the back of the desk, he removed a key... a skeleton key. "That!" he announced and handed it to his mother.

"My word!" Kristyn exclaimed. "It's a key!"

Now Tyler examined the area where the key had been, "There's a rusty tack here, it must have been hanging from it." He took the key from Kristyn's hand and remarked, "That's why we didn't see it, what with the cobwebs and it being the same color as the desk. How on earth did you see it Nathan?"

"It moved," replied Nathan.

"Well, if it hadn't moved, it wouldn't have been seen. Someone made a point of hiding this key very, very well."

"It's a strange looking sort of key. I have never seen one like it before. I wonder if it is the key to the attic?" questioned Kristyn.

"Well, this is known as a skeleton key," explained Tyler.

"Skeleton key? I don't understand what that is," said Kristyn. "I have never heard that term before."

"Skeleton key, also known as a pass key or even a master key. It could be for a door, a cabinet, a chest or even a security type box. This type of key was once used in Europe and America during and after colonial times. This house must be about two hundred years old, so it's likely that those types of locks, known as level or rim locks, were used. The term 'skeleton key' derived that name because of its resemblance to a skeleton. Yeah, I know, it is hard to see that," said Tyler, when Kristyn raised her brows questioningly. "Their use has been phased out since around nineteen forty and they are rarely found, unless it is in an historical house such as this."

"My grandfather changed the knobs and locks in the house; they are all like what you will find in newer homes today. So, why did he keep this key? It has got to fit the attic; it still has the older style lock."

"Well, let's finish this up and I'll slide the desk back in place, then you will be done in here."

A few brushes with the broom with eyes alert to anything that might be hidden, but seeing nothing more, Tyler pushed the desk back into its space. Reaching out his hand towards Nathan, who had been asked to hold the key, Nathan placed it into his hand with a big grin. Tyler ruffled his hair and said, "Let's go see what's in that old attic."

Moments later, the three stood in front of the daunting attic door. "Ready?" asked Tyler, looking at mother and then child. The pair nodded. First Tyler tried the knob just to check if it was locked. When there was no response, he inserted the key.

Chapter Five

Locked Out

Tyler turned the key; no response, then he turned it back the other way and a click was heard as the level lined up, permitting the bolt to be released from the junction in the opposing section of the lock. Turning the crystal doorknob, Tyler pushed on the door and it opened easily. He released the breath he was holding and heard a sigh from Kristyn. Everyone was anxious with expectation and felt relief when the lock gave way.

Once again, the narrow stairwell was revealed, leading upward into the gloom. Cobwebs undulated faintly from the draft of air rushing in from the hall.

"Looks like we need the broom in here as well," observed Tyler.

"I'll get it," volunteered Kristyn.

While she was gone, Nathan said, "That is where the light went."

Not wanting to discourage him, Tyler replied, "I expect so."

Taking the broom from Kristyn upon her return, Tyler said, "I'll do the honors," and began knocking down the dangling webs, moving upward one step at a time leaving clear footprints in the dust, which rose briefly then resettled. As Tyler reached the top of the stairs, he disappeared into the darkness and all that Kristyn could see was his lower legs.

"We have another problem," he shouted back down. "There's another door here and the key will not unlock it," Tyler emerged back into the light as he was speaking.

"I don't remember another door," said Kristyn. "But Grandpa always went into the attic, I never went there alone. It was just a little too creepy for me, when I was little, that is. I remember a doorway but no door. How odd is that?"

"I guess as children we don't always take note of things and I suppose a door would have no special meaning for you. You probably never actually saw him open it. But there's one there and it is shut and locked. Double indemnity I imagine. I wonder what was so important in an attic that it had two doors and both locked."

"The light doesn't want you in there," piped up Nathan.

Both adults looked at him, then at each other, with questioning expressions, as if he might be right. "It's late, and I must get some supper together," said Kristyn, "We can check into this another time. Mr. Doyle, will you stay for supper?"

"Well, I would consider it an honor *if* you will call me Tyler."

"Done... Tyler. And I prefer Kristyn."

Tyler helped entertain Nathan and even lent Kristyn a hand in the kitchen but for the most part, he and Nathan got to know each other. Nathan hadn't been around men too often, as his daycare providers were all women, so to have a man take up time with him was a real treat.

Doing their modest meal, Kristyn and Tyler exchanged general information. Kristyn told of her education, how she met, and married Nathan's father, of their very brief marriage before he left for Iraq and then his early and tragic death, having never even seen his son! Kristyn controlled as best she could the tears that always formed when she thought of Nathan Lance.

Tyler expressed his condolences at her loss. He saw the darkness that swept across her features when talking about her husband. Her pain was deep and it was real and she was still suffering.

He also related to Kristyn the story of his own engagement, that had ended when his fiancée met another man and broke off the engagement. "She claimed that to be the wife of a preacher's son would be too restricting, whatever that is supposed to mean."

Kristyn saw the disappointment on Tyler's face and realized that he had missed out on love but, that also he knew deep down that this woman had not been meant for him. She so wanted to touch his face and tell him that she understood. But *this* was too new and they were still strangers and so she controlled the impulse.

Tyler continued his story but the empathic look from Kristyn did not escape him. His minister father had hoped his only son would follow him into the ministry but Tyler had declined in favor of a more hands-on, tangible career. He had started his own contractors business a few years ago, after learning the ropes from a friend of his parents. They had taken a great deal of time to teach Tyler properly the ins and outs of the construction business. So far, his company had proved profitable even with the economical environment of the day. People did not feel confident in buying new homes so many were opting to remain where they were and just improve what they owned. During his training, Tyler had also taken a course in engineering.

"Yeah, the engineering course was necessary, have to know the basics. Can't rebuild if you can't build to begin with."

"Well, in that case," said Kristyn, "Are you interested in a job?"

Tyler raised his brows questioningly, "You mean this place?"

To which Kristyn nodded, "You can begin with replacing the window upstairs that was broken somehow. Right now I have a piece of plywood nailed over it, what do you say?"

So arrangements were made that Tyler's crew would begin the small renovation that the house needed.

"How would you like that Nathan?" Kristyn asked of her son and Nathan grinned.

"I can help too" he beamed.

"Always need a good hand," replied Tyler.

They finished up supper and cleared away the dishes.

"I guess I need to go," said Tyler glancing at his watch. "It's almost seven; it's been a busy evening. Are you and Nathan sleeping downstairs again?"

"Yeah, but I would like to get back into the bedrooms. I don't see any real danger up there. I mean I spent the day upstairs cleaning up, without incident. So as soon as you can repair that window, I'll feel secure enough to return to our rooms."

"Well my father was very serious about spirits. Although I am not as convinced as he, we do need to investigate further before you trust things upstairs again. Maybe after the attic is opened, we can sort through any happenings, we just might find logical explanations for them."

"How are we going to get the door open?"

"Well, there's a locksmith, should be easy enough. I'll check into it for you if you like," replied Tyler.

"It all seems so silly now, in the light of day. Nathan's light is probably no more than a moving car headlight beam. I think getting a locksmith is the best idea I have heard all day!"

"I'll have a man here first thing in the morning. He will be in a company truck, with my logo on it, so you will know that I sent him."

They walked to the front door with Nathan holding onto Tyler's leg as if he did not want him to leave.

Tyler turned to Kristyn, and said, "I would like to see you again..."

"Me too," declared Nathan.

Laughing, Tyler bent down, scooped Nathan up, held him and tickled him, "But of course, you're the main reason." Then Tyler looked pointedly at Kristyn.

"I would like that too," she whispered, and then smiled as their eyes met and chills shot down Kristyn's spine and she physically shivered.

Seeing this, Tyler said, "Are you cold?"

"No, no, just a chill, like someone walking on my grave. You know that old saying?"

"Yeah, that's an uncanny sensation alright. I'll call. Are you in the book?"

"No, I haven't had a land line connected yet, but here's my cell number."

They exchanged cell phone numbers, and as Tyler returned his cell to its holster on his belt, he reached into his pants' pocket and retrieved the key, "Here, I almost forgot this," and handed it to Kristyn. "Keep it; it might fit some other lock in the house."

"Thanks," she said taking the key and folding her fingers around it, sensing warmth where it had been in contact with Tyler's body.

"Well, good evening," he nodded at Kristyn, "Oh before I forget, and I think I already had, Dad said to remind you of the Wednesday night church services; they have a meal first and service afterwards. We all would love to see the pair of you there."

"I will do my best to attend."

"Great, Mom will be there. She just missed you Sunday what with the sudden storm and all."

After a few more words, Tyler got into his truck and headed the black pickup down the road. Kristyn and Nathan watched until he had left their path and had turned onto the main road. Kristyn turned to Nathan, "Bath time young man!"

****

They stayed another night in the den, the window upstairs had not been repaired and until it was, they would not return to their bedrooms. Tuesday morning began quietly; Kristyn received a call from Tyler informing her that Franklin was on his way to her house to repair the window and to be on the lookout for him.

Franklin arrived fifteen minutes later. He was a black man, much older than Kristyn expected. He was medium height and stooped just a bit, thin, and probably over seventy years of age. He had on a dark green cap with Tyler's logo embossed across it and when he removed it, she saw that he was nearly bald and sported a white goatee and mustache. He wore old faded bib coveralls and a tool-belt, and high-tops black work shoes.

"Morning, Mad'm," he greeted her, as he approached the steps of the front porch. After a few words of greeting, Kristyn took Franklin upstairs to the job.

"Well, there it is," she said pointing towards the piece of plywood that she had nailed across the bottom half of the window.

"Shain't take me so awful long," stated Franklin studying the makeshift repair that Kristyn had attempted.

Laughing, Kristyn said, "I know, I'm not much of a carpenter."

Setting down his toolbox, Franklin replied, "You did good, Mad'm, you did good." and proceeded with the repair.

"Well, I'll leave you to it," said Kristyn and she went back downstairs. Between seeing to it that Nathan was kept occupied with some home schooling projects, something the child's daycare had started to get him ready for kindergarten, and her household chores, the morning's agenda was full.

While sweeping the front-receiving hall, Kristyn saw Franklin coming downstairs. "My goodness, are you finished already?"

"No Mad'm, gotta git my jacket from de truck," he replied now heading out the front door.

"Why would he need his jacket," Kristyn wondered. "Unless..." Propping her broom against the wall, she hastened upstairs. Upon reaching the landing, she immediately felt the cooler temperatures but as she walked towards the broken window, it grew even colder. She breathed out and saw her breath, just the same as before on Saturday.

"I know," said Franklin as he emerged from the stairwell. "Don't make any sense. I think that maybe you had the AC too high, but they ain't none on up here. So, I reckon to myself, I best git my jacket. These old bones hurt a bit when they git cold. Yer got several panes broken," continued Franklin, gingerly touching a shard, "they's gotta come out and new glass put in. Shain't take me so awful long, though," he paused, "I'll patch the screen too, but it needs replacing. I'll tell Mr. Doyle, 'cuz some younger fellow gotta to git out on the roof thar and put back de screen from de outside. It might can be done from in here, but de whole 'sembly would have to come out then and that'll take a might longer."

"Do you have the correct size glass pane needed with you?" asked Kristyn.

"Yea' Mad'm, we try to be prepare for all situations and we pritty well know 'bout the *Whitaker* house, what is what with it and all."

"*Whitaker House?*" asked Kristyn. "Why is it called that?"

"Well, if I can recollect, 'cause it's been known by that name since I was a boy. This here house was built some hundreds years ago by a man, named *Whitaker, James Robert Whitaker.*"

"But my grandparents and my grandmother's grandparents before them, owned this house and the surrounding land and their names were Harrison and Morrison," reasoned Kristyn as she shivered and wrapped her arms about her body. After all, she had on a tank top and shorts and it was freezing. "So why would the name of *Whitaker* still be attached to this house?"

"Cain't answer that one, Mad'm" replied Franklin.

"Well, it's too cold for me right now. I can't stay up here any longer; maybe you can finish up here and tell me more later."

"Sure thing Mad'm. Ain't gonna take me no time, no time tat-tall!"

Kristyn eyed the attic door and subconsciously fingered the skeleton key that she now wore on an old light chain about her neck. "I bet it's hot up there," she spoke softly.

"What's that you say Mad'm?"

"Oh nothing, just that I bet it's hot in the attic."

"I s'pect so, Mad'm, I s'pect so."

"I think I'll just check something. Franklin, can I borrow your flashlight?"

"Sure thing Mad'm," he answered and handed her the light.

Even though it was still unbearably cold, Kristyn decided to endure it a little longer. She removed the key from around her neck and stepped precariously towards the attic door.

'What's wrong with me?' she chided herself. 'It's only a door,' and inserted the key. The level clicked and the lock gave way and she pushed in to open it. It felt immensely warmer and she reveled in that warmth, feeling the chill depart. Aiming the light up, 'Well, at least Tyler got all the webs down.' she thought. Finally, as she swept the light further upwards, it focused on the door at the top of the steps. 'Yes, there's a door.' Kristyn realized that she hadn't believed really that there was a door, although she also knew Tyler had no reason to fabricate its existence. 'I'm just going to have a quick look see...'

She proceeded up the stairs, she felt her heartbeat quicken as she advanced. 'Why am I acting like this? Kristyn, get a hold of yourself.' Now she stood on the narrow landing with the door within reach.

She tested the knob, 'Maybe it isn't locked,' but it was, so she inserted the key. At first it did not respond, so, exasperated, she twisted the knob at the same time that she turned the key and the door unlatched! But it was still closed, so Kristyn, pulled, but the door latched back. 'Well, that was smart!' So, she repeated her actions and heard the level release; she pushed, and the door swung away from her, into the attic.

Chapter Six

Access to the Attic

Inhaling deeply, Kristyn allowed her eyes to adjust to the dim light. The only locale she saw clearly was wherever she shone the light. Without leaving the shelter of the doorway, she slowly directed the beam around the huge attic.

The attic was full! There was so much stored up here! *'How will we ever sort through all of this?'* she asked herself. Some of the items, like the old spinning wheel, were at least a century old. There were baby things; some very old, like a cradle, a rocking horse, an old fashioned baby carriage and other miscellaneous items for a baby or a very young child, that must date from the nineteenth century. Why were these very old things still up here? There must be possessions in here from the first owners; would that be the Whitaker family of whom Franklin spoke?

Then there were the boxes! Boxes upon boxes! There was a rocking chair, almost identical to the one downstairs but not in such good condition. One rocker was broken off at the back, and it was missing an armrest.

Her eyes adjusted more and Kristyn warmed up. When she realized nothing sinister was afoot, she took tentative steps into the attic, stepping first onto the dusty planks of the floor.

'How many years has it been since a living soul ventured into this isolated section of the house?' she thought. 'Probably not since Grandpa made his last excursion up here!' she answered her own question.

Silently she walked about; occasionally a plank squeaked, sounding much louder than it should amid the quiet of the attic, which set her nerves on edge. She was already apprehensive about entering the attic and those little squeaks just frayed her nerves even more. Additional items became clearer as she drew nearer to them. She saw a metal strongbox with a locked lid and a tag hanging from it and written on it was *'Alyssa / Alyce'* underlined in red marker. Kristyn recognized her grandmother's handwriting. *Alyssa* was her mother's name and Alyce was Kristyn's middle name. *Maybe some of Kristyn's things were kept in there also. What else could it be?'* So this box held mementos from her mother's childhood. *'I wonder why this box is locked. If it contains only childhood mementos, the box would not be locked like this. Something else of importance must be in it. Grandma never shared these things with me. Perhaps, they were too painful to go through.'*

Kristyn decided she would browse through them later, after they were taken from the attic. Up here in the heat, with poor lighting, was no place to search through the strongbox.

Standing, she continued her investigation of the attic. Now her eyes fell on the two dark windows of the attic that faced the rear of the house; two more faced the front. They were recessed within the gables that were mounted on the roof outside. There was nothing more unusual than the cobwebs swaying about everywhere. However, just as she turned to search elsewhere, an item materialized out of the murk, just beneath one of the rear windows. It was a rather large trunk! *'What? Where did that come from?'*

It was a wooden trunk, faded brown in color with leather bindings, which wrapped completely around it in two places. It was dusty and presented yet another mystery to Kristyn.

Still scanning the interior she thought, *'Still can't see why the attic would have two locked doors.'* More discarded furniture, chairs, a three-legged table, a bookcase still filled with books, a full-length mirror with a crack traversing from one corner to the other.

'I guess Grandma and Grandpa didn't have anyone to give these things to; after all they left their furniture here as well. I must hire someone to clean out this stuff. Some can go to antique dealers but most will probably end up at the landfill.'

Because Kristyn had been so cold upon entering the attic, she endured the heat that accumulated up there for a while but now it caught up with her and beads of moisture formed on her brow. Wiping them away with her forearm, she whispered, "I need to get out of here. I knew it would be hot and it is!"

As she turned toward the door, a movement caught her eye, 'Not mice!' she thought. But she had spoken too soon, no, what caught her eye was not mice but light, yes, a bright light reflecting on the wall, lighting up the entire back side of the attic and illuminating the two back windows and the trunk! Kristyn stared, while trying to make sense of what she was seeing. Now the light began condensing until it was a sphere hovering over the trunk. At that second, someone called, "Mad'm! Era you up here?"

It was Franklin and he stood at the door. "Era yer alright? Yer's been up here a spell."

Turning towards him, Kristyn responded, "Oh yes, Franklin. It is beginning to heat up and I was on my way down," she replied, walking towards him and the door. Glancing behind, she saw the orb had vanished.

"I got some worried; I mean I am done with the window and yer still up here. Funny thing too, it warmed up a bit after you left and I had to come out of that jacket. One sec, I'm freezing my butt off and not two seconds later, it is as hot as blue blazes! It's crazy, I tell ya. Just crazy!"

Kristyn looked once more behind her, "Just my imagination," she said softly.

"What's that you say, Mad'm?"

"Oh nothing," she replied. "Let's get out of here!"

Allowing Franklin to exit before her, Kristyn pulled the door to, inserted the key and felt as well as heard the clicks as the level fell into place. She tried the knob and was satisfied that it was locked. She repeated her actions out in the hall on the second door. She then replaced the key on the light chain around her neck. She wrapped her fingers around it, a habit she had developed since she first started wearing it. Somehow she gained comfort, possibly from the gesture.

"See here, Mad'm," said Franklin. "Tis good as new!" as he proudly showed off his craftsmanship.

Surveying Franklin's repair job, Kristyn smiled at him, "You did a splendid job, Franklin! How much do I owe you?"

"Oh, Mr. Doyle handles all of thet. I gits paid by the hour, jest look in the mail fer your bill. Well, g'day to you Mad'm and I 'vise you not to go into that attic on hot days like today and you shouldn't go alone anyhow!"

"Franklin, do you have a moment that you can spare me? I'll fix you a glass of iced tea or a soda."

"I've always got me some time for sweet iced tea, Mad'm."

****

Downstairs, Kristyn sought out Nathan and now, in her spacious old fashioned kitchen, Franklin, Nathan and she enjoyed a light lunch of tuna fish sandwiches, on toasted wheat bread and fresh iceberg lettuce. There was a freshly opened bag of potato chips and, of course, the promised iced tea.

"Gotta thank ya, Mad'm," said Franklin between bites. "I shor didn't 'pect lunch."

"I hadn't realized that lunch time had come. Time flew while I was up in the attic," replied Kristyn.

"Mama, you went into the attic and didn't tell me!" exclaimed Nathan, his eyes opening wide when learning of this visit which he so wanted to experience. "When can I go?"

Smiling at her son, Kristyn patted his hand and said, "When Mr. Doyle comes, all of us will check into it."

"Did ya see the light, Mama?"

Kristyn hesitated, *light*. Yes, she had seen a light but was it something supernatural or paranormal, or resembling what Nathan had described? She couldn't honestly answer that question so she only said, "No, Nathan, I saw no light."

"Yer didn't, Mad'm?" injected Franklin.

Two pairs of eyes look pointedly at him and he continued. "Well, I done and seen that whole wall lit up when I went to fetch you. Yer shor yer didn't see it? 'Cuz you were looking right at it."

Now Kristyn felt the attention focused on her; she looked at her son, and before she could deny it, he exclaimed, "You did see it!"

Kristyn released the breath she was holding and nodded, "Yes, I did see some sort of light but there was nothing special about it. It could have been light reflected off of the windshield of a passing car. The sun is so bright; you know, that even reflected light from glass can be blinding."

Nathan stared at her, nodded, and then smiled, "You saw it Mama."

"Okay, Nathan I saw *the light.*" Kristyn then focused her attention on Franklin, "Franklin, why is the house known as the *Whitaker House*?"

Swallowing another bite, followed by a long drink of tea, Franklin cleared his throat and then began his narrative:

'As far as the story was related among the black folks of the area, which weren't generally known by the whites, and he stressed that point, the first owners possessed slaves. Well that was nothing new; after all, this was the South and even North Carolina had their wealthy slave owners.

'Sometime before the War Between the States broke out in 1861, a story arose of a three-headed monster, supposedly kept hidden in the attic of this house by Joseph Whitaker, a great grandson of James Robert Whitaker. But this creature wasn't always kept under wraps and had been spotted by the residents of the time rambling around inside of a high fence at the back of the main house.

The slaves especially reported this and some said that certain slaves were its keepers, providing care for the monster. The rumors continued that, at times, this monster escaped its keepers and would stalk the children of other white families.

There was a name given this monster by the slaves, *Dudu-Mtu!,* which is Swahili, meaning 'insect human or man.' This creature was described in many different ways. They said that it had three heads or three faces. It was reported to have many extra limbs, six or eight or ten were reported. Also, that it did not or could not walk but crawled instead, like an infant.'

"Why haven't I heard about this creature before now?" Kristyn asked when Franklin paused in his narrative.

"Don't know that Mad'm. But this *Dudu-Mtu* is still seen in the swamps 'round these parts."

Continuing with the Legend of the *Dudu-Mtu*, Franklin lowered his voice to little more than a whisper. "They say that on stormy nights that you can hear it cry. It puts you into mind of a baby crying. Those that searched for this baby, weren't never heard from again. And when the moon is full, folks claim to see this critter crawling through the swamp! They say it is trying to find its way home, back to the *Whitaker House.*

"But personally Mad'm, I don't think there is such a critter! Even if there ever was one, it's long dead by now. Mamas tell their little ones about this critter to make them b'have themselves. They say, 'You be mindful now or the *Dudu-Mtu* will crawl out from under yer bed and carry ya off!'"

When Franklin was finished with the urban legend, he looked at mother and son.

"Well, that makes for a good fairy-tale, but there's not a bit of truth to be found," declared Kristyn.

"You sure, Mama?" asked Nathan.

Gathering her five-year-old son close to her, she answered, "Yes, I am sure. Didn't you hear Mr. Franklin say that mothers told that story to make their children be good? That's all it is. Now, lunch is finished and I think you need your afternoon nap! In fact, I think I'll lie down awhile too."

"Thank you Franklin, you have enlightened me quite a bit," said Kristyn, as the three stood up and Franklin shuffled towards the front door.

"Well, I do hope I ain't scared the youngster none. T'weren't my intention, jest got carried away a bit, I s'pect," replied Franklin, now at the front door. He retrieved his jacket and toolbox, which were by the door and made his way to the truck.

Chapter Seven

The Shadowman

Napping peacefully, mother and son were curled up together on the hide-a-bed in the den. The television was on but its volume was low. Both had dosed off watching an old black and white movie. Everything was still and the mantel clock ticked quietly; everything seemed well.

A noise broke through to Kristyn's mind, an incessant beat. She opened her eyes, felt comforted for the moment, for Nathan lay within her arms but she didn't know why she had wakened. Apprehension surged through her. Then it registered! The noise wasn't loud but it was non-stop and coming from upstairs. She sat up, waking Nathan when she removed her arm from under his head.

"What's the matter, Mama?" he asked sleepily.

"Shhhh, listen!" she whispered.

As they sat still and listened, the banging continued. "It sounds like a door closing!" said Kristyn. After a moment, she swung her legs onto the floor, pulled Nathan to his feet, took his hand and then headed for the front entry hall. They stood and listened. "It's coming from upstairs," said Kristyn. "Could there be someone up there," she wondered aloud.

Dare she go check, or call someone? The banging continued in tempo. "No, that's not someone; they wouldn't make a steady noise like that for so long. Maybe a window is opened and the wind is blowing. Yes, that's all it is. I'll just go to the head of the stairs and see."

Quickly Kristyn and Nathan climbed the stairs, no sooner had she reached the top than she felt the cold and Nathan shivered. Coming fully into the corridor, she was horrified to see the attic door opening and closing, repeatedly. It wasn't exactly slamming shut but had still made enough noise to disturb her from her slumber.

"What in the world..." Kristyn exclaimed. Exhaling, her breath formed a cloud and drifted away. Not yet fearful, she walked to the end of the hall, just past the window, which Franklin had repaired only hours before, only to see it broken again, in the same manner as before, The hanging plant had not been replaced however, so it could not have been the cause this time.

Taking note of this, she then turned her attention to the attic door; she reached out her hand to grab the knob but the door slammed shut with an ear-busting bang! Unperturbed, she tried the knob and as she suspected it might be, the attic door was locked! She fingered the key around her neck; it was warm from having been against her body, 'Should I go up there?' she wondered.

As if he read her mind, Nathan exclaimed, "No Mama!"

Looking down at him, Kristyn raised her brows questioningly.

"Not now, Mama. That's not the light!"

"What..." she began.

"That's the dark, Mama."

Where would Nathan conceive of such a notion? Was he mentally in tune with whatever the light was? As this thought penetrated her mind, a movement once again caught her attention. As the pair watched spellbound, around all four edges of the attic door, a smoky mist seeped out and gradually formed an irregular pulsating cloud in front of them. A free-standing shapeless shadow!

Stifling a scream, Kristyn scooped up Nathan and rushed towards the stairwell with him on her hip all the while sensing the shade pursuing her! By now, the unexpected appearance of the shadow, Kristyn's reaction to it and their hurried flight downstairs, had Nathan trembling and near tears. Kristyn ran outside onto the front porch where she sat down on the glider, pulling Nathan next to her. Her breathing was rapid and beads of perspiration formed on her brow. Reaching for her cell phone, she quickly called the one person she felt could help her at this very moment.

****

"Hello, Tyler Doyle speaking," said Tyler into the mouthpiece of the bluetooth headset of his cell. He was on another jobsite and walking about when Kristyn's call came through. At first, he was confused, for he did not recognize Kristyn's high pitched voice but he did recognized panic when he heard it. "Hold on!" he demanded. "Who is this?"

Listening intently to her, he replied, "Don't go back inside. I'm on my way!"

****

Twenty some minutes later, a dust trail was seen as Tyler's black Fork pick-up sped up the dirt path, which led to Kristyn's house. It came to a halt right in front of her porch, having crossed the lawn and the stone path up to her doorsteps.

Kristyn, seeing him, waited for him on the top step as he came up. Suddenly, she was in his arms; an action that startled them both! But she felt safe and secure as she reciprocated the embrace. For a long moment, they just held each other, then Tyler freed one of his arms from around her waist, as he bent down to pick up Nathan who had wrapped his arms around both his mother's and Tyler's legs.

"Thank God, you both are safe! Now, come over here and tell me again exactly what happened," indicating that they should sit.

"It was the shadow man," said Nathan, before Kristyn could begin. "I saw that shadow man in my bedroom one night." Then Nathan cupped his hand over Tyler's ear and whispered, "That's the dark."

Then Kristyn picked up the story and in short, no nonsense sentences, explained what she had seen. "I wasn't scared of anything, not the door opening and closing on its own, nor the fact that the window that Franklin had just fixed this morning was broken again. No, it was the dark mist that came out of all edges of the attic door and then formed a shadow that stood right there, like a, ahh... like a man! It meant to harm us; I felt its anger, its rage! It was at that second that I became frightened. I grabbed Nathan and ran downstairs with him, and I just know that the Shadow Man came after us. I don't know that it did, because I did not take the time to look, I just sensed it. But after I got downstairs, to the receiving hall, I no longer sensed it. I don't think it will come down the stairs."

"That's cause it's scared," said Nathan.

"Nathan, how do you know this?" asked Kristyn.

Nathan shrugged his shoulders, "I don't know."

"So, the window is broken again," stated Tyler.

Both Kristyn and Nathan nodded.

"What were you doing when this began?"

"Napping," was Kristyn's one word reply.

"Did you do anything different today than usual?"

"No," said Kristyn thoughtfully.

"Mama, you went into the attic," volunteered Nathan.

"You did what?" asked Tyler. "You went into the attic?"

"Well, yes... I did. I had forgotten that."

"How...?"

Kristyn looked down at the key round her neck and held it out for Tyler to see, "With this."

"You mean the key unlocked the door at the top of the stairs?"

"Yeah, it did."

"What did you do in there? Did you disturb anything?"

"No, I walked around up there for almost an hour," she explained, "but I only looked. Then Franklin came looking for me, and we both saw the light."

"Yeah, the Light," grinned Nathan.

"Explain things to me," said Tyler.

Kristyn related the morning's events to Tyler, she even told him of the *Dudu-Mtu* of which Franklin had told her.

"I have never heard that story before," said Tyler, "but then, I am not from around here. My folks come from Alabama, which has its own set of urban legends."

"What are we going to do," asked Kristyn.

"First thing is to get Dad here. He will be most interested in this turn of events."

****

Pastor Doyle arrived within minutes of receiving Tyler's call. He explained, as he approached them from the driveway, "I've just left the hospital. Janet and Russell have a new baby boy. He's fine, so just a routine visit with new parents. But I was already on this road, which is why I got here so quickly. I could tell how upset you were, so, just what went on?"

Between Kristyn, Tyler and a word or two from Nathan, Pastor Doyle quickly understood the dire situation in which Kristyn now found herself.

"So, the first thing I need to ask," said Pastor Doyle, "is, 'how safe do you feel here?'"

"I grew up in this house," answered Kristyn, "it is the only home I know. Right now, I feel pretty safe downstairs, but after this afternoon... I don't know how I feel."

"I asked, because we can find a family in the church who will take you and Nathan in for awhile, until..."

"Until what, Dad?" asked Tyler. "We need to deal with this, and soon. You know what I am getting at!"

"But son, the Church does not deal in exorcism, not in the same manner as does the Catholic Church. At best, I can bless the house, and pray with the family."

"Before anything more is said," injected Kristyn when it became apparent that father and son were disagreeing on what should be done now, "I will not leave this house. I will not be forced from my childhood home. I will not allow this... thing... to win so easily."

Both Tyler and Pastor Doyle looked at Kristyn; Tyler, as if he was seeing her for the first time. "Good girl," he grinned at her. "I agree with you, you should remain here and I'll stay also."

"Son! You cannot do that!" exclaimed Pastor Doyle. "You would compromise her reputation! It is not seemly for a man and woman to reside under the same roof without the benefit of marriage! This I forbid!"

"It's okay," soothed Kristyn. "I will not need a guardian. Whatever this thing is, it will remain upstairs! It will not come downstairs. I think there is something in the attic that I might have disturbed or maybe it sees my entrance there as an intrusion on its own and it is attempting to warn me off. I saw an old trunk up there, which I think holds a clue because the light first appeared near it. Let's bring it down to look inside."

"Right," said Tyler. "I'll stay until bedtime, then I'll leave. Just remember, I am only a phone call away. Oh yes, I have made arrangements for the barn to be cleaned out tomorrow, do you still want to go through with that?"

"Yes, I see no need to alter my plans to clean up the place and get it back in shape. Shall we go inside and see if things have settled down?"

"If you plan on remaining here, I guess we better check things out," answered Pastor Doyle.

With Tyler leading, they entered the receiving hall. Tyler stood still for a long moment, then motioned for them to follow. The welcoming coolness of the AC reminded them of how warm it was outside. It was late afternoon, probably the hottest time of day, and to be lounging around outside in the heat was none too comfortable.

"I'll get some iced tea, if you would like to sit down in the living room," offered Kristyn.

"I'll give you a hand," said Tyler, "Dad, you take Nathan in there and we will be back in a bit."

****

In the kitchen, neither of them spoke, Tyler knew where to get ice as Kristyn poured tea into glasses. Both were lost in their own thoughts and Tyler didn't want to frighten Kristyn any more than she already was, with his major concern; that a demonic presence might be residing in her home!

Minutes later, the four sat at the big round coffee table in Kristyn's living room. Tyler and she, with Nathan between them, sat on the Queen Anne sofa while Pastor Doyle sat in her grandfather's favorite armchair. Kristyn had also brought some chips and cookies as a snack.

After a blessing on the food, there were some discussions about Kristyn's sleeping arrangements downstairs and she assured them that they were quite comfortable in the den. "But, I do need to get fresh clothing from upstairs," she continued.

"Tyler and I will take care of that for you," said Pastor Doyle. "I wish there was a way of closing off the exit from the stairwell, but I've seen the layout and it isn't possible. But maybe a spiritual barrier can be established."

"Such as..." said Kristyn.

Before Pastor Doyle could reply, Tyler explains, "He means a Bible. We can lay one on a stair step. If we are dealing with a demon, and it's likely we are, it will avoid the Word of God or Jesus, who is referred to as 'The Word.'"

"Also," added Pastor Doyle, "when you feel its presence, just say God's Holy name out loud, Yahweh, and the demon will flee. Demons must obey when a command is given them in Christ's name."

"You sound so serious about it being a demon," said Kristyn.

"Until we learn different, that is all I am prepared for," replied Pastor Doyle. "I know that some people believe in ghosts or the spirits of the dead but there has never been concrete proof of the departed still roaming the Earth. In Corinthians, we are told that the dead are asleep and know nothing and on that, I must rely. We are dealing with Satan and his demons, the fallen ones, and I think that some evil person once resided in these premises and somehow has invited the evil ones into this place."

Now Kristyn interrupted with, "Franklin, who repaired my window upstairs this morning, told me a tale of a *Dudu-Mtu* which was some sort of monster... with three heads or something to that effect and that its master was a wicked plantation owner, a hundred years or more ago. It's an urban legend in these parts and I don't know any more than that. But could the owner, his name was Whitaker, have instigated this evil presence here?"

"We probably need to look into the property's history," said Tyler. "I'll have my secretary do that for us. She is from this area, plus she used to teach at the schools here. She is retired now, which is why she only works part time for me. Kristyn, you say that you grew up in this house, right?"

Kristyn nodded and waited to learn what he was getting at.

"Was there any sort of activity here when you were a child?"

"None," she replied emphatically. "What do you have in mind?"

"That would set a time line kinda, of when all of this paranormal activity began. I am thinking it is rather new and we need to keep that thought in the back of our minds."

After a long moment of silence while everybody considered this, Tyler then looked at his father and said, "Dad, ready to go check out the upstairs to get what Kristyn needs?"

"I'm going too; you will never find exactly what I need. Pastor Doyle can wait here with Nathan. We'd best try, it'll be dark soon."

****

So Tyler and Kristyn headed upstairs. Upon reaching the landing, they waited and looked around but everything appeared normal. Tyler held up the Bible and said, "I command you in the Name of Christ, the Son of the living God, Yahweh, to retreat!"

They waited another moment or two, all was quiet and the temperature was warm indicating that the entity was not there... for the moment. It did not take Kristyn long to gather together clothing for her and Nathan and within minutes they were once again in the den.

"I'm going to bless the house now. Stand in a circle and hold hands," instructed Pastor Doyle.

With the four of them holding hands and heads bowed, Pastor Doyle said a prayer of protection over the house and another blessing for Kristyn and Nathan. At the phrase, "In Christ's name, we do pray." a screech came from upstairs. It was loud and it was frightening. The shrieking continued and Pastor Doyle shouted, "I command you in the name of the living God, Yahweh, to cease your lamentations!" The shrieking stopped but now the shattering of glass was heard and then the slamming of a door.

Nathan cried, "Mama! I'm scared!"

Kristyn picked up her son and soothed him, "It's alright Nate. It went into the attic." She looked at Tyler, "It reacted to the prayer, didn't it?"

Tyler nodded his head and said, "That's how it appears."

"Yes Kristyn," said Pastor Doyle," that's what has happened. The fallen ones can't bear the name of God as it is spoken in prayer. It gives them pain and sorrow. It is because they can no longer exist in His Holy Presence. It is also why they must obey a command given in His Name. I think you will be safe though; so far, it has only appeared and is trying to frighten you away. The prayer has forced the evil to retreat, and as long as the barrier is there, it will not cross it. Son, after I bless this Bible, set it midway on a step of the stairs."

Tyler took the Bible and laid it halfway up the stairs, after a short prayer and a command, in Christ's name to the entity to stop its activity.

"That is all I can do for now," sighed Pastor Doyle as he scanned the area, as if searching out any hidden entities. For now, the house was at peace and quiet and darkness had fallen outside. As it was late, both father and son decided to leave at about the same time, even though Kristyn had a hard time convincing Tyler that she was fine and promised to call should anything arise.

Tyler lingered a while after his father drove off; still not happy with the fact that he was leaving mother and son in this house alone. The two of them stood on the front porch listening to the serenade of the crickets. Tyler said, "Time to go. You promise to call?"

To which, Kristyn nodded. Nathan waited for her at the screen door.

As Tyler made to step down the first step, he halted, turned and looked at her. He saw the fear in her face that she was trying so hard to hide. Without saying a word, he stepped closer to her and cupped her chin to look him in the eye, "It will work out," he said and placed a light kiss upon her closed lips.

This one act caused Kristyn's heart to beat faster. He said nothing more, for his eyes said it all. He released her and left.

****

During the night when no eyes saw, a light projected down the stairs. The sphere moved through the air, it alighted upon the Bible and the pages turned until it stopped upon a page of scripture; then the orb departed.

Chapter Eight

The Barn

Wednesday dawned bright and sunny with the promise of another sweltering July day. For a moment, Kristyn lay still, as she listened to the hum of the dawn; the farm's one lone rooster crowed again and songbirds repeated his greeting of the day. The sun peeked over the horizon casting long beams towards the earth, painting the sky a bright crimson color.

The den's one large picture window faced west but still it was unmistakable that the sunrise was on them.

Nathan still slept next to her. She knew she needed to get the day moving but so wanted to just lie there, safe and secure. But then she knew that security was not hers just yet.

The events of the previous evening leaped to the front of her mind. First, the ordeal with the shadow-man, as she now thought of the black mass that had confronted her and Nathan. It brought a deep-seated fear, which she had never encountered before. Not even the death of her husband and grandparents, had brought this unfounded dread, for she knew it was the fear of the unknown, of a world that she had never thought existed, of a different time and space. Was not life itself difficult enough, why must she deal now with a paranormal world? A world of shadows and secrets. But a newfound strength rose up in her breast and she thought, '*That is what it wants. It wants us out of this house and I will not be forced from my home so easily.*'

Then another event of the previous evening also invaded her thoughts and the kiss that Tyler had unexpectedly bestowed upon her. '*I think that kiss stunned us both!*' she thought. The tenderness and the caring of that one kiss spoke volumes about the man, as well as herself. She hugged that memory to her, and lingered in the warmth that spread through her body.

But there were things to do and they would not get done with her lying in bed. Later, with a steaming cup of sweetened coffee, with cream, in her hands, she stepped out on to the back porch to view the rising sun for herself. The sky was a rich crimson color with a splattering of lilac and gold. An old saying leaped to her mind, '*Red sky at night, sailor's delight! Red sky in the morning, sailors take warning,*' and she wondered how long before a summer storm would hit.

****

About nine, Tyler arrived with a fleet of trucks, well, if three trucks constituted a fleet. He had brought a good number of his crew with him, including Franklin.

Kristyn's heartbeat quickened as she watched Tyler walk up to her. He smiled, as did she, but they did not touch.

"Good morning; how was your night?" was the first question he asked and Kristyn knew he had spent a restless night worrying over her.

"Uneventful," she replied. "Can I offer you and your crew coffee, tea or I can make a batch of lemonade..."

"Tea or lemonade would be great, whichever is easier for you."

So tea and lemonade along with chips and cookies were soon placed on the round deck table, just inside of the screened-in back porch, out of the sun and away from insects.

Tyler made a quick inspection of the house. The Bible, although still on the step where he had placed it the night before, was now opened and he assumed that a breeze had flipped through the pages. A quick walk through of the entire downstairs revealed nothing out of the ordinary. Satisfied, he gave a brief report to Kristyn. He also informed her of the plans to open the barn and other activities to be carried out during the day.

Tyler assembled a few men, giving them instructions on what tools to bring and what their job most likely would be. His thoughts were mainly to search for any dead animals, because of the stench that Kristyn had reported. Tyler wasn't sure what to expect from a building that had been closed up for nearly ten years. He knew of the reported trespassers some years back and that they had supposedly camped out in the barn but there had never been, to his knowledge, a thorough investigation of this event. The trespassers had left in a big hurry and since no one lived on the property at the time, no more attention was given the matter.

Tyler and his crew gathered at the barn's small entry door, like an army about to attack. Each man carried either a shovel or a rake.

The barn was more a weathered grey than red, with two doors at ground level and a large window/door at the top. The largest of these ground level doors closed off the area where farm equipment, like a tractor would be housed and the smaller door, the one that Kristyn had opened was the main entrance. It was at this door that they now stood.

Tyler took hold of the wooden lever, which acted as a handle; he pressed down and pulled to open the barn door. Stale air with a lingering scent of death greeted them.

"We really need to get this barn opened up and ventilated," said one of the crew. All were agreed on that.

"Maybe so," said Tyler, "but we are going in anyway. Put on your mask, it will help some."

With flashlight in hand, Tyler stepped on to the cinder block that was the only step and entered. He waited for a moment as clouds of dust formed close to the floor from the invasion of fresh air. This part of the barn was used to house tools but not many remained here. The floor was partially covered with old straw from decades before. Breathing through a painter's mask, he still sensed the unmistakable smell of decay. The stench was weak, which meant it was old, and most likely opening all of the barn's doors would eradicate it altogether in a few days.

Now, his eyes focused on the doorless opening that led to the larger open section of the barn. He motioned for his men to follow him inside and told a couple of them to open the larger outside door. So now, they stepped down on to the dirt floor of this part of the barn. As the two men made their way towards the larger door, Tyler aimed his light about. Still housed here was an antique tractor; now a faded red color with rust invading critical areas of the engine and crippled by one deflated tire. Also hanging on the walls was gear for hitching a horse to a plow. Other remedial tools of unknown function were either hung on the wall or propped against it, or lying on the ground.

Tyler detected the stench of decay, stronger here, but could not see any carcasses. Of course, by now, it could well be only skeletal remains. Now, a burst of blinding sunlight filled the barn as the two workers pushed the big door open, while simultaneously, a flock of blackbirds made a mad dash for the opening.

Amid flying feathers and irate birds' calls, they made their exit, as the men ducked to avoid collision with the frightened flock.

Fresh air gushed into the barn, illuminating the dust clouds stirred up by the flight of the birds. Revealed also, were dangling cobwebs and hanging from one large beam was a huge spider's web with its solitary occupant.

Tyler began giving instructions as to what each man should do but he had to admit that except for the odor, there just wasn't much in the barn that needed removing. He made his way back to the house to discuss with Kristyn further repairs to the house itself.

****

"Alright," continued Tyler. He and Kristyn sat at her small kitchen table with lemonade and chips, as he went over the list they had made out together. "Repair again the window up stairs...."

As they continued this evaluation, Franklin knocked on the back screen door, and called, "Mr. Doyle?"

"Come in, Franklin," called Kristyn. Somehow, from the excited tone of his voice, she knew something was amiss.

Franklin shuffled in with cap held in both hands in front of him; he politely nodded in Kristyn's direction and then addressed Tyler, "Mr. Tyler."

"What is it, Franklin? You seem upset, what's wrong?"

"Well sir, not sure I otta say so beforth the Missus."

"She will need to know, no matter, so what..."

"Well sir, we done an' find some graves!"

Their astonishment at this news was revealed by Kristyn's sharp intake of breath and Tyler suddenly standing. "You mean human?" For what else could

Franklin mean for him to make an issue of telling his boss about it.

"Yes sir! Human graves. I ain't right sure how many they is, but they's a few."

With that news, Tyler knocked over his chair as he made a hasty exit. "Call the sheriff," he called back to Kristyn.

****

Upon seeing the skeletons that his men had unearthed, Tyler ordered all of them out of the barn. The graves were shallow ones and lined up along the outside wall of the barn. As far as he could make out, there were three obvious ones. So far, the skeletons had only been partially unearthed, as the men had continued to search for others.

Not wanting to see what was before his eyes, but staring at it anyway, Tyler made out the brown and grey of the bones. The skulls were grotesque with vacant eye sockets and gaping mouths, bony fingers reached from the earth. They lay still in their pits, an unnerving testimony to the violence enacted upon them in life!

The smell of dirt mingled in with the smell of old decay that was even stronger now, infiltrated Tyler's senses. He could bear it no longer and tore away to search out Kristyn. With everything that had already happened at the house, how would she hold up under this? He found her waiting at the backdoor with Nathan clinging to her leg and Franklin at her side with a reassuring hand on her shoulder.

Tyler knew that Franklin had a soft spot for this lady because he had remarked how gracious she was to him, inviting him to eat and talking with him like a friend. Franklin was getting on in years; his wife of forty-seven years had died ten years ago and his four grown sons had scattered about the country.

Franklin lived alone and it was through some friends that Tyler had come to know the old black man and built a strong friendship with him. Franklin was his most reliable and trusted employee.

Tyler escorted them all back into the kitchen where he answered Kristyn's question. He could not give details, for Nathan clung to his mother and as badly as this would affect Kristyn, her young son was even more vulnerable. His answers were brief and non-descriptive.

"Don't you worry none, Mad'm," Franklin sought to assure Kristyn, "Mr. Tyler here, he and I ain't gonna to let nothin' happen. Even if I've gotta sleep on the front porch."

Tyler chuckled at this remark, saying "Hopefully, it won't come to that," and gave Kristyn a quick hug, as a way of reassuring her that he would be nearby. Kristyn responded to his embrace by squeezing him back, then released her grip.

"I've called the sheriff's department and they are sending someone straight away," said Kristyn. "I guess we can wait for them at the front of the house."

Tyler called his father and then they retreated to the living room.

****

The crew awaited the sheriff's arrival on the front porch. The conversations were whispered as if they did not want to speak aloud the horrors they were imagining.

Pastor Doyle pulled into the drive right behind two sheriff's cars, which had arrived with sirens blaring and lights flashing. The scene was one of organized chaos.

Tyler met his father and the officers at the front and, without invitation, they entered the foyer. As Tyler watched a few moments longer, two deputies began to debrief the crew and one deputy, accompanied by two of the crew, made their way towards the back yard.

****

After the formalities and introduction, Sheriff Brown started right away talking with Tyler, who had volunteered that it was his crew who had made this gruesome discovery.

"What time of day did you first become aware of the human remains, Mr. Doyle?" asked the sheriff.

Before Tyler could answer, he felt an arm go around his arm and looked down to see Kristyn. It felt good to know she was leaning on him, even though they barely knew each other. "Franklin is with Nathan," she explained. "He said Nathan didn't need to hear this and of course he doesn't, but I felt I did."

"And you are the granddaughter of the Morrison's?"

"Kristyn nodded.

"I'm Sheriff Brown, Miss...."

"Mrs. Spencer. But please I prefer Kristyn."

"Certainly. I am the one who ran off the trespassers from the property some years back. I'm sorry, but we didn't know how to get in touch with you and I didn't put any significance to it at the time, and since they were gone, so... anyway, I wish I had investigated a little further. As far as I could tell at the time, the house hadn't been broken into, and I saw no other damage. So, I closed the book on the case."

"I understand, Sheriff," Kristyn responded. "We still don't know if the trespassers are connected with the graves in the barn.

"No, we don't but all possibilities will be investigated."

"Mr. Doyle, what else can you tell me?"

"There's not much more than what you know
already. I ordered my men out of the barn when we
realized that it was possibly a crime scene. Nothing
else was touched and we waited for you in front."

"That was wise," said the Sheriff. "I'm going out
there now for a quick look but I'll have my deputies
guard the crime scene around the clock while the crime
lab does their investigation. One last question, have
there been any strangers around or maybe activities
that you can't explain?"

At that question, Kristyn and Tyler both looked at
each other and Tyler replied, "What do you mean,
exactly?"

"Well, obviously there haven't been or you would
know instantly if there were."

"I've only been back in the house a little over a
week," added Kristyn, "and the only people that have
been here are ones I hired to help clean the yard and
the house."

"I'll need the names of those, just in case they
might have seen something that you would not have."

"They were the Efficient Maids and Jordan Landscapers."

The sheriff wrote this down on a pad that he
removed from his shirt pocket, "Well, I thank you both
for your cooperation. I have Mrs. Spencer's cell
number, and I need yours also, Mr. Doyle. My
department will stay in touch should we need any
further information. Now, I am going to look in the
barn."

"Is it alright if I go with you?" asked Tyler.

"I don't see why not... this time, but after the crime
lab begin their analysis, no one will be allowed beyond
the *CSI* tape."

****

Pastor Doyle sought to comfort Kristyn, who sat on the Queen Anne sofa with Nathan huddled close to her side.

"I think keeping this from Nathan was wise. Franklin is a great fellow; he visited our church a few times but I don't think he attends any church regularly," he spoke softly.

"I see. I think we need a glass of tea," said Kristyn. "Tyler's crew must be thirsty standing around outside."

Pastor Doyle said, "Do you mind if I have a look around downstairs while you get that?"

"Of course not. What are you searching for?"

"I'm not sure; just want to see what's what. That's all."

Some minutes later, Pastor Doyle returned and he had the Bible that had lain on the stairs all night and most of the day, in his hand. He held the Bible open and carried it in both hands. Kristyn gave him a puzzled look on seeing this way of carrying it.

"It's curious," Pastor Doyle began. "Did anyone disturb this, I mean open it or anything of the kind?"

Shaking her head negatively, Kristyn replied, "No; why?"

"Well, when Tyler left it on the stairs, it was closed. But see, I have found it open. Now, I kinda take these things as a *sign*... and was surprised that it was open to the book of Ecclesiastes, the first page of the book. What is notable to me, is the first chapter, verse eleven, one, one, one.

"It reads:

'There is no remembrance of former things; neither shall there be any remembrance of things that are to come with those that shall come after.'

"Of course, there are several verses on these pages but the Book of Ecclesiastes is a book not known for joy. Most who read it, come away feeling a little depressed. But this one verse just jumped out at me, it drew my eye as if a light had focused on it."

After a thoughtful moment, Kristyn looked Pastor Doyle in the face, and said softly, "It wants to be remembered!"

Closing the Bible, Pastor Doyle nodded an affirmative.

Chapter Nine

The Orb

The rest of the day became a beehive of activity. Kristyn found herself on the outside looking in. When Franklin left with the rest of Tyler's crew, Kristyn kept Nathan close and entertained him with coloring books, and his favorite toys but even so, he would cease his activity and sort of stare into space, then resume his play.

Once, when he looked up with a preoccupied expression, Kristyn asked, "A penny for your thoughts, Nate."

"I am thinking about the Light, Mama."

"Why?" Kristyn asked, sitting down on the floor next to him.

"The Light is happy and the Light is sad."

Kristyn contemplated his words for a moment and thought she understood what he meant. The verse in the Bible lent character to the Light, as if it was a conscious entity. And, somehow, this 'entity' was in sync with Nathan. Not having any wisdom for him, not any he would understand, she smiled gently at him, kissed his brow and continued her watch. From the kitchen she could easily see the men working inside of the barn.

Additional official vehicles arrived and soon yellow plastic ribbon was wrapped completely around the barn as lawmen in uniforms, men in business suits and men in light blue workers' uniforms mingled in and out of the barn. Then came a dog, a bloodhound, "Why did they bring in the dog?" she asked Tyler, when he came into the house to check on her.

"It's a cadaver hound," he explained. "They are specially trained to search for human remains. They won't send an alarm for any other dead animals, only human."

"Have they found any more than the three?"

Looking at her, Tyler sighed, "Yeah, how many is unsure. I am only getting bits and pieces from overheard conversation. Dad has a church service tonight, the usual Wednesday night assembly, so he has left and Mom is with a church member who is in the hospital but both said to tell you, that as soon as they can, they will come to the house.

"Tonight, Dad will let the congregation know what's going on and pray on it. So, expect visits and calls from them, they will want to know how to help. Don't be hesitant about asking for help. That is what we do as a church family." Tyler paused, then continued, "I told him that I was staying over tonight..."

Kristyn quietly laughed at that statement, remembering the Pastor's objection when Tyler suggested this before, "He vetoed the idea again, didn't he?"

"Well, no he didn't. You must remember that the deputies will be on guard day and night to keep the crime scene from being compromised by the inquisitive. So, I think we will be well chaperoned. Besides, I want to stay upstairs tonight. I want to see what is what. Also, I have asked for one of my employees to come and stay here at the house tonight, but only one without family. He should be back by dark."

"That's good," she agreed. "But I just don't know about the upstairs; what with the shadow mist I saw yesterday. How dangerous is it?" she added, with anxiety mounting in her voice. The shadow, she perceived it as malevolent.

"Well, I'll use the tactics I used last night. You know, using the power of the Holy Spirit to command the entity in Christ's name and I'll keep the Bible closed. It is a material representation of Christ, the Word. If I can experience what you and Nathan did, then I'll have a better understanding of the situation. Maybe this entity will make contact..."

"Entities..." corrected Kristyn. "There are more than one, the Light and the Dark, according to Nathan."

"Yeah," Tyler sighed. "Maybe tomorrow we can go back into the attic, since you were able to get the key to work."

At that moment, a light tap was heard at the kitchen door. They looked up to see Franklin standing there. "'Cuse me, Mr. Doyle."

"Franklin, are you staying the night?" asked Tyler.

"I is that, sir. Most of de other fellows done got plans or family and I ain't got none. 'Sides the Misses and I is friends, and friends always helps ones another."

"Thank you, Franklin," Kristyn smiled at him. "I'm glad you are staying. Nathan really likes you, and well, so do I."

"Thanks yer, Mad'm."

It was decided that Franklin would take the sofa in the living room. Somehow, Kristyn felt a sense of security at the prospect of both men staying overnight and knowing the deputies would be outside.

****

The sun setting brought night to the farm. Also arriving was the thunderstorm that the dawn had promised. The wind picked up and the first clap of thunder was heard in the distance. It didn't take long for the rains to follow. In a way, a summer storm was welcome; it would clear the air of dust and bring down the temperatures. With the onset of the storm, everyone left, except for a lone sheriff's car, with two deputies remaining to watch over the crime scene.

Kristyn stood with Tyler on the front porch, after settling Nathan down in the den with Franklin for company, to watch a little TV before bedtime. As is usual with these storms, this one moved away as quickly as it had come. Now the evening was cooler and the grass stood straight following the drink of water. Rivulets of water ran down the driveway, towards the drainage ditch at the main road. The night sounds of crickets and a lone bullfrog penetrated the otherwise quietness. They did not speak, just watched as the moon took her place in a velvet sky. The retreating storm clouds marched across her face as the night exchanged places with the day.

Then breaking the silence with the question that everyone was asking, Kristyn said, "Were those people murdered?"

Tyler looked down at her, "That's the general consensus. I heard the term, *serial killer* or killers, from the sheriff. Also, the sheriff remembered the trespassers from a few years ago, and a dating of the human remains will confirm or disprove whether it happened at about that time. I can only imagine what actually happened here and it is atrocious."

Kristyn sighed, laid her head against Tyler's upper arm and said, "I do not want to know. My beloved childhood home, the only place on this Earth where I felt loved and secure has now been turned into a macabre site of death. After all this, I might sell."

Turning to face her, Tyler gently took her by her upper arms, "I understand how you are feeling. How else would you feel? But this will pass. You will find love and joy and security again. Maybe not here but somewhere, with someone who cares deeply for you and for Nathan."

For a long moment, they looked into each other's eyes. Kristyn's heart began to race and she willed it to remain calm, but it did not heed her will, just its own. The meaning in Tyler's words was all too clear. He was saying it without using words, because their involvement was too new, but he was telling her he cared intensely for her, in more ways than one.

Gathering her close so that their bodies pressed together, he tilted her face up to his, and slowly sought her lips in a burning and passionate kiss that started Kristyn's blood racing. They were lost in this fiery embrace and time and movement stood still. When he released her, she lost her balance after being supported totally by him, and he chuckled, "Easy there. Can't have you falling."

To which she replied, "I think I already have."

A grin spread across his face, "Me too."

****

Later, Tyler slept in the Master Bedroom, for it had not been used since Kristyn had moved in. It took a few hours after he had lain down on the old fashion four-poster bed to drift off but now he slept soundly.

Outside, the two deputies kept watch while sitting in their cruiser. But before long, their heads nodded and they too dozed.

Kristyn and Nathan slept soundly too, probably for the first time in days. She had shut the door of the den, which led into the foyer within feet of the stairs.

Franklin, being an older man, had more difficulty going to sleep or staying asleep for more than an hour or two at a time. He had left the door of the living room open and the stairs were across the foyer from him. The downstairs bathroom was beneath the stairs and he found himself using its facilities several times during the night, which was the norm for him.

Thus, Franklin was the only one awake, and returning to the living room saw a glow radiating from the top of the stairs. Franklin was barefoot and dressed in a white T-shirt and his work pants, not wanting to disrobe completely in someone else's home. Thinking that maybe Tyler was up, he walked to the base of the stairs and looked up and called, "Mr. Tyler, era that you up thar?"

There was no response. Franklin then took a couple of tentative steps up the stairs and saw the light, which was a glow spreading across the wall. It wavered, acting like a flickering candle flame and this intrigued Franklin even more and, without hesitation, he headed up the stairs.

As he neared the top, he was bathed in the pinkish glow of the light. Reaching the landing, he saw the Bible, laid there earlier by Tyler, but it was still closed. He then looked down the hall to his left, which was in the direction of the two smaller bedrooms, the bathroom and the attic. Tyler was in the Master Bedroom, to his right.

Now the light began condensing until it was a hovering orb, about the size of a basketball. It emitted a soft pink, flickering glow. It appeared crystalline and was separating into several spheres, then rejoining again. Franklin stood frozen as he watched this orb and it watched him. Then a voice whispered, seemingly within his mind, "Come for us."

"What dat you say?' Franklin whispered back.

The orb grew brighter then began to shrink; it became as small as a pinhead, and now lay on the floor, a flattened version of its former self. It slid along the floor until reaching the attic; it then slid beneath the attic door.

Now Franklin reacted and hurried to the Master Bedroom, where he walked in because the door was slightly ajar. He heard the deep rhythmic snores from Tyler. The room was dark, he called softy, "Mr. Tyler!"

There was no immediate response, so Franklin called him several more times. Tyler jerked to a sitting position, coming fully awake but confused. It took a moment for Tyler to remember where he was, and then he responded with, "Who's there?"

"It's me, Mr. Tyler," Franklin replied.

"Franklin," said Tyler, swinging his legs over the side of the bed. He too was still dressed in his jeans but no shirt. "What's wrong? Kristyn? Nathan?"

"It's the Light, Mr. Tyler. It's in de hall. And it just went into de attic."

The remnants of sleep vanished; Tyler reached over and turned on the bedside lamp. "The attic?" Grabbing his shirt, and slipping his stocking feet into his unlaced sneakers, Tyler hurried out into the hall and looked towards the attic door. But everything was dark. Too excited now to just return to bed, he all but ran to the attic and grabbed the doorknob, but of course, the door was locked. "Kristyn has the key," he mumbled. Well, he would not awake her tonight; he turned and looked at Franklin, "I guess this will have to wait. Come on, I'm going back down stairs, I'm too wide awake to lie back down."

****

Kristyn awoke to mumbling sounds. She sat up, startled, for the sounds were human voices coming from another section of the house. Then she remembered that she had houseguests and that they were probably already up and active. The drapes were drawn over the window in the den and the foyer door was closed, so it was still quite dark. The tick-tock of the mantel clock was the only other sound she heard which meant that it was not yet daylight, for the rooster had not made his usual proclamation of the dawn.

What was the time? It was way too dark to see the hands of the mantel clock, so why were Tyler and Franklin up? Tyler's name in her thoughts brought back the memories of their passionate kiss the night before. It had been an eternity since her husband had last made love to her and, since his death, she had not entered into a relationship even though the offers had been there.

No, life was painful and she had built a wall around her damaged heart; she was cool and distant from any male who approached her. Her facade said, "Stay away," and after a few attempts by suitors, they did. So why now did she give in to this new emotion? What had lowered her defenses? Was it Tyler's rugged good looks? She remembered how she had first reacted on seeing him, an action which shocked her, one for which she was unprepared. And even though her logical mind sent warnings, she failed to heed them. He was tall, attractive and gave off a strong male musk that had seeped through logic and caught her unaware. Had she healed? She felt the wall around her heart crumble; was she ready to allow herself to love again, to allow herself another chance at happiness?

The memory of his strong arms around her, holding her close, had instilled in her a burning, a yearning, a fire that was stoked and smoldered even now, a fire rekindled. His kiss had awakened another world into which she was falling and she almost had, when he released her from the embrace.

These thoughts of passion were a bit too much to contend with and she thrust them to the back of her mind. Then, swinging her legs over the edge of the bed, being careful not to awaken Nathan, she threw on her housecoat and tiptoed to the door. She eased it open and stepped into the foyer. Light came from both the living room and the bathroom and was enough to guide her. Hearing murmurs from the living room, she headed in that direction.

"Well, good morning gentlemen," she greeted them upon entering, for they were engrossed in their discussions and were unaware that she had joined them.

Now, on hearing her, both men looked in her direction, "Good morning yourself," said Tyler, standing and approaching her.

Kristyn's heart betrayed her with a skipped beat but she managed to hide, or at least she hoped she hid, her reaction to his presence.

"Did we wake you?" he asked as he took her hand, which gave her goose bumps, leading her further into the living room where he indicated for her to sit on the Queen Anne sofa.

"Yes, you did, but it's okay," she replied sitting down.

"Morning, Mad'm" Franklin now repeated his greeting.

"Morning Franklin. I hope this sofa was comfortable."

"Yes Mad'm, it serve de deed," he smiled showing his golden tooth in the front.

Returning his smile, she then looked at Tyler, "What's going on? Why are you two up at four am?"

At first neither answered, but looked at each other as to whether or not they should tell her what had just transpired upstairs. They took way too long to answer so that Kristyn became alarmed, "What is it? There's something up, so you might as well spill the beans!"

Franklin, who was in the armchair, looked at Tyler, who nodded that he should inform Kristyn of recent events. "Well, Mad'm, I done and seen that light again."

"You have? Where? Down here?"

"No Mad'm, I seen it up de stairs. I checked it out and what I see then was a bit scary. It was a shiny floating ball up there in de hall. It then shrunk and 'came no bigger than a straight pin head and then slid underneath de attic door."

"That's when he woke me," jumped in Tyler, "I attempted to go into the attic but it's still locked and you have the key. I was too wide awake after that to go back to sleep, so Franklin and I have been comparing notes. I still have not seen anything, only you three have. As soon as it's good and light, we will go into the attic."

"That sounds like a splendid idea," said Kristyn, "I want to take a couple of things down from there, a metal box that holds items that belonged to my mother and a trunk that I think has a link with the light."

"Good," returned Tyler. "You just let me know when you think it would be a good time."

"The very early morning hours would be best because of the heat," she said.

"Beat the heat," Franklin chimed in.

Kristyn smiled, and replied, "That's the idea," then stood. "Since we're up already, how about some coffee?"

"Coffee, you bet. I'll give you a hand," said Tyler, following her out into the kitchen. "Just tell me where and what and I'm at your bidding." he said, with a big grin.

Returning his smile, Kristyn gave general directions on where to find cups, sugar and cream as she prepared the coffee maker.

Fifteen minutes later, Tyler called Franklin into the kitchen for coffee. It didn't take long before the conversation turned to the human remains found in the barn.

"To me," said Tyler setting down his coffee mug and looking first at Kristyn and then at Franklin, "and from what I have overheard, this is the work of a serial killer if not killers! I overheard something about missing persons and some unsolved murders around about in the last several years. After we check out the attic, I will do some research on the net and see what I can come up with. We aren't going to get much out of the sheriff at this point but I expect that the media will soon get wind of this and we will have another set of problems."

At that statement, Kristyn looked at Tyler with an expression of surprise, "Yes! You are right! That notion hadn't crossed my mind. There's just too much going on - and now to have to deal with the media! You know how pushy these newspeople can be. I've seen it enough on television."

"Well, I'll stay here with you, if that'll ease your mind some," promised Tyler.

"Me too, Mad'm," said Franklin.

Kristyn smiled.

Chapter Ten

The Trunk

It wasn't long before they heard the crow of the rooster, and the first rays of the sun peeked over the horizon. Daylight had arrived and so did the forensic lab van, more sheriff and SBI vehicles, all seemingly arriving simultaneously. It was going to be a busy and, probably a depressing, day.

Nathan wandered into the kitchen still in his pajamas, sleepily rubbing his eye with one small fist, he said, "Mama, what's going on? There's a bunch of cars and trucks outside."

Nathan had not been told what was found in the barn and Kristyn so wanted to protect him from that horror. "Guess what, Nate?" she replied as she took him by the hand and led him to the table. "Those nice people are going to clean out the barn for us. What do you think about that?"

"I like that, Mama. Are they going to take away that stinky smell?"

"That they are, Nate that they are."

****

After arranging with Franklin to entertain Nathan and to protect him from the events outside, Kristyn and Tyler headed upstairs.

"It looks so peaceful and normal up here," said Kristyn. "But looks can be deceiving as they say. Well, let's get to it. Here," and she handed the key, still on the chain, to Tyler, "you do the honors."

Tyler took the key without comment; silently they approached their target, the attic door. "Ready," Tyler asked.

Kristyn nodded her reply. Tyler inserted the key and the door swung inward to reveal the stairs. He turned on the flashlight and took the lead upwards. Kristyn followed. Now the second door, same results as the door swung inwards and the murkiness of the attic was revealed.

It was about an hour after sunrise but dark shadows still obscured much of the attic's contents. For a full minute, Tyler directed his light around the attic. Neither spoke as they viewed this huge expanse of space, which was the attic. Kristyn, of course, knew what to expect but even so, more items of interest appeared.

"There's a lot up here," Kristyn said.

"Yeah, I can see that," agreed Tyler, as he took his first steps into the attic. "What's your plan for this?" he asked as he swept his hand in a circular motion to take in the entire contents of the attic.

"I've not really decided," Kristyn replied, "but I do want to take two things down from here so I can go through them. The box and the trunk."

"Well, let's see, where is that box?" asked Tyler and Kristyn led him to it.

It took Kristyn some minutes to locate the strong box, what with the size of the attic and recalling that she had only been up there once. It just happened to be centrally located so that it became lost among the other boxes but at last, they located it. Squatting down next to it, Tyler inspected the lock, "I wonder," he said. He took the skeleton key and inserted it into the keyhole, and the lock opened!

"Good gracious!" gasped Kristyn.

"Another reason for hiding the skeleton key so well," said Tyler. Tyler lifted up the hinged lid, to reveal papers in folders, which were expected, and a scrapbook. Also, there were different mementos, such as a diary and faded dried flowers, a couple of tins and a number of other items that you might expect to find in a keepsake box but not necessarily in a locked strong box!

"Let's get this near the door, so we can find it later," said Tyler, lifting the box on to his shoulder and leaving Kristyn standing there. Seconds later, he rejoined her and without speaking, began exploring for himself the attic's contents.

As with Kristyn a few days before, Tyler took in what appeared to be a hundred years or more of items. "All this couldn't belong to just your grandparents. There's several families' belongings here."

"I don't know for certain, but I do know that Grandma's parents and grandparents lived here too, since from the Civil War era. I guess they just didn't want to throw out the other things. I don't know. But I do know it must be sorted through and some of it probably needs to be destroyed. I mean old papers and cardboard boxes can be fire hazards."

"That's true," agreed Tyler. "After things have calmed down in the barn, I'll have my crew set about removing all of this. This attic is big enough and almost finished like the rooms so if you wanted, it could be remodeled and added living space constructed."

"I doubt I'll do that and I am considering selling," Kristyn answered with a shake of her head.

"Yeah. What with the findings in the barn and all. For a sec that had slipped my mind. Let's see, the trunk?"

"It was under one of the rear windows," Kristyn replied, pointing in that direction.

They each began walking towards the rear of the house, when Kristyn gasped and grabbed Tyler's hand. She didn't have to say anything else, for, as they watched, an orb materialized above the trunk. Its pinkish glow pulsated and it separated into three spheres and then joined again. A faint rhythmic sound, like several beating hearts came from the light. The orb didn't move but hovered in place over the trunk.

Frozen in their tracks, Tyler uttered a low curse, "Well, I'll be damned."

Kristyn glanced at him, shocked. After all, he was a preacher's son and swearing just was not done, but he had, and she thought it best to pretend she had not noticed.

"Did you see that? It almost separated into more than one. What's up with that?"

"I've no idea. This is the first time I have ever seen anything like this. What to make of it? Paranormal? That's for sure. Ghosts? Demon? Or angel? Dad should see it. It just might change his mind on some things."

The orb remained in place, the heartbeats grew louder and then the orb began bobbing slowly over the trunk, almost touching it.

"Do you want us to see what is in the trunk?" asked Kristyn, not knowing why she spoke to it, but deep down she felt a connection and that this orb was not the malevolent entity that the grey mist-like shadow was.

"Come for us," was plainly heard by Kristyn and she roughly grabbed Tyler's arm. "Did you hear that?"

Looking down at her, the expression he wore plainly said that he had, even as he nodded. Tyler usually was never lost for words, but words failed him now.

"Is it communicating with us?"

"Yes, I would say so!" Tyler answered, finally finding his voice. "Can we look in the trunk?"

This time, the orb brightened. "I'd take that as a 'yes'," whispered Kristyn.

As they walked towards the trunk, the orb ascended higher and began dispersing, becoming a white light covering the back wall, where it faded into the murkiness.

The trunk was dusty and when Tyler went to lift the lid, he was unable to do so. It was locked. Then he saw the keyhole. "It's locked," he said. "I wonder...." so he took the attic key and inserted it into the keyhole and the latch sprung up, releasing the lid. "Well, I'll be..."

"I wonder if Grandpa knew of this?" said Kristyn. "He must have. The desk was one piece of furniture that was his; he told me he had inherited it from his grandfather. But if the key fits the attic door and now this trunk, then Grandma knew of it. So, which one hid the key?"

"I think perhaps both knew and since you said it was your grandfather that came into the attic, he must have had possession of the key. Why they would hide it like that is another puzzle."

For a long moment, neither said anything but just looked each in the eye as the possibilities sank in.

"Are you ready for this," Tyler asked now.

Kristyn nodded. Tyler lifted the lid. The first thing they saw was rags, old and brown from age. Both Tyler and Kristyn began removing them, slowly and carefully, lest there be something important wrapped in them, which proved to be the case. One ragged bundle when unwrapped did contain a book, very old and tied shut with twine. Tyler laid it to one side. Another bundle contained a scrapbook, also tied up. This too they laid to one side. Crammed in the bottom were newspapers and a couple of magazines. Another cigar box held tickets for long ago shows, pieces of ribbon and some coins, very old and probably rare. Tyler dug through them but turned up nothing more.

"Let's see if I can lift it by myself," and so saying, he grasped the trunk by the two handles on each side and lifted it a few inches. "It's heavy enough, but I think I can get it to the door for now."

"Here, let me to help," said Kristyn and between the two of them, they carried the trunk and its contents to the attic door. It took two trips, but they got both containers out into the hall and downstairs into the dining room.

****

Forensic technicians invaded the barn early in the morning. The coroner had come and gone and it was assumed that the remains would be transported to the state lab for expert analysis.

The family stayed inside and mid-morning, Pastor Doyle and his wife arrived. Tyler and Kristyn, on hearing their car drive up, went outside to greet them.

Mrs. Doyle was a lady in her late fifties; her hair was a deep dark brown with a white streak just to the left of center. She wore it pulled back in a bun. Her eyes were velvet cobalt, the same as her son. She was a tall slender woman, but shorter than her son and about the same height as her husband.

'So, that's where he gets his height and eyes,' thought Kristyn to herself.

Mrs. Doyle had in her hands a small white furry bundle, a kitten. Upon greeting Kristyn, she explained, "Tyler told me that your son wanted a pet. He asked if I knew of anyone in the church who might have a litter of kittens or puppies. I only found a litter of kittens. I hope you don't mind, but I took the liberty of choosing one for him. What with all the fuss going on around his home, he might need this for companionship."

"Oh, you just don't know the good you have done. Nate is going to be thrilled. Please, come in. I'll make a fresh pot of coffee."

They all went into the den with Nathan and Franklin. "Nate, come see," said Kristyn as they waited at the door. Kristyn didn't need to tell Nathan. His young eyes were quick and he saw the kitten right away, helped by its mewing and clamoring to get down.

"Mama, is it for me?" he asked with wide-eyed wonder.

Mrs. Doyle responded, "It certainly is. Hello Nathan." As she spoke, Nathan reached to take the kitten from her and she gently released it into his small hands.

Looking at Mrs. Doyle, Nathan said, "I prayed to God for a kitten. Mama said He would get me one. Are you one of His angels?"

Mrs. Doyle smiled and kneeled, "Yes, sometimes I act for the Lord as an angel when His other angels are busy. Do you like the kitten, Nathan?"

"Oh boy, do I," he said as he stroked the kitten's fur and cuddled it close.

"What's his name going to be?" Mrs. Doyle said to him then.

"I have a great name," Nathan replied. "I'm naming him Casper. That's cause he's white, you know like Casper the friendly ghost."

"I see, I think it is a perfect name for him. And, we checked, it is *a him*, a tom cat."

"Nathan, go stay with Franklin, while we talk," said Tyler.

"Okay, I know what y'all talking 'bout," he surprised them with that remark. Had their attempt at concealing the proceedings been successful?

The adults looked at each other and, not really knowing how to reply, Kristyn said, "Never you mind, Nathan, at what we are discussing. You don't need to know everything."

"I seen those bones out there in the barn. I seen 'em when they bring 'em out and put 'em in that van."

"Well, you just take your mind off all of that. Take Casper and get to know him," said Tyler.

So Franklin volunteered to stay with Nathan in the den. Franklin obviously had grown fond of the child and had taken to telling him stories and playing games.

****

Later, out of earshot of Nathan, which was not easy these days, Kristyn spoke, "How did Nathan happen to see that? They should have placed the remains in body bags. How did he see bones?"

"I know the time he is talking about," answered Tyler. "They brought the remains out into the sunlight to examine them better. The lighting in the barn isn't the best even with aid. There must have been something unusual and they needed a better look. But my question is, where was he at the time? The kitchen? It's the only room that opens directly into the back yard."

"It must have been, probably when I wasn't paying close enough attention. After all, I hadn't told him not to go into the kitchen or to look outside. Oh well, just calls for a closer watch on him. But it's bad," said Kristyn with a sigh. "I'll get the coffee. Want to help?"

"Sure," Tyler answered.

Alone in the kitchen, Tyler gently took Kristyn's upper arm, as she went to make the coffee. "Hold up a second," he said, as he turned her to face him. "I know all of this is weighing heavily on your mind and that Nathan is being exposed to undesirable scenes, and I wish I could protect the both of you from those horrors. This is what I want you to know. That I am here for you both; you don't have to face this on your own. Mom, Dad, and the entire congregation of the Church are supporting you. If we can't see what you need, just ask."

Kristyn sighed and felt the tears form in her eyes; her chest became heavy with emotion and all she could do as she felt the tears roll down her cheeks was nod. Tyler drew her to him, close against his broad chest and she laid her head against him and heard his strong heartbeat. She wrapped her arms about his waist and closed her eyes as she took in the strong scent of his aftershave and his own masculine musk.

Tyler rested his chin upon her dark blond hair, took in her fragrance and felt the warmth and the softness of her slim body in his arms. "I could stay this way forever," he whispered into her hair. Kristyn inhaled and Tyler felt the rise and fall of her breast against him, stirring him, he pushed her gently from him and as he looked into her eyes, he found himself sinking into their depths and, as if it was written, he brought his mouth down on hers and their bodies and souls merged.

"Ehh, excuse me," a female voice came from the doorway.

Tyler looked up, without releasing Kristyn, although she attempted to pull away. "Hey, Mom," he greeted his mother. He was not ashamed of his feelings for Kristyn and he was not hiding it. Although the open showing of sexual affection was not for the public eye, this innocent embrace was something of which he was proud.

"I'm sorry son, but I was wondering if you and Kristyn needed help. But I'll return to the living room," she said with a knowing smile, a smile that said she approved.

By now, Kristyn had regained her composure and spoke, "That's okay, yes, please, your help is appreciated."

****

Now, in the dining room, with the trunk and the strongbox both sitting on a chair, everyone gathered around the table for coffee and coffee cake.

"It could well be that the trespassers of a few years ago are responsible for these deaths," this from Pastor Doyle as he took a sip from his cup. "Has anyone learned any more at all about this?"

"No, you know how hush-hush information is, about ongoing investigations. I've asked Bernice to research the history for me and I hope to be hearing from her soon," said Tyler. "But first I want to look at this journal and scrapbook we found in the trunk."

Tyler took first the scrapbook and cut loose the twine holding it shut. As expected, there were photographs here, very old photographs. The first were pictures of Joseph and Naomi Whitaker, owners of the Whitaker House at the time, before and during the Civil War. These pictures had been inserted into small brackets on all four corners of the photograph and below the photographs were handwritten captions, naming whoever was in the photograph and the month and year.

Photography was still in its infancy at this stage in history, although the ability had been around for a century or more. It was just impractical due to the size of equipment and chemicals needed. But in the 1850's, cameras were more portable and some men traveled about the country making their livelihood from photographing clients who were often just the rich. Any photographs that these men took on their own, of the era, were for their own private collections. These often ended up in museums whenever found.

A wealthy family would engage these early photographers and have many family pictures taken. Evidently, this was the case with this family album. Flipping through its stiff and yellow pages brought the expected family shots. There were pictures of the farm, showing acres of cotton and field hands working there. At the main house, there were many photos of the household slaves. Women of color dressed in the costume of the day, wearing kerchiefs over their heads and big white aprons. Small children of color, some almost naked were captured in motion as they ran to hide from the camera's eye.

There was even a group photograph of the household slaves, posed in front of the main house; there were eleven people in this shot. Then there was another photograph of the field workers, but they were not posed. They sat on barrels, on rocks or tree stumps around a large cooking fire as they ate their noontime meal. None seemed aware of the photographer as he took this photo. These men looked haggard, weary, dirty, and were dressed in rags. Not a smile was seen on their faces. This told a sad story, one of enslavement and of despondency.

The dates written below these photographs dated between June of 1851 and October of 1851, which would indicate that the photographer spent the summer and fall at the plantation taking these pictures.

"I don't see anything unusual in this album; these are great pictures of a bygone era and probably have historical value but that's about all," elaborated Kristyn. Just then another page was turned, then this one photo jumped out at them and proved to be one of several.

As all gazed upon this next photograph, Kristyn said, "What am I looking at? Is this some sort of Halloween mask or costume?"

Tyler carefully removed this one picture from its holder; he stared at it a long time, then said, "Unless this is an accidental double exposure, it looks like a head with three faces, almost."

It took a long while studying the photograph to know what they were seeing. It was a baby, or babies? Several other photos showed more of the baby, it was nude, female, and had one head but three faces. They were complete faces, a face centered on the head, and the other two in profile on the left and right sides of the head. All three faces looked completely normal, if you looked at each face alone; it was as though you were seeing a pretty and normal child.

A study of the torso revealed three, as though placed back to back and joined. Each torso faced the same direction as its corresponding face. But there were only four arms and four legs! At the junction of the legs were the genitals, three and female.

No one spoke, as more photographs of this child were shown, all were infants, taken that same summer. In the pictures, the child's eyes were opened and the baby looked alive. But there were no more pictures of the child any older than newborn.

Mrs. Doyle had been silent but now offered her opinion, "This is a conjoined set of triplets. And it probably died soon after birth and most likely its poor mother did as well."

"De *Dudu-Mtu*," said a voice and everyone looked up to see that Franklin, holding Nathan's hand, was standing over them and that they had both seen the pictures!

Chapter Eleven

History of House

A loud knocking on the front door made everyone at the table flinch. 'Who on earth could that be?" exclaimed Kristyn.

"I'll check," replied Tyler, already heading for the front door. Opening the door, Tyler was dismayed to see a group of reporters waiting on him and cameras going off as pictures were taken. Tyler knew that it would be best to give a statement and hopefully that would satisfy them for a while. He stepped out onto the front porch and quietly closed the red door behind him.

As if on cue, the small mob clustered around Tyler and began shooting questions at him, so rapidly that each question was lost in the mayhem of chatter. Holding up both of his hands in a signal saying 'STOP!' the reporters quickly quieted.

"I'll take one question from each," said Tyler and one reporter stepped forward.

"Mister...?"

"Doyle, Tyler Doyle," supplied Tyler to the unasked question.

"Mister Doyle, we understand that there have been unearthed in the barn, numerous skeletal remains. Are you aware that these remains could possibly be from a rash of missing persons reported around the county for the last four or five years?"

"I concede that is possible," replied Tyler as he looked to another reporter, "yes, your question?"

"Has the sheriff revealed to you how many skeletons have been found?"

"No," and Tyler looked at a female reporter this time.

"Mr. Doyle, is the owner of this property going to remain here?"

"For now, yes," Tyler looked at another male reporter.

"Was the owner aware of the possibility of criminal actions having occurred here?"

"No, and you know as much as we do," said Tyler. "These skeletons were found by my crew doing a cleanup of the barn. There had been unusual smells coming from the barn from the first day that Mrs. Spencer moved in, and that is all anyone knows. The sheriff has taken over for the county and the coroner has the remains, so I suggest if you want more news, that you seek them out. Good day."

Although more questions were fired at his back, Tyler determinedly re-entered the door and closed it firmly behind him.

Returning to the kitchen where everyone waited upon him, he said, "That's just the beginning."

"I wonder if this will be on the local news tonight," speculated Mrs. Doyle.

"No doubt," sighed Kristyn. "While you were running interference with the media, your accountant called; she has that information you requested and she is emailing it to me. I'll get the laptop set up."

"Missus, is it okay to take Nathan outside?" interrupted Franklin. He and Nathan had sort of melted into the background when the commotion started with the media. "Little fellow is justa itching and he wants to play with his new kitty. I'll take him on de far side of the house, that way he'll be outa de way of the police and those newspeople."

"Not a good idea," said Tyler. "I don't think you can safely keep him away from the media, it looks like they are parked out there and I even saw a satellite truck coming up the path when I came back inside. Why don't you take him onto the back porch? It's screened in and should anyone bother you, we are right here to help."

"Yeah sir, Mr. Tyler, I cans do that. C'mon Nate. I'll get us a soda pop, if that be okay with your mama."

Kristyn smiled and nodded her head and then squatted down next to Nathan, "Are you okay, Nate?"

Nathan nodded, then unexpectedly he asked what everyone had hoped he had not comprehended, "Mama, did that baby have three heads? I ain't ever seen that before. Is that a monster?" All the while, he held his new kitten close to his chest, where the kitten purred as it slept in his arms.

Kristyn lowered her head for a moment. How to explain something like this to a child when even she found it hard to understand?

Pastor Doyle on seeing Kristyn's dilemma, came to her rescue with an explanation, "Nathan," he began, as he too squatted next to the child, "Sometimes, these things happen that we do not understand but God does. He had a purpose for that child and that child will be in God's Kingdom. Understand?"

Nathan nodded his head and then just as quickly shook it, showing his confusion.

"Well, I tell you what," continued Pastor Doyle, "as soon as we know for certain we will tell you. Now, you go with Franklin and take good care of... Casper... is that his name?"

Nathan nodded.

"I just bet he's hungry and we brought cat food for him. Franklin, check my car and get the litter box, litter and food, and set it up on the back porch for now."

"Sure thing," said Franklin, and he went to do so.

As they awaited Franklin's return, the conversation stayed on mundane things, like the heat and what to have for lunch, but Nathan was a clever five year old and well he knew things weren't as they should be.

When Franklin returned, he said, "Those newsfolks sure is pushy. But I managed and said I was going to call the police if they didn't leave me be." With that, he took Nathan's hand and led him to the back porch.

Now that Franklin was entertaining Nathan, the rest felt more secure about investigating further into the trunk and the strongbox.

Kristyn retrieved the laptop and arranged to receive the email that Bernice had sent. Soon they had the information.

"She sent it as an attachment," said Kristyn. "Here, I'll bring it up full screen. I can print it out if you like."

After a long study of the document, which was a PDF file, Kristyn said, "It seems to have dates and copies of deeds, showing the original boundary of the property and here it shows how it has diminished in size, as acreage was sold off over the years. It once occupied about half of the county!" exclaimed Kristyn, looking at Tyler who sat next to her at the dining room table.

"Go ahead and print it out, Kristyn," he said, "it's kinda hard to see on the screen. These maps, blow them up some."

Kristyn sent the file to her printer, which was a wireless connection and soon the document, ten pages of it, was in their hands. A simple breakdown of what was in the document follows:

The man that had originally built *Whitaker House in 1804* was cruel, not only to his slaves but also to his family. For two centuries, the house had retained that reputation although, after the Civil War, in 1865, the Union seized the property for non-payment of taxes and sold it. That is how the house came into the hands of Kristyn's great, great, great, great grandfather, who had migrated from Michigan to take advantage of seized cheap property. *Carpetbagger was* the name given to people who came south seeking their fortune. This applied to Kristyn's ancestors.

It wasn't a noble act but it was what it was and was how her ancestor, Sam Harrison had acquired the *Whitaker House*. Stranger still was the fact that he had married the youngest daughter of Joseph Whitaker. The girl was the lone survival of a family of three boys and two girls. Roberta and Sam had three sons and it was the oldest son that inherited the property. This kept the bloodline of the Whitaker family going, although now it was the Harrison surname instead of Whitaker and with the marriage of Kristyn's grandmother, Julia Harrison, who was an only child, to Kristyn's grandfather, Clyde, who was a Morrison, the property once again changed names, but still had the original Whitaker blood-line. Kristyn then realized she was of that descent. Her mother was a Morrison, who married a Young, Anthony D. Young, Kristyn's father and Kristyn's maiden name.

"Look at this," said Tyler, "Roberta, had an older sister, Naomi, who died nine years before the Civil War. And here, the sister was married to Albert Joyner; he was killed during the war, as were all three of Joseph Whitaker's sons. She died during childbirth. A postmortem cesarean section was done by the midwife but the child was stillborn."

"That must have been the conjoined triplets, although it doesn't say so. But the pictures showed a child that looked alive to me, didn't it seem that way to you?"

"It's hard to say from the photograph, its eyes were open on one face but the other faces couldn't be seen that well."

Mrs. Doyle eyed the journal and picking it up, said, "I wonder if there is something in here about the child. It looks like they were stored together for a reason." She handed it to Pastor Doyle, as he reached out for it.

"Should I read it? he asked, looking from one to the other.

Before anyone could answer, Franklin appeared at the back door and cleared his throat to get their attention. Not waiting to be asked, he said, "Nathan and I are going to play hide and seek out in the front hall, if that be okay?"

Kristyn stood and walked over to him, "That is a good idea, Franklin. And thank you so much for helping out with him."

"Why, you more than welcome, Ma'am. C'mon Nate," Franklin called to the child. Nathan came in and then Franklin said, "Can we get a chair to use for homebase? I wants to put it next to de front door."

"Of course," smiled Kristyn.

They waited until Nathan and Franklin had left the kitchen and Tyler had closed the door to the dining room and explained. "So that Nathan can't surprise us again. I know Franklin will knock before he enters."

"A good idea," agreed Kristyn and the rest nodded their approval.

"So, let's see what's in this journal," said Pastor Doyle as he cut the twine with his pocket knife. It was a plain brownish color more from age than its true color, which was most likely white.

"These pages feel a little brittle to me," said Pastor Doyle as he carefully laid the journal down on the kitchen table.

Feeling the journal, Tyler agreed, "Yeah, they are. We should be careful in turning these pages." As he spoke, he opened the journal. It was handwritten, which they expected and was going to be difficult to read. "We need a magnifying glass," he said.

"I'll get one," said Kristyn doing so.

They placed a lamp on to the table and focused its light directly on the journal, "That helps a great deal," said Mrs. Doyle.

Tyler read quickly what he could make out, "There's no mention of the baby here, it is just dealing with the running of the plantation. This is more of a ledger than a journal." After turning through about half of the ledger, it only revealed the cost and schedule of the plantation.

"I'm not sure we are going to find anything," he remarked. "But the pages are becoming easier to read, I guess because they are newer and sort of protected from the elements, buried deep within the book like this."

He continued to thumb carefully through the pages. "Wait, listen to this. 'Funeral cost for Naomi Joyner. $300.00 for a casket. $50.00 for services'. She was buried at the Church's Cemetery. Plot number 409. It doesn't record anything about burial for her baby. Unless the child and mother were buried in the same coffin and grave. I know that was often done when a woman and her baby died during birth."

Still they continued looking through the ledger and a few pages from the back, where it was again difficult to read, they found the listings of all the sons that had died during the Civil war; the breakdown of costs of burial, the dates and plot numbers of each one. The dates varied during the war and even recorded a memorial stone for one son whose body was never found. All of them were buried at the Church's cemetery.

Then from the front of the house, they heard, "Ready or not, here I comes!"

Kristyn laughed and said, "I guess Franklin was 'it'. I hope Nathan hid well. He needs this activity to help to burn up some energy. So, I guess that is about all there is to know in the trunk. While Nathan is occupied and we have about an hour before I'll make sandwiches, let's open the box. It has my mother's things in it. I wish that I remembered her. But I don't remember either of my parents. I do recall their funeral, though. How odd is that?"

"That's probably because of something occurring that was so different from your normal routine that it sticks out in your mind," said Mrs. Doyle, reaching over and patting Kristyn's hand.

Chapter Twelve

Hide and Seek

Franklin, with Nathan's help, managed to get the litter box filled and Casper fed. Nathan sat on the floor next to Casper, sipping his cola and stroking Casper's soft fur as the kitten ate. True to the curiosity of a child, Nathan looked up at Franklin and with a puzzled expression, asked Franklin a few disturbing questions.

"Why doesn't Mama want me to see those pictures of the babies?"

"It's not that Nate, your Mama thinks they will upset you."

"But I ain't upset," he insisted.

"Well, I's know that, Nate, but mamas are like that you know."

"Yeah, I know. I know about the light and I know about the dark too, and I know that the light is scared of the dark. I know that the dark wants the light to stop."

"Stop? Stop what, Nate," asked Franklin, getting the impression that this child was more in tune with the activities going on than the rest of the adults knew.

"The dark is scared too," added Nathan, not answering Franklin's question. "It's scared the light will get away and leave the dark all by itself up there in that attic."

"Ummm, I see," said Franklin. "How comes you know so much?"

"'Cuz I felt it. The light let me know. I don't know how.... it's like appearing inside my brain."

"Oh, I can see that," said Franklin. Franklin thought that perhaps Nathan was dwelling too much on that subject and so suggested a game to play. "Wanna play hide n seek?"

"I ain't played that before. Is it fun?"

"Why sure, tit is, I played it bunches of time when I was your age."

"How?" asked Nathan, rising and sitting down at the table and then resting his head on his arm as he looked up at Franklin.

"Well, one of 'us will be 'it',"

"It? like in tag?"

"Yeah, that's it. The person that's 'it', hides they eyes so they cain't see, and they counts. While they counts, the others hide somewheres. After '*it*' is done counting, he shouts, 'Ready or not, here I comes.' Then, he tries to find'em. Now, if you is hiding, and you sees your chance to run to home base without being tagged by 'it', then you is safe. But now if 'it' finds you and say, 'tagged my base on so an' so, then 'so and so' is 'it'. Then de one's that is 'it' calls out, 'Olly Olly Oxen free!' Then that means, somebody done and been tagged and they are 'it' so everybody that's still hiding, can come to homebase and not be 'it'. Do that sounds like a fun game to yer?"

"Unhun," replied Nathan bobbing his head up and down. "When can we play?"

"Why right now, if yer like."

"Who's gonna be 'it' first?" asked Nathan.

"Let's flip a coin and see," said Franklin taking a quarter from his pants pocket, "Choose heads or tails when I flip it."

Franklin placed the quarter on his fist atop of his thumb, then flipped the coin into the air and while it spun, Nathan shouted out, "Heads!"

The quarter then landed on Franklin's forearm where he slapped his hand over the quarter, more to keep it from falling off his arm than anything else. Lifting his hand, Franklin said, "It's heads alright, and I guess that makes me 'it'"

Nathan grinned and said, "Oh boy! Now what?"

"We gotta find a homebase. How about out in the hall there next to de front door? I'll take a chair out there and that will be homebase."

"Okay," agreed Nathan.

Franklin stepped into the dining room, leaving Nathan with the kitten, then Nathan heard him call him and he joined the rest of them in the kitchen. Soon he and Franklin were in the front foyer and the game began.

"Now, I'm gonna set this here chair right here, next to de front door, then I's gonna count, let see, how 'bouts fifty? That otta give yer plenty of time to hide. One thing though, yer cain't go outside. Your mama wouldn't like that. Yer can hide anywhere in here, okay?"

Nathan bobbed his head up and down indicating he understood.

"Alrighty then," said Franklin. Franklin placed both hands over his face and then laid his head against the wall, "One... two... three...." He began counting slowly.

Nathan looked around, trying to decide which way he should go. He couldn't hide in the living room, it was too open, neither the dining room nor the kitchen, he knew his Mama didn't want him in there right now. That left the den, and he thought, 'I think I can hide in there,' and turned in that direction.

"Best hurry, Nate," said Franklin when he realized that Nathan hadn't moved yet.

"Okay, I'm hiding now," and headed towards the den but right at the den's door was the staircase. He looked up at the stairs, and at the top of the stairs was the orb. In his mind, Nathan heard his name; he grinned and headed up the stairs.

"Six... seven... eight... nine... ten..." continued Franklin.

With the runner on the stairs, Nathan barely made a sound as he headed up the staircase. Now on the second floor, he stood and looked around.

"Twenty-one... twenty-two... twenty-three..." Nathan heard Franklin still counting, his voice sounding far away and barely audible.

Nathan froze; as he watched the orb bob up and down, and another thought entered his mind, "Follow us." Then the orb floated towards the attic door. This time the orb did not diminish in size or go under the door but waited as Nathan walked slowly towards it.

"Thirty-nine... forty... forty-one..." Franklin's voice drifted up to Nathan. Although Nathan couldn't count all the way to fifty, he did know that his hiding time was running out, and he considered that the attic would be a great place to hide. So, he followed the orb.

Nathan was now standing within a few inches of the orb, the orb shrank, as it had before, and slid under the attic door. "Forty-six..." Nathan placed his hand on the knob, "Forty-seven..." he pushed open the attic door, "Forty-eight..." he entered the stairwell. Here the orb waited, "Forty-nine..." the door closed behind Nathan.

But the stairwell was not dark, the orb's soft glow lit it up, the orb now waited for Nathan at the top of the stairs and he proceeded up them. But this staircase was a steep incline and the steps just a tad deeper than the staircase in the front foyer, which made Nathan crawl up the stairs, leaving his prints in the dust. Nathan drew near, the orb diminished in size and went under the main door to the attic. Without waiting, Nathan pushed on the door, it opened and he entered the attic; the door closed behind him.

"Fifty! Ready or not, here I comes," shouted Franklin but this declaration was unheard by Nathan.

Chapter Thirteen

The Strongbox

Kristyn reached towards the box and Tyler, antici-
pating her actions, quickly lifted it onto the table. She
smiled at him and said "Thanks."

"All you need do is ask," he said with a wink that
sent chills down Kristyn's spine.

He proceeded to lift up the lid, which he hadn't re-
locked. He eased back the lid until it caught on the
hinges, then a quick glance at the contents revealed
once more the album and the file folders, about three;
he lifted them out and set them on the table. There was
a first year baby-book, and next came clothing, infant
and toddler sizes, only something was very strange
about them. They were female outfits but why were
they sewn together in such a fashion?

As Kristyn held up one small garment, her heart
skipped a beat! "Oh no," she cried.

All of them stared at the little dresses, the dresses
had been split at the front bodice and then the end was
sown to an identical dress, making one!

"That is for conjoined twins," declared Mrs. Doyle.

"But this box contains things belonging to my
mother," said Kristyn. "I don't understand."

Tyler sighed and placed his arm about Kristyn's
shoulder. "Maybe these will tell us what is going on,"

and he picked up a manila folder, opened it and laid it flat onto the table.

The folders revealed Kristyn's worst fears:

Julia Morrison was delivered by caesarian section of a set of conjoined twins, girls. They had been named Alyssa and Alyce. Both children survived until the age of twenty-eight months, when separation surgery was attempted. It had been a hard decision because the twins had only one heart and that meant one would die. Not to separate the twins, meant both would die and soon. They wouldn't know until the surgery began which girl would survive. As it turned out the heart was Alyssa's and so it was determined that Alyce would die. The operation took twelve hours with two sets of surgeons performing the surgery.

So, that was where Kristyn got her middle name, from her dead Aunt.

"This is hard to take in," Kristyn whispered. "No wonder Grandma never shared this with me. And she went to her grave with the secret. I wonder, did my mother know?"

"Wait, here it is, your grandmother wrote this,

"'Alyssa does not remember Alyce but she does remember the operation. I have decided not to tell her of her sister. There is no need in her having the burden that I have. The scar, which runs down the center of her chest, will be explained as surgery for a valve replacement in her heart. This will explain things to her for all the follow-up treatments she must undergo. My heart is heavy. I loved both my daughters and the decision was a difficult one. But as they grew older, the one heart would be too strained and both would die at a young age. Clyde and I felt we had no choice. But at least we did not have to decide which one would die. God took that burden from us.'"

"Why then, did my mother name me Alyce, if she did not remember? Only my grandparents knew."

"Maybe we will learn more," said Pastor Doyle.

And they did. In another medical folder was another handwritten note from Kristyn's grandmother;

'Alyssa and Tony are having a baby." Further down, 'A baby girl was born yesterday. I have had my first look at my new granddaughter. She looks so much like her mother, same coloring; it breaks my heart for I remember Alyce! This baby girl, they are naming her Kristyn May, but I suggested that her middle name be 'Alyce,' I said it was a family name and it is. They are thinking it over. Has God returned my Alyce to me?'

Another handwritten paper, 'They have named my granddaughter, Kristyn Alyce Young', my heart beats with joy.'

Another handwritten paper; "My hearts breaks. How can I bear this pain? My only child and her husband have been killed instantly in a head-on collision on the interstate. A big 18-wheel truck lost control and flipped onto the oncoming traffic of the opposite lane, right in front of their car. They were pronounced dead at the scene. My granddaughter was with her grandfather and me. As Anthony's parents are not willing to take her, I will raise my granddaughter."

Several more minutes were spent going through the strongbox, where Kristyn saw that her grand-mother had also stored in this box items from Kristyn's early years, which she had spent with her parents. There was her Christening gown, and some infant toys, a lock of Kristyn's hair, all inside of her first year baby book, with pictures of Kristyn as a baby with her parents holding and playing with her. Kristyn realized that she had never seen pictures of herself with her parents. All the pictures that her grandmother possessed had been of Kristyn alone, professionally taken pictures in studios. There was one picture of Kristyn next to her parents' caskets; she stood on a stool as she gazed into the caskets, for a last 'goodbye' to her mother and her father. Kristyn didn't remember that event. She was not yet three years old. Memoranda stopped at the age of four and Kristyn knew that was when she went to pre-school. All other mementos were kept downstairs in albums that she now had.

There was another album. Kristyn's heartbeat speeded up, 'What would be in it?'

It proved to be exactly what she expected; it was photographs of Alyssa and Alyce from newborns up to and after their separation. They were Thoracopagus conjoined twins. Two bodies fused from the upper thorax to the lower belly. The heart was always involved in those cases.

The babies were perfectly formed and faced each other where their upper bodies were attached. These early pictures showed the babies nude. Each had that baby fine hair almost white in color, the same as Kristyn's hair.

There were pictures as they grew, wearing the little dresses created for them. Evidently the babies learned to walk, for there were photographs showing them standing and holding onto each other.

Then there were photographs just before the babies underwent surgery, lying face to face on the gurney as it was pushed to the OR. Then the lone picture of Alyssa, lying asleep, alone in the big hospital bed. She was hooked up to all kinds of equipment. The year was 1966. The surgery was complex but not complicated; as it involved only one organ howbeit, a vital organ, for one baby would certainly die.

Next were several pictures of Alyssa from several months after the operation, showing her rapid recovery. Tyler picked up a white envelope. Inside were pictures of Alyce after the operation. She was dead of course; two pictures were of her in the hospital, she was all bandaged, but was not hooked up to machines as was her twin sister. The next three pictures showed her in a yellow dress, her hair combed and with a ribbon in it. Her eyes were shut and she looked asleep, but she lay in, not a bed, but a coffin. Then the lone photograph of the grave immediately after the funeral, all covered in flowers. There was no head stone.

How many people knew of the co-joined twins? It had to be quite a few. Had there been some sort of conspiracy to keep it hidden? There must have been and surely the pastor knew of it and many in the congregation also. Perhaps because Julia and Clyde did not want Alyssa to know, the parishioners kept the family secret. Kristyn's grandparents had always attended the Church, as did her mother as a child and later Kristyn herself, until leaving home for college.

A short note by Kristyn's grandmother was found, it read, 'My beloved daughter, Alyce, wait for us in Heaven, we will see you again.' Another document in a manila envelope, a certificate of death, dated May 5, 1966. It also revealed a burial plot in the Church's Cemetery, plot number 1575. Also in this envelope was Alyce's birth certificate, and on it was revealed she was a twin, born on January 12, 1964.

"I wonder if it was on my mother's birth certificate that she was a twin. I have it somewhere in my personal files, along with Daddy's and both of their death certificates. Hold on, I'll go look."

Kristyn went out into the foyer; the documents she wanted were in her dresser in her bedroom upstairs. Deciding not to mention that fact to anyone, for she wouldn't be up there that long, she headed upstairs. Upon reaching the top of the stairs, she looked about for a moment, everything was quiet and a little warm, so she felt no threat and headed to her bedroom, where she retrieved the folder from the bottom drawer of her dresser. She then quickly returned to the kitchen. It didn't cross her mind that she saw neither Nathan nor

Franklin, just assuming that Nathan was well hidden and that Franklin was busy searching for him.

Returning with the folder, they quickly searched it to reveal that her mother was listed as a single birth!

"Somehow, my grandparents had this changed," exclaimed Kristyn.

"Well, it can be done," said Pastor Doyle. "You know when you adopt a child, there is a change in their first as well as their last name but, most important, is the change in who the parents are. In this case, I guess, they had the twin births changed to a single birth. Your mother never knew!"

"But now I am more confused than ever," said Kristyn. "First the conjoined triplets and then just a few generations later, conjoined twins, both in the same family, is this trait inherited?"

"No, no, my dear," said Mrs. Doyle.

"Siamese twins are a freak of nature, an accident at conception, not inherited," said Tyler.

"Yes, I know that fraternal twins are, but this makes me wonder. In identical twins, the fertilized egg divides into two sections, and continues growing as separate embryos from there. Scientists suspect that external stimuli might affect cases of identical twining. It is only a theory of course, they cannot anticipate when it might happen and afterwards nothing shows up to reveal what element or forces acted upon the ovum creating the twins. It might be something like magnetism, is what one scientist suspected. High magnetic fields acting like a separator so that when the egg begins to divide and multiply, they can't stay clustered together, or, in the case of Siamese twins, the force isn't strong enough to cause a complete split and the ovum continues growing, creating conjoined twins."

"I hadn't heard of that before. How did you learn this?" asked Mrs. Doyle.

"I'm sorry, it was in a medical journal I read some time ago," explained Kristyn.

"Well," said Tyler, "we know now why the strong-box was locked and why the key was hidden so well."

Tyler looked Kristyn directly in the face and she at him, and Tyler read her expression as one of bewilderment, as well as comprehension.

At that moment a knock sounded on the kitchen door, and, without waiting for an answer, Franklin pushed the door open and announced, "I cain't find Nathan!"

Chapter Fourteen

Nathan is Lost

All eyes focused on Franklin and for the longest moment, there was no reaction, then they all spoke at once, "How?" Or, "He's around you just haven't found him." Or, "Where have you looked?" "Did you tell him to come out?"

"I done and searched all downstairs. He cain't go outside 'cus I was at de front door and you all were here at de back door...."

Kristyn looked at Tyler and whispered loudly, "The attic!"

Now, there was a mad rush toward the kitchen door, but Tyler won the race and was bounding up the stairwell way ahead of the rest. Kristyn wasn't far behind and arrived at the attic door only seconds after Tyler.

Tyler turned the knob expecting it to be unlocked and was brought up short when it wasn't. "It's locked," he exclaimed in disbelief, looking at Kristyn. "He couldn't have gone in there."

"Yes, he could have," replied Kristyn as she took the key from around her neck and handed it to Tyler. "The door seems to be unlocked whenever Nathan is near it, like 'they' want him in there!"

Taking the key, Tyler wasted no time in unlocking and shoving open the door. In the dim light, they could just see Nathan's small handprints in the dust of the steps as they led upwards, into the attic.

"We need a light," Tyler called and Franklin handed him his. Tyler focused its beam on to the steps, and Kristyn gasped when plainly to be seen, were Nathan's prints going all the way up. They followed them to where the prints disappeared into the attic!

Tyler tried this door; again, it was locked. Using the key, Tyler unlocked the attic door and pushed it open. Everyone had come upstairs and now everyone entered the attic. Kristyn stood next to Tyler with her arm wrapped around Tyler's left arm, as he used his right to shine the flashlight.

"Nathan," Tyler called out first, no response.

"Olly Olly Oxen free," shouted Franklin, the signal that the game was over and all of those hiding were safe and could come out from their hiding places.

Everyone held their breath, as they waited for Nathan to appear from behind the clutter in the attic. Nathan did not!

"Nate, it's Mama," called Kristyn. "Nathan, you hid very well and Franklin could not find you. You are safe, you can come out now."

Still nothing moved among the clutter and the boxes, stacked nearly to the ceiling, and Nathan did not appear.

"Franklin," said Tyler, "get the crew back here to the house, we are going to empty the attic. Dad, get the sheriff."

Both men, without further ado, left to carry out the orders. Tyler was left with his mother and Kristyn, with Kristyn clinging to his arm. He walked further into the attic and the women followed. Slowly they made the circle around the boundary of the outer wall, searching, moving boxes and lifting up boxes, still no Nathan. They repeatedly called him, enticing him to come out, but it was a fruitless effort.

Kristyn felt tears filling her eyes and then over-running onto her cheeks, she wept silently. Tyler could feel the rise and fall of her chest against his arm and felt the silent sobs. He freed his arm from her hold and wrapped it about her. His mother too, placed her arms around Kristyn.

"Kristyn," said Mrs. Doyle, "Let's let Tyler continue searching, we are only hindering him. The crew will be here before long and they will carry all of this out onto the lawn, if he is in here, Tyler will find him."

Kristyn looked at Tyler for his response, "Mom's right, Kristyn. Why don't you wait in one of the bedrooms? It is getting really hot up here now, it's almost the afternoon."

"That's what I know," agreed Kristyn with a low sob. "He can die up here!"

"That's not going to happen!" declared Tyler.

"Of course not, dear. We are going to find him. He's in here somewhere, perhaps he has fallen asleep."

Then Franklin appeared at the door, "Mr. Tyler, de crew's comin' up de path. Want me to fill'em in? I don't say nothing 'bout this on de phone, only that you wanted'em."

"Yes, Franklin, do that."

"And de sheriff is on his way up here now. He was out in the yard, but dem thar news folks are askin' questions again. All over me dey were. De sheriff made'em leave me be. Okay, I'm gonna go an' tell de crew now." Franklin helped Mrs. Doyle escort Kristyn to the exit. Kristyn was hesitant about leaving her son but the gentle pressure on her arms from both Franklin and Mrs. Doyle, ensured that she did leave.

As the trio emerged out into the corridor, they met Sheriff Brown and one deputy coming up the stairwell from the foyer.

"Good afternoon, folks," greeted Sheriff Brown. "Can you direct me further to Mr. Doyle?"

Mrs. Doyle replied, "Yes, go to that last door, the one which opens into the hall, inside is the stairs, it's up there."

"Thank you," the sheriff answered, as he proceeded down the hall.

****

After Franklin and the women left, Tyler called out to Nathan again, "Nathan! It's Tyler Doyle. If you can hear me but can't speak, can you make a noise or move something, so that I can find you."

Tyler waited, seconds passed with no noise or movement, then he heard his name, "Mr. Doyle!" It was the sheriff.

Tyler made his way back towards the door and greeted the sheriff, "Morning, Sheriff Brown."

"I'm afraid it is afternoon," corrected the Sheriff. "Man, is it hot up here!"

Tyler then took note of the increasing heat. If Nathan was indeed in the attic, then ventilation was needed or the child might not survive!

"Can you tell me any more than what your employee did? He only said the child was hiding out in the attic. All I can say is, if he's in here, we best find him fast!"

"I know," agreed Tyler. "Let's step back into the hall, it is a might cooler there."

They did that, then, as they waited and discussed the situation more, Tyler's crew emerged up the stairs. Tyler wasted no more time in giving directions to his crew, as his mother and Kristyn peered around the door from Nathan's room, which was closest to the attic.

"First, get the fans, and position them in strategic locations to best ventilate the attic. Open the attic windows and if they cannot be opened, break the glass;

136

we can repair them later. But we must cool the attic down or the child will die from the heat."

Several men left immediately to get the fans set up. Several more headed into the attic to open windows. The rest remained to hear more directions.

"The rest of you can begin to carry the things outside. Don't leave it here in the hall, there is too much of it, carry it outside onto the lawn. Okay, let's getting moving!"

Tyler's crew set to work. The men who went first into the attic found it was necessary to break the windows, and the rush of fresh, cooler air was already lowering the temperature but not quickly enough. As the remaining crew proceeded to carry out boxes, the men arrived with the fans and feet of extension cords. Two fans were set up, one at the back and one at the front, between the windows. The fan at the front of the house blew into the attic, drawing in fresh and cooler air. The fan at the back of the house was set to blow out of the attic, which created a continuous movement of air throughout. It did not take long to feel the results.

The accumulation of stuff in the attic was beyond belief, as it often took two men to carry one item. And although the fans helped, the temperature was already well into the nineties! Kristyn and Mrs. Doyle brought up iced water to keep everyone cool and hydrated.

Kristyn and Mrs. Doyle kept their vigil at the attic door in the hall. Kristyn wanted to go back into the attic but she could not find the stairwell empty long enough to enter. So, she, Pastor and Mrs. Doyle, waited in the hall. Pastor Doyle had led them in a prayer, and the prayer remained in Kristyn's head, repeating it over and over again.

'Dear God, please protect him. Please let us find him.'

The spinning wheel came down the steps and then out into the yard, then the rocking chair, the broken table, the children's hobbyhorse, the stroller, the cradle, out they came. Now, the cracked mirror, and as the two men walked by Kristyn with the front facing her, she screamed.

Everybody reacted, the men stopped and looked at her strangely, as she stammered and pointed at the mirror. Tyler rushed out into the hall. Pastor Doyle came from the head of the stairs; they gathered around Kristyn and looked at what she was pointing at - the mirror!

To everyone's shocked amazement, the reflection in the mirror was not of the hall and the people looking into the mirror, no, it was Nathan!

Chapter Fifteen

The Mirror

Nathan looked around the attic. For a five year old, it was a placed of intrigue! The boxes stacked about were way over his head and finding his way through them was like navigating a maze, a maze of boxes and old furniture. He had lost sight of the orb but now it loomed above him, twinkling like a star.

"Hey," Nathan said.

The orb bobbed, but no thought formed in Nathan's mind, no words came from the orb.

"What's the matter?" he asked. But as soon as he spoke, the orb beamed brightly and in an instant, vanished! Panic entered Nathan's thoughts then. He was alone and it was dark and it was getting warmer. Nathan ventured further into the attic. Tears formed in his eyes as he tried to find the door from the attic. He could not see without the glow from the orb, it was murky and foreboding. The bit of light penetrating from the windows was swallowed up by the gloom.

Nathan looked up, the stacks of boxes loomed over his head, like towering mountains, hiding his way. Feeling his way through them, he came into the center of the attic, where it wasn't quite as cluttered. But the darkness was overbearing, and it seemed to come together into a point of a shadow, where it then grew into the misty shape that he had seen that first night in his bedroom and later, he and his mother had seen out in the hall. The Shadowman!

Fear seeped its way through Nathan, overtaking him completely; his heartbeat quickened and he could hear it pounding, like drums in the distance, a rhythmic beat with an ever-increasing tempo. Nathan held his place, afraid to move. Maybe the Shadowman could not see him. He was small after all, and it was dark too, so Nathan waited and held his breath. He watched this being of mist and shadow waver, changing its shape slightly as it had done that first night. Then at the crown of this entity, where you would expect to find a head and a face, eyes opened. They exuded an infrared ray. Light radiated from the eyes like light from a torch! This now spread an eerie red glow about the attic. Nathan remained frozen.

The Shadowman's eyes seemed to shift, as if searching, then focused upon Nathan. It saw him! Nathan made to run by turning around and heading back the way he came, but at every turn, the Shadow-man appeared in front of him, blocking his escape. Then with flat, misty arms, it reached for him; Nathan felt the chill as he was encircled by this shade. The Shadowman lifted Nathan off the floor, higher than the boxes. It then opened its mouth, which appeared as an empty orifice in its blackened face, and Nathan was engulfed by the shadow, making him one with it as he was swallowed. The Shadowman then, with Nathan as a part of itself, circled the attic, but they traveled over the clutter, near the ceiling. Nathan began shivering as the warmth left his body; the Shadowman was draining him of his body heat!

'That's why it's so cold when it is near. It is taking away our warmth.' this terrifying thought flashed through Nathan's mind. Nathan understood, as well as a five year old could understand, that he had been gobbled up by the Shadowman and yet he was fully

aware, so he must not be dead! So what was he now? How could he get the Shadowman to spit him out? Nathan grew colder, then as numbness settled in his extremities, he started to shiver, he grew colder still, he closed his eyes and he felt the blackness and the cold, then, oblivion!

****

Nathan sat within the mirror, his small legs pulled up to his chest, with the ankles crossed. His forearms were folded atop of his knees and his forehead rested upon his arms. Kristyn and the others looked intently at the reflection in the mirror and realized that it reflected the interior of the attic and not the hall; they reached out and touched the smooth cool glass.

"How can this be?" asked Kristyn with broken words, when her tears were so near and she was trying desperately not to cry. For crying wasted energy and solved nothing and her son needed her. He needed her to be strong and to have a clear head, so she brushed her tears away.

"*That* is impossible," declared Sheriff Brown, yet his eyes told him different. "How can I issue an Amber alert on this?"

"Take the mirror downstairs, I am going back into the attic and see if I can spot this exact location which it reflects," stated Tyler.

Two men took the mirror, followed by Kristyn and Mrs. Doyle. Franklin and the sheriff followed Tyler back into the attic. The attic was only about a third empty and as they searched, it became apparent that the reflection in the mirror no longer existed. The environment had changed and it could have been facing the front as well as the rear of the attic expanse.

"I don't know what to make of this," said Tyler.

"I'm right there with you on that," agreed the Sheriff.

Franklin nodded his head in silent agreement.

"Although we have found Nathan, sort of, I still want everything removed from up here. Something is hiding, what, I don't know. But there's a couple of centuries represented here with this stuff; there has got to be a hidden clue and I don't intend to miss it!"

So the crew continued with their emptying of the attic. Piece by piece, the attic's contents were relocated to the front lawn. The afternoon waned, and darkness fell, yet the work continued. The men took short breaks, a couple of men at a time, so that the removal of bits and pieces never ceased.

Tyler and two men would do a thorough inspection of every single item brought down from the attic. This took a great deal of time, but was necessary in order to spot anything significant, which might be vital in learning more of the mystery of the attic. Then came an enclosed and locked mahogany bookcase. The men summoned Tyler back to the attic.

"Mr. Doyle," explained the youth, "This case is too heavy to move. See, it has books in it," as he indicated the glass doors.

"Empty it, to make it lighter," said Tyler in puzzlement. Why didn't they just go ahead with that without asking him?

"That's just it, the thing is locked," said the teenager. "I wonder how it was gotten into the attic in the first place, filled like that."

After playing with the lock a bit, Tyler realized that it had a keyhole similar to the ones on the doors, the trunk and the strongbox. Well, it was worth a try, so he took the skeleton key, and inserted it. It was a perfect fit; he turned the key, and felt as well as heard the click as the case doors unlatched. The men started unloading it, placing the books into several cardboard boxes, with

Tyler inspecting each item. Also found were several old faded ledgers. Tyler took possession of them, remembering what was written in the one that was found in the trunk. He would go through them on his own, just in case they were significant. He decided to take them downstairs, to see what was going on with the mirror, and to console Kristyn.

"Is there any change in the reflection?" he asked.

Kristyn joined him in front of the mirror, where they wrapped their arms about each other's waist.

"Just a bit," answered Pastor Doyle. "It's getting darker, just like here, so I guess the mirror is reflecting real time. Also, things are disappearing from the mirror. I guess that's when the items in the attic are removed; they then disappear from the mirror too. But Nathan remains as you see him, very still, we can't even make out if he *is* breathing!"

"I don't know what to do," said Kristyn. "Is he alive? Asleep? And where is he?"

Franklin came over to Kristyn; he placed his hand on her arm and said, "I ain't real sure but us old folks thinks he is between worlds."

"What is that suppose to mean?"

"Well, it's like when someone's asleep or maybe knocked out, they ain't aware of de real world and they are in a dream-like world. I don't claim to understand it, but I knows of a lady, some might even call her a witch, but she ain't no witch like you automatically thinks of, no sir. She just wise in the ways of nature and the spirit world and she knows how the *darkside* works. I can fetch her if you like."

"I don't think so, Franklin," interrupted Pastor Doyle. "The Bible does not hold with consulting witches. We will just continue with our prayers. So forget this woman."

"Yeah sir, I'll do that," said Franklin. He hung his head and left the room.

Kristyn thought on the idea a little longer, and then dismissed it. What to do? At that moment, Sheriff Brown entered the living room where they were gathered.

"Mr. Doyle, I've gotta go, I've received new information about the investigation out in the barn, and they want me back at the department as soon as possible. Those news folks have left for now, but my men in the cruiser will remain overnight again. Is the attic emptied yet?"

"Not quite, the boxes are out but there are still a few pieces of furniture left. I know it is dark outside but it is cooler now, so the men are going to finish it up tonight. I don't know where to go from here."

"Wish I could help there, but a boy in a mirror is out of my expertise," said the sheriff. "There's the chance that we will be leaving the barn, if there's no more to be found, although the yellow tape will remain up for a while. Is there anyone I can call in to help with the missing boy, missing, although we can see him. I am as confused as anyone on this."

"I don't know either," said Tyler, shaking his head.

"Good luck, I'll be back in the morning, unless you call me before," with that the Sheriff departed.

****

Franklin lingered out on the front porch; he stayed out of the way of the younger men who were finishing up with the attic. The summer night was warm and the sky clear. There was a slither of a moon in the sky and many stars swept across the heaven. His thoughts were on Nathan; the child had been left in his charge and the child was now a prisoner. Franklin solely blamed himself, he should have stipulated that Nathan should not go upstairs, and especially not into the attic. Although not a word of blame had been directed his way, he felt it, nonetheless. Franklin just knew that Miss Lilly Jenkins could make contact. Miss Jenkins was near ninety but was spry for her age and sharp as a tack in her mind. She would know what to do. Not saying a word to anyone, Franklin took the truck that was allotted to him, and left the farm.

Chapter Sixteen

Some Answers

No one wanted to leave Kristyn alone, so arrangements were made for Tyler to remain overnight and his parents would return early the next morning. As Tyler's parents stood at the mirror, looking at Nathan in the position he had been in from the beginning, Pastor Doyle said, "I know we need to pray, but from my experience in this house, I don't think it should be said out loud and I think silent prayer will be just as effective; shall we bow our heads..."

Kristyn buried her face into Tyler's arm; he held her close as his father silently prayed for protection and intervention.

"Well, I'll be back first thing in the morning," said Pastor Doyle as he and his wife left, and soon the darkness swallowed up their car as it sped away. Tyler and Kristyn watched it go and Tyler said, "I'll take the sofa, I don't know where Franklin has gone. It isn't like him not to let me know his whereabouts."

"I think his feelings might have been hurt, remember the witch he spoke about and what your father said."

"Yeah," sighed Tyler, "I remember."

****

Later, Kristyn covered the mirror with a blanket. Although she knew that the image reflected in the mirror would or could not feel cold or heat, it still made her feel better however, as though she was tucking Nathan into bed.

Tyler told Kristyn 'goodnight' as he placed a light kiss upon her lips, "Call me if anything happens, and I mean anything. I know neither of us will sleep but we need to try."

Kristyn nodded and held back her tears. It took hours of tossing and turning before either one fell into a restless sleep.

****

The next morning, as promised, before dawn Pastor Doyle returned, with Tyler letting him in. Kristyn awoke on hearing their voices and soon coffee was brewing as the three of them gathered in the kitchen. They were sipping their first cup and flipping through the albums from the trunk and the strongbox, when there came a loud banging at the front door. Tyler answered the persistent knocking.

"Good morning, Sheriff," said Tyler when seeing him, "it must be something of importance..."

"It is," barked Sheriff Brown not allowing Tyler to finish his sentence. "Where is everyone?" Without waiting for an invitation, the sheriff entered the foyer.

"Out in the kitchen. Won't you come in? What's up?"

The Sheriff, already familiar with the home's layout, walked determinedly through the dining room. He glanced at the mirror, now uncovered. It had changed a bit and now reflected an empty attic. Nathan, however, had not moved.

In the kitchen, they were having breakfast and coffee, but it didn't look like Kristyn was eating and the others lacked enthusiasm in their morning meal. Tyler entered behind the sheriff. All eyes looked surprised at the sheriff's grim expression.

Before anyone could speak, the sheriff pulled a large manila envelope out from under his arm. "We have the results..." he began as he laid documents out onto the table along with photographs.

"We were surprised to find that some of these remains are close to three hundred years old. We want permission to continue the excavation on the outside of the barn. The graves inside are recent, within five years, which matches up to the timeframe that the farm has been closed and within the scope of the trespassers.

"Three are women, thirties, fifties. The other two are older men. We do suspect the work of a psychopath.

"The older graves are those of slaves, and we think that this must have been a cemetery for the slaves. None of the graves have markers. Most of the older bodies were buried without coffins, only burlap shrouds. The most recent ones were buried along the wall, those that Mr. Doyle's crew unearthed, without shrouds or coffins. It looked like animals had attempted to dig those graves up because they were close to the surface, thus keeping the stench very strong."

Everybody remained silent as the sheriff looked at each one, and seeing the confusion on their faces, he continued.

"As I said, mostly slaves' graves, except for this."

He then pointed to several photographs. As they looked closely, Kristyn whispered, *"The Dudu-Mtu!"*

"From what we can decipher from the forensics, and from the urban legend around for over a hundred and fifty years, this set of Siamese triplets did not die at birth but lived until their early teens."

"So, that would add credence to the legend?" whispered Kristyn. "I am related to them."

Sheriff Brown looked at her from under his brows, "How so?"

"We have the ledger that gives this information, plus the records that Bernice found in the archives at the courthouse," explained Tyler. "We also have a photograph album with pictures of the triplets at birth."

"Can I see it?" Sheriff Brown asked.

As the album was still on the kitchen table where they had been going through it again, Pastor Doyle handed it to the sheriff. He took it and slowly flipped through its pages and when coming to the photographs of the triplets, he let out a low whistle and exclaimed, "Well I'll be a monkey's uncle." He stared at them a long moment and then said, "These should be given to a museum for their medical rarity section."

"I had considered that," replied Kristyn, "but that is the last thing on my mind right now. It can wait until after Nathan is released."

"Yeah, it can," agreed the sheriff.

"Well, we are keeping this case open; will you, Mrs. Spencer, give us permission to dig outside of the original crime scene?"

"Of course," Kristyn replied.

Sheriff Brown handed her a document he took from the envelope and said, "Read over this, and sign it, if you agree."

Kristyn gave the document a brief glance and signed and dated it where indicated.

"I'm afraid you are going to have to put up with us and the media a little longer. They haven't gotten wind of this yet, but the coroner's conclusion is public knowledge, and they will sniff it out like bloodhounds and be parked once again on your doorstep. I apologize for that, but there is only so much we can keep secret. I must leave for a while but the forensic people will be back as soon as I file this consent form. I am using all avenues to locate your son, even though... Well, I haven't given up on him. I'll see you folks soon. Good morning to you."

A sniffle was heard and all eyes were drawn to Kristyn. Tyler placed his arm about her shoulder, "Try not to worry, we will get Nathan back, I promise."

The sheriff made his farewell, and quickly left. Outside, the deputies began their examination of the crime scene.

****

Kristyn sat in a kitchen chair in front of the mirror. Nathan was as he had been from the beginning, no signs of movement; they could not even tell if he was breathing! Tyler entered and tucked under his arm were the three ledgers. Sitting down at the kitchen table, he summoned the rest of them.

"What is that?" asked Pastor Doyle.

"I made a point of checking every item that was removed from the attic, and one thing that caught my attention was the enclosed bookcase. It was locked and as I suspected, it was the skeleton key that unlocked it, another reason why the key was hidden so well. There are valuable volumes there, worth a great deal of money but what caught my eye more than that was these older ledgers, three of them. When I found myself unable to sleep last night, I went through them. *And* I think we will find the answer as to why the barn was built on top of a cemetery.

"To make a long story short, the original homestead had been moved at least once, relocating further away from the creek, the main source of water. Most times a home was built as close to water as possible. There's a record here of a fire severely damaging the second home, which was far grander than this one, and was the original *Whitaker House* that everyone knew. It was burnt by Union soldiers, and it was Sam Harrison that rebuilt and repaired the house and built the barn at the same time. Roberta wrote that the triplets died right at the war's end and before she met and married Sam Harrison. She was living with the triplets in the damaged home and it was she, with help from loyal slaves, who buried them in the backyard. By that time, as land was valuable, the slaves' cemetery was long ago forgotten or deliberately overlooked and was leveled as part of the yard of the main house.

"But look at this ledger, it concerns the triplets. The triplets were named, Abby, Bella and Callie, in order from the left to right. They were cared for by Roberta, Naomi's younger sister after Naomi died giving birth. That was about nine years before the Civil War. The triplets were delivered by caesarian section after the death of the mother. They were not expected to live and their father, Albert, wanted to allow them to die by starving them. Roberta kept them alive and hid them in the attic whenever her father, Joseph was in the main house, as he did not want to look at them. Albert, the triplets' father left the plantation after his wife's death and later was killed in the war.

"It looks like Roberta was about eleven or twelve at the triplets' birth. Two female slaves took care of the girls and stayed with them at all times. The ledger reads like a diary, with almost a day-to-day account of the girls' lives. They never could sit nor walk, but instead crawled about on their stomach using their eight arms and legs to propel them forwards.

"They even got loose from time to time and rambled the fields and down by the creek which was a small swamp at the time. They were seen by the slaves of neighboring plantations and the name *Dudu-Mtu* was given to them. They were feared and when their grandfather, Joseph, learned of this, he then used the triplets as a means of control over his slaves.

"He was the one that began the legend concerning the powers the triplets were supposed to have. The legend went like this; any disobedient slave would be captured by the *Dudu-Mtu* and eaten.

"I think that the tale became twisted and more added to it and then used as a scare tactic for children. But there was never any proof that the triplets ever harmed anyone!

"It was Roberta who kept this diary, but I didn't figure that out until about now in the story. She loved the girls and tried very hard to make their lives easy. Then the year before the war ended, the triplets died. It doesn't say how, just that they died."

Completing his narrative of what he had learned from his study of the ledgers, Tyler now looked at Kristyn and his father.

At first there was silence as this story sunk in. "How did they get buried in the barn?" asked Pastor Doyle.

"They were buried in the back yard, with a marker and Roberta kept up the single grave.

"The story ends there, and is where the ledger we found in the trunk merges the two stories, repeating in the fourth ledger some of what was in the third."

"That clarifies a great deal," said Pastor Doyle. "It doesn't however give any insight as to why Nathan is trapped like he is. I have no idea how to go about releasing him. We have offered up our prayers, but maybe a fast will instill more passion, and God will intervene."

"A fast?" questioned Kristyn.

"Yes, when we sacrifice of ourselves when praying, God perceives it as a request which is of utmost importance to us. Christ fasted for forty days and prayed continually, as he resisted the temptations of

Satan, while in the desert. A fast does not weaken us as you might assume, but strengthens our spirituality and shows our sincerity."

"Yes, I can see that," said Kristyn, nodding her head slowly. She sat down at the kitchen table, and lowered her head onto her arms as great sobs erupted; there was no consoling her.

Pastor Doyle was dismayed to see her sorrow and had no recourse for her, but he needed his wife here and so looked at Tyler and said, "I'm going to go get your mother to stay with her while we search for a solution. I won't be gone long."

Tyler nodded his head towards his father, then sat down beside of Kristyn, and took her into his arms.

Chapter Seventeen

The Spiritualist

Franklin awaited his moment. He sat inside of the diner with a young woman, contemplating on how to approach Kristyn, for it was she and Nathan who had propelled him into this action, an action he knew would be frowned upon. They ate breakfast and sipped iced tea, and gazed out of the large window, keeping a vigil, waiting for their opportunity. Then what they were waiting for appeared out on the highway, Pastor Doyle's car. This was Franklin's signal for action. He had driven by Kristyn's home just before eight that morning and had seen that Pastor Doyle was already at the house, so he waited here, at the *café*, with the granddaughter of Miss Lilly.

"There he goes, Miss Ruby. Are you ready?" he looked at a woman in her mid-thirties. She was of mixed race, a product of a white father and a black mother; her mother was Miss Lilly's daughter.

Miss Ruby Jenkins had never married. Her ethnicity was oblivious, with her lighter skin tones, amber eyes and reddish hair, a strikingly beautiful woman, who quickly caught the eye of anyone near her! She wore a white sundress of eyelet material, with a blue-green sash tied at her waist and a matching hair-scarf worn gypsy style.

Miss Ruby Jenkins had the gift; her mother did not. Her grandmother, Miss Lilly Jenkins, had raised her from the age of twelve, after Ruby had accepted the offer to become a High Priestess, taking the required oath.

Ruby's parents had not married either and she wasn't even sure if her white father knew of her existence, although her grandmother had told Ruby whom she thought her father might be. He was a high-ranking government official who was now married with a family, although not at the time that he was with Ruby's mother.

Miss Lilly Jenkins had schooled her granddaughter in the art of spirituality and spiritual healing as well as alchemy. Her methods were questionable by some but for those people who sought her out, there had never been any complaints.

Ruby's grandmother was not in good health these days and so when Franklin asked for help, Miss Lilly consulted with her granddaughter to see if she would be willing to help and of course, she agreed.

Now they quickly left the diner, and ten minutes later, were pulling up at Kristyn's home. Franklin arrived at about the time the deputies were becoming more involved with the forensic team, in widening the crime scene's yellow tape to enclose the entire back yard and the area behind the barn. Also, the media were back with satellite trucks and three times the number of reporters as before.

Franklin led the way to the front door, ignoring the reporters who rushed towards them. He knocked twice on the closed red door and waited.

"Franklin!" exclaimed Tyler as he opened the door wider, an unspoken invitation to enter. Franklin stepped to one side and nodded for Ruby to precede him. Tyler stared at the woman, trying to decide who she might be.

Kristyn joined them in the foyer when she heard Franklin's name. "Franklin," she cried as she hugged the old black man. "I'm so glad to see you! I was worried, after yesterday…"

Then she realized that there was a beautiful woman of African descent with him, and spoke to her, "I'm sorry for being rude, won't you two please come into the living room." and she led the way as she spoke.

Somehow, Kristyn knew who this was and so waited for Franklin to explain. Tyler also suspected who she might be and for some reason was pleased that Franklin had gone against Pastor Doyle's wish in not bringing a witch into the situation.

"Ma'am, Mr. Tyler," began Franklin, "this is Miss Ruby Jenkins, she's the granddaughter of Miss Lilly." Not waiting for Tyler to object to him bringing her, he rushed on with the introduction, "She's *not* a witch…"

"Indeed, I am not," Ruby declared. "I am a spiritualist, or a more correctly, a *Necromancer*!"

Kristyn smiled and as a tear formed in the corner of her eye, she said, "I would not have cared. All I want is my son."

Ruby took Kristyn's hand in hers and said, "Allow me to educate you a bit about myself, then I think you will feel better. My profession has a few practices in common with the Wicca Religion but we believe in the one true living God, the God of Abraham. We *do not* believe in a god and goddess, which are represented by the sun and the moon as in Wicca. Much that we know comes from the lost books of Solomon. My ancestors can trace their lineage back to Solomon by way of the Queen of Sheba who bore Solomon a son, Makeda.

"My family is descended from the Priesthood of the Ethiopian Church. We are a little known sect of the Church known as the Emancipated Priestesses. We are married to Christ much in the same way that the Nuns of the Catholic Church are, only we are allowed a consort, though we remain single. We bear only female children, who at the age of twelve, are given a choice of becoming a Priestess. Not all girls choose to become one. But should they have children or marry, their firstborn female is always given the choice and the firstborn only can acquire it. My mother chose not to become a Priestess, so the power was never activated in her.

"I did choose to accept and after my marriage ceremony to Christ, I came under the tutelage of my grandmother, Miss Lilly Jenkins. It was she that passed the blessing on to me. There are only five hundred of us worldwide. I will carry on, as will my daughter; she has just now reached the age of consent and her training has begun by my grandmother and myself."

The room was quiet as this story unfolded, and Kristyn asked, "I think that's a remarkable account and, as hard as it is, I do believe you. I had heard of the relationship between Solomon and the Queen, of course; it is written in the Book of Kings and in Chronicles. It doesn't say there was a son, though. But this lost book, it isn't in our Bible is it?"

"No," Ruby replied, "it is not. It is one of the many books not accepted into the Canon; it *is* in the Holy Book we use. These books are known as the *Apocrypha* books."

"Can you tell us more," asked Tyler who was very impressed with the knowledge and carriage of this lady.

Ruby smiled and replied, "I am pleased that you are interested. Everyone is familiar with the Wisdom of Solomon but most are not aware of his control over the spirit realm, especially those of demonic persuasion. He had spells, or incantations that he used to seek help from the spiritual realm. He was an alchemist as well and we have the recipes of his potions and his incantations. Now, time is precious, please show me the child."

Tyler responded first, and said, "This way," and led them into the dining room where the cracked mirror reclined against the wall. "Here, see for yourself."

Ruby stepped nearer the mirror, knelt down and stared hard into it. She touched the fracture, then looked back out into the dining room, and said, "It does not reflect this room. What room does it reflect?" she asked looking at the three of them.

Together, they replied, "The attic!"

Looking their way as she stood, she said, "The mirror must be taken back into the attic, for it was there that the child was imprisoned." As she spoke, she removed from her shoulder bag, a book. It had strange symbols etched into the front of its leather jacket.

"This fissure here," she said as she slid her finger along the crack in the mirror, "is a portal. It is how he was taken into the other realm."

A gasp came from Kristyn. Seeing her distress, Tyler drew her close to his side, "How...?." She asked.

"How? That is the unanswerable question, one, we as mortals, will never know or understand. But it is what it is. I am searching my book of incantations, so while you carry the mirror back, I will go through this for the best spell or potion, whichever is needed."

Together, Franklin and Tyler carried the mirror back up stairs, as they did so, there was a knocking at the front door. Kristyn eased it open only a crack to see who it might be. To her dismay, she saw the media cluttering her front porch. Not wanting to take the time to talk now, she said quickly and rather rudely, "I cannot talk now, will you please leave my porch." She pushed the door closed, twisted the deadbolt and hurried back to where Ruby sat at her dining room table, slowly flipping through her copy of the Book of Solomon.

Kristyn sat down opposite her at the table. She did not speak, for she did not want to break Ruby's concentration as the woman was obviously reading. Ruby looked up, stared a moment at Kristyn, rubbed her brow and spoke, "I think I have found the potion and ritual needed to invoke the entity which holds your son in the space between worlds. As a flesh and blood mortal, he could not enter the spirit realm, so there has been a separating; his spirit has crossed over, his physical, flesh and blood body, is still in this world. The image in the mirror is just that, an image, only we cannot see it except by way of the reflection in the mirror. Yet this being wants something more from him," Ruby paused.

"What does it want from a five year old?" asked Kristyn anxiously.

"I am unsure for this particular occasion but generally they want energy and innocence, an unmarred soul. They go about acquiring it in different ways." Ruby removed a small notepad and pen from her shoulder bay, "Excuse me for a moment, I need to concentrate."

Ruby returned her focus to the Spell Book, and you would think that she was alone in the room when she turned her attention to it; she had the ability to block all others when she needed to!

Kristyn eased her way from the table. Wanting something to do that was useful, she began cleaning up the kitchen from their morning breakfast. She had to hand wash the dishes and made a mental note to purchase a dishwasher. Also, she needed to buy a washer and a dryer;. appliances that she had left behind in her furnished apartment.

Mundane chores, why did she bother, when the only thing of any value was lost to her? Yet she continued with the clean up, finally taking the broom and sweeping the kitchen. She had barely taken note of Tyler and Franklin returning; they stood at the kitchen door without speaking then left the room quietly. It was plain that Ruby should not be disturbed and that Kristyn too was mentally, as well as physically, occupied.

Kristyn's final task was to carry out the trash, a chore she had given Nathan, a chore he did with pride because it earned him his five dollars a week allowance. It was now two days and it had not been taken care of, so she did it now.

Carrying the bag to the back porch, she was startled to be greeted by the kitten! Casper was hungry, he hadn't been fed since the day before and both his food and water dishes were empty! Purring loudly, the white cotton ball wrapped himself about her ankles. Setting her burden down, she bent and scooped up the kitten.

Rubbing his softness next to her cheek, the tears she had been holding back now flowed freely. She sat down and let the tears come; she did not want to be comforted, she wanted, she needed, this release of emotions. She cried silently, drying her tears with her hands, and all the while, Casper purred in her lap as she stroked his silken fur.

Just that repetitious motion brought a kind of comfort. After all, this kitten was the last thing Nathan had held, had cared for, had loved. Time passed; how long she did not know but something then broke through her veneer of grief; a mumble, her name, they were looking for her.

"I'm out here feeding the kitten," she called with just the least bit of a tremor in her voice. She entered the kitchen carrying Casper.

"Come here, Miss," said Ruby.

Kristyn took the chair next to Ruby. "You have found what should be done?" she asked.

"Yes, I have found what is needed. We first must have a circle of protection about this house. That will be done by twelve young men, wearing white hooded robes, with the leader carrying the Holy Bible. As they circle the house at sunset, each in turn will pour plain salt creating a circle of protection. Each will carry a scented candle. As they march, there is a chant that they will speak continuously until the ritual is complete.

"Then, we must have a sacrifice... an animal sacrifice. It should be a creature owned by the victim. Also, we need ash from a fire, which was used in a loving home, preferably the victim's home. We need earth from the grave of a close relative, preferably one that has died recently. And many candles of which some need to be scented; pine for cleaning, vanilla for sweetness and cinnamon to sooth. The unscented candles are for clarity."

Kristyn stood with Casper in her arms and he purred softly; the thought that rushed through her mind, she just as quickly discarded. How could she allow him it to be sacrificed? So she said nothing.

"I'll tell Tyler," she said and went to find him.

Franklin and he were in the front foyer, looking out the window at the commotion outside, with the media and the authorities. Evidently, the media was instructed to take a further location from the crime scene.

"Tyler," she whispered.

Both men turned their attention to her.

"Miss Ruby needs some things, can you help get them?"

"Sure, just say," responded Tyler.

Kristyn supplied the list and Tyler wrote them down. Just as they had finished, there was a knock at the door.

"It's Mom and Dad," said Tyler glancing out the window and then unbolting the door to let them in. Quickly they entered; all the while fighting the barrage of questions thrown at them. At least the media did not attempt to enter the house; they stayed on the ground at the base of the doorsteps, amid all the boxes and items out on the lawn, exiles from the attic.

"It's become a battlefield out there," stated Pastor Doyle.

"Indeed, it has. I see Franklin is back, we saw his truck," said Mrs. Doyle.

"Yes, he and a friend arrived just after you left this morning, Dad," said Tyler.

"Oh? Who?"

"Come on into the dining room, Tyler replied as he and Kristyn led the way.

As they entered the dining room, there stood Franklin with Ruby. "This is Miss Ruby Jenkins," said Franklin.

"The witch?" exclaimed Pastor Doyle.

Chapter Eighteen

Barn's Investigation

Just then, a knock at the back door drew everyone's attention, "I'll get it," said Tyler. It was mid-morning, and the heat was already unbearable, it was August now and the dog days of summer were in full force. There stood two men, both dressed in white cover-alls, which weren't so white any longer. One man appeared to be in his mid-forties, with sandy colored hair, a large mustache and sunglasses. The other one was only slightly younger, with coal black hair, brown eyes and a deep tan.

"Good morning gentlemen, how can I help you?" asked Tyler.

"Good morning. Forgive this disturbance of your morning. I am the lead forensic investigator, Sergeant Murphy and this is my assistant, Officer Langston. We need to fill you in on what we've found so far," said Sergeant Murphy.

Tyler held the door open further, "Won't you step inside?"

"Yes, thank you."

Both men moved in front of Tyler in the direction he pointed. "These gentlemen want to share some information with us. I hope it's okay, but I've asked them inside. It's mighty hot out today."

Pastor Doyle responded, upon seeing the look of despair on Kristyn's face. "I'm sure it's no problem. Please come in, have a seat," and he indicated the kitchen chairs. "Would you care for some iced tea?"

"That would be nice, if it's not too much trouble," said Sergeant Murphy.

Pastor Doyle looked at his wife who replied, "It's no trouble."

'What now?' Kristyn thought. Another interruption to stall the release of her son. Although her heart was not in it, Kristyn's sense of hospitality kicked in and she uttered, "Here, allow me."

Mechanically, Kristyn went about the motion of getting glasses, filling them with ice and handing them to Mrs. Doyle to fill with tea. Only minutes later, they sat around the small kitchen table, listening expectantly to this news. It was hoped that it would be declared complete, and the forensics personnel and the media would leave, and allow Kristyn to concentrate on retrieving Nathan. The wish was too much to ask.

"....further evidence shows a wide-spread use of the land to hide the bodies. The barn needs to be demolished, which is why we need to see you. Who owns this residence?"

"That would be me," said Kristyn with just a touch of exasperation in her voice. "Why demolish it? Not that I really care, most likely I will do so myself."

"Well, we really want to go over the structure board by board, just to see. I think we have two crime scenes here, a recent one, and another dating from around the time of the Civil War and forward until today. We keep finding, side by side, human remains, people who met their demise at different times, as much as one hundred and fifty years' difference. Not natural deaths either. There was something going on here for a longer time than we first thought. We kinda suspect ritualism in play."

"What do you mean by that?" asked Pastor Doyle.

"He means sacrifice, human sacrifice," came a feminine voice. Ruby stood in the doorway from the dining room; they had forgotten her and Franklin for the moment.

Both forensic men now looked at her. "What do you know of this?" Officer Langston asked.

Ruby slowly entered the room, "It is an outlawed form of voodoo. It is practiced by a sect that has lived in this area for some time now. They are of African descent, West African to be precise. This would include the countries of Togo, Benin and Nigeria. My people are from East Africa, Ethiopia, and we practice an entirely different religion. I am Christian, whereas they be of *Vodun* or,as the west pronounces it, Voodoo. My grandmother, Miss Lilly Jenkins, she is near a hundred years old, and has told me stories of this cult, located in various sections of the old South. Their beliefs have become corrupted and no longer resemble true Voodoo. No one knows the primary location of their meeting place and people suspect that they worship demons and sacrifice humans to them. I am sure you can learn more in research online or even better, in the archives of this area at the library or city hall."

Sergeant Murphy nodded his head and said, "*That*, we suspected and we think this barn may be it, the primary site for their ceremonies."

Now everyone's attention focused on the Sergeant, as he continued, "I will tell you what has been found so far, but this is confidential. We can't leak this to the media or our case will be sabotaged and we will never find out who is behind these grisly murders. But it is a cult that is of the African-American community, members must not be of mixed blood, only true bloods are allowed. Ancestral research is done on new applicants, and they must pass. Our experts in this field have already dove into it and found out this much.

Also found was a surprising abnormality. Now prepare yourselves for this; we also found the skeletal remains of a set of Siamese triplets that had been sacrificed as well."

"Oh no!" exclaimed Kristyn coming quickly to her feet. "We found ledgers in the attic about them. It only said that they died, not how. We just assumed it was from natural causes."

"So, you folks know of them. I thought it would come as a surprise. However, no, our results clearly reveal that the center triplet was sacrificed ritually and that the other two were allowed the torture of slowly dying by poison from the decaying body, which took over a week. They did not die at the same time."

Tyler retrieved the ledgers and showed the accounts of the triplets' lives and their photos to the two men.

"Then this ledger has recorded only the partial truth. You know what this means?" asked Tyler looking around the room.

"It means that either my ancestors were in on it or knew of it and hid the fact," said Kristyn despairingly.

Tyler nodded, and went to stand next to Kristyn, where he placed his arm about her shoulder. He could feel that she was on the verge of collapse and how she was getting through all of this was beyond his comprehension.

"Well, we know how upsetting all of this information is," said Sergeant Murphy. "I asked Sheriff Brown about those trespassers and he confirmed that they were young black men, about four of them that he actually saw, could've been more. They could be members of the cult, we are checking into that. That was about three years ago and as far as we know they have not returned. The most recent remains that we've found were from around that time frame."

"And you think that more will be revealed by tearing down the barn?" asked Pastor Doyle.

"Well, as it stands right now, all we've done is excavate the graves but we have our suspicions that more are there. Do we have your permission?"

"Yes," replied Kristyn. "When will you begin?"

"As soon as you sign this consent form," said Sergeant Murphy taking from his shirt pocket a folded typewritten sheet of paper. He laid it out flat on the table; it was very simple with no fine print, just instruction and spaces for signatures and witnesses.

"Today then," stated Kristyn as she looked up at Tyler, who nodded sending the message that it would all work out.

She picked up the paper and read the short instructions. She quickly signed it and watched as Tyler and his father witnessed it.

Sergeant Murphy took the sheet, re-folded it and placed it back into his pocket. "Heavy equipment will be called in now. We will keep it as tidy as possible and we will take care to clean up afterwards. You should have no worries along those lines. Good morning to you." Both men exited the back door.

The group remained silent for a long moment, as the news sunk in at what had transpired on this farm.

"But I lived here my entire life; there were never any such activities going on, I would have noticed," said Kristyn, as she looked around the room.

"Things can be hidden," said Ruby.

"I suppose they can, but for almost eighty years my grandparents lived here and farmed this land. I don't see how," Kristyn's voice had the tone of disbelief.

"Before we draw any conclusions, why don't we wait and see what is uncovered in the barn," said Tyler, keeping his supporting arm around Kristyn's shoulder. "Right now we have more pressing things."

Now Pastor Doyle looked at Miss Ruby Jenkins, "You say you are a Christian?"

"Yes, that I am," she replied and took time to explain how. Afterwards, Ruby paused as she observed Pastor Doyle's facial expression.

"I can only say I have never heard of your sect before - women priests? Not customary in traditional Christianity, I am at a loss and do not understand," said Pastor Doyle with a shake of his head.

"I do not need to understand," blurted out Kristyn, pulling away from Tyler. At the moment, she did not want a comforting touch unless it came from her son. "We have wasted so much time! Ruby, I have given Tyler the list of things needed, what now?"

"Now we wait until dark."

"I see," sighed Kristyn.

"It will take some time to prepare, we need the young men and can we have the debris on the front lawn removed?" said Ruby. "It is in the way and evil spirits might harbor among the boxes."

"I'll take care of that," said Tyler. "I have a storage facility at the work yard. Franklin," he said looking at the old black man, "You know what to do."

"Yes sir, Mr. Tyler that I do," and he hurried from the dining room as he dialed numbers on his cell.

"Dad, how about seeing if the Youth Group has twelve young men who will help us tonight."

"Sure son, what do I tell them?"

Tyler explained as quickly as he could. "I'm on it," said Pastor Doyle.

"We need ash from a loving home," Ruby reminded them.

"I'll check the fireplace in the living room. Grandma always burned a fire in it even after the heating system was installed. So, I'm pretty sure there's a bit there. Do you need a great deal?"

"No, a handful or so, it must be mixed with the blood of the sacrifice," Ruby explained. "Then there's the soil from the grave of a loved one."

"Nathan's father is buried at the cemetery behind the church," said Kristyn. "My parents and grandparents are there too, which would be the best?"

"The father," answered Ruby. "The soil will also be mixed with the blood and ash."

"I can have the caretaker of the cemetery gather the soil for you," said Pastor Doyle. "He lives on the grounds so it shouldn't be difficult for him. He has all the records and location of the plots."

"It sounds like that just about covers it," said Tyler. "So, I'm off to town to pick up the rest of these things. I'll be back as quick as I can. I'm confident my crew can have the lawn cleared this afternoon."

Chapter Nineteen

The Preparations

Soon there was a buzz of activity outside of the house on the front lawn, as Tyler's crew brought in a large moving van and began loading the boxes and other items into it. As it was about one o'clock in the afternoon when they began, it took until four o'clock to complete and take away. Kristyn took a pail from the back porch and went into the living room. She knelt at the fireplace; fond memories returned to her from her childhood. She remembered the hot summer days when she sought coolness within the stones of the fireplace. There was always ash there even after Grandpa had cleaned it, and there was now. Using the hearth shovel, she scooped some up and dropped it into the pail. She took her treasure to the kitchen and sat it on the floor by the door.

Ruby sat at the dining room table still reading her copy of the Book of Solomon. Kristyn did not speak and left the lady to her study. Kristyn picked up Casper from his bed where he slept and carried the kitten with her to the foyer. Here she watched from one of the long windows that framed the front door, as Tyler's crew loaded the attic's contents into a large moving van. Also, there came on a flat-bed truck, two backhoes, which were driven to the back of the house and unloaded, then the rig left. She watched as a cameraman and several reporters talked with Sergeant Murphy. She wondered briefly what sparked their interest now, the crew removing the items from the front lawn, or the backhoes taken around back, most likely both.

All the while, she held onto the kitten who accepted this attention as his just due.

"Miss," a voice came from behind her, it was Ruby.

Kristyn turned and faced her with a questioning look.

"I need a private place to prepare myself, with fasting and prayer; do you have a private room?"

"The bedrooms upstairs are the most private areas of the house," Kristyn replied, "but it is up there that all of the activities occur. How would you feel about using the master-bedroom?"

"I think it will do nicely, do you mind showing me?"

"Of course," replied Kristyn, as she turned from the events outside and preceded Ruby up the stairs. At the landing, Kristyn paused, looked at Ruby, smiled as she stroked Casper whom she still carried, and said, "There is the master bedroom, there is no AC in that room but if you leave the door open, the cool air from the other two bedrooms will cool it. I'll switch them on for you now."

As Kristyn headed in that direction, Ruby replied, "There is a presence up here, I feel it powerfully."

Kristyn stopped and replied, "Yes, there is." She said no more and turned on the AC in both rooms then rejoined Ruby, "Do you still want to stay up here alone?"

Ruby nodded, "Yes, I need isolation just now. Don't worry; I will do very well on my own."

Kristyn smiled, nodded and said, "I believe you will." Without another word, she went back down stairs just in time to see Tyler entering the front door, with a posse of reporters on his tail. "Sorry, no comment at this time," he called to them and shut the door as he set down the large cardboard box which he carried.

"Looks like you escaped this time," said Kristyn as she joined him.

Tyler looked down into her face and saw the worry plainly written there, "Yes, I did. How are you?" As he spoke, he gently took her by the shoulders and pulled her close to him. He felt her sigh as she allowed this embrace; she rested her head against his chest and listened to the steady beat of his heart.

"I am living a nightmare," she responded, "a bad dream from which I cannot awake."

"I'm having the same nightmare," he said. "Can I get you anything? Tea, a sandwich? It's nearly five and you missed lunch..."

"Did I? I don't recall. This day has been a blur. It's passing quickly but yet it seems like it will never end. We must wait for darkness, is what Ruby said."

"Speaking of her, where is she? In the kitchen?"

"No, she is upstairs in the master bedroom."

"Why?"

"She is fasting and praying, is all she would say and she wanted complete solitude."

"But that's where..."

"I know, and she sensed it but wanted to stay anyway. I was just coming down when you came in. How is everything coming?"

"I have everything she requested, some of it is still in the truck but I brought in the candles, didn't want to chance them melting in this heat. The men have the lawn cleared I see, now the reporters have more room," he smiled at his own joke.

Kristyn half-heartedly returned his smile and just nodded her head in the affirmative.

"Come into the kitchen and I will fix you a sandwich," said Tyler as he took her upper arm and gently guided her in that direction. Kristyn allowed this mentoring as she felt drained and knew she needed to eat although her hunger was not for food.

****

Ruby stood alone in the darkened master bedroom and surveyed her surroundings; the drapes were drawn to shut out the afternoon's heat. The old fashioned four-poster bed was the dominant piece in the room. The roll top desk was an antique and seemed to have an ambiance about it. She listened to the retreating steps of Kristyn as she went back down stairs, then there came muffled voices rising up from the foyer. Then those too faded and vanished. Now the only sound she heard was the machinery from outside. A glance out the window revealed a backhoe beginning the demolition of the barn. They had said that they would start immediately and they had.

Ruby began her preparations; she placed her satchel upon the bed and removed from it a sheer lace veil, that she used to cover her head and face. Next, she removed a smooth red stone the size of a goose egg, with a glossy surface reflective like a mirror. It was used for Scrying, or a method of communicating with spirits and for seeing into the immediate future. She placed it on the desk. Next, she laid the Book of Solomon and the Holy Bible gently next to it. The Bible's leather binding was black and on the front cover was a symbol etched in silver. Next, she removed a red cinnamon scented candle, which was commonly sold during the holidays.

She struck a match and lit the candle as she placed it on the desk. She closed the door. It was still warm in here for it hadn't been long enough for the AC to cool the other bedrooms, much less get this far down the hall. It would have to do; she needed the privacy and the darkness to aid in preventing outside distractions and interference. She made use of the chair and sat down. She opened the Book of Solomon; she flipped deliberately through its pages, as though she knew where the verses were located which she needed. She was no longer searching for answers or instructions, she knew what was needed; she just needed the special prayer. Finding it, she adjusted her head cover, moved the candle close so that its yellow flame flickered on the rice paper of the book. Her lips moved as she silently read the verse. Then cupping her hands together, she laid her forehead upon them, shut her eyes and began whispering the prayer. The prayer soon turned into a chant.

Behind the darkness of her lids, Ruby felt the chill enter; it crept up from the floor at her ankles, slowly rising up her entire body where it shrouded her. Still she prayed, still her eyes remained shut, and colder she became. Soon, chill bumps appeared on her uncovered arms and legs; still she chanted, only now her words were no longer whispered but rose in a crescendo, until she was screaming them. But she did not open her eyes.

****

Kristyn and Tyler sat at the kitchen table where they were eating a bacon, lettuce and tomato sandwich and drinking iced tea. Then the stillness was shattered by the relentless chant coming from upstairs. It grew in intensity and became more of a scream. Both of them jumped from their chairs.

"Ruby!" they exclaimed together, immediately they headed towards the foyer, and then ran up the staircase, with Tyler leading. Not waiting to knock on the bedroom door, he pushed it, but it would not open. He looked at Kristyn with a puzzled expression. She returned his look with a shrug of her shoulders. He tried again with more force. This time the door flew open and a shadowy mass rushed out and flew down the hall, where it crept beneath the attic door. Tyler stared long and hard after the shade. So, that is what Kristyn and Nathan saw that day. He must admit it was unnerving and he felt a chill rush over him when the shadow fled.

Returning his mind to Ruby, he and Kristyn hurried into the room. They felt the cold and the murkiness of the darkened room. Ruby was slumped over at the desk, with her head resting on her folded arms and the book.

"Ruby," whispered Tyler as he took the woman by her shoulders and gently pulled her to a sitting position. Her eyes were squeezed shut and she still whispered the chant. "Ruby," he spoke louder, "Come out of it," when he realized she was in a trance.

Still no response, Tyler shook her roughly, "Ruby! Come out of it!" he shouted.

This time she ceased the chant and whimpered, "Is it gone?"

Tyler looked at Kristyn and they both looked around the room then at the open door, Tyler replied. "Yes, it's gone."

Tyler felt her relax as the tenseness in the muscles of her upper arms let go. She opened her eyes and stared hard at Tyler; she shook loose his grip and made to stand, but her legs were shaky and she sat down again.

"What happened here," Tyler asked.

It took a moment for Ruby to compose herself, then she answered, "I was preparing for tonight, but this entity considers this upstairs area his domain, not just the attic. It attacked me and had I not had the protection of the Firestone, it would have carried me away as it did your son. But it is not as strong out here as in the attic, and I am not an unprotected five-year-old. Help me stand please, I feel weak. It was trying to possess me."

Between them, Tyler and Kristyn escorted Ruby back down stairs and into the living room.

Ruby felt the warmth return to her body and slowly her strength also. "Thank you," she said, looking at them both. "We are dealing with evil, a demonic spirit. Had I not been in deep prayer when it attacked, I might not have been able to resist it. What time is it?"

"It's almost seven," said Kristyn. "We have about two hours before sunset."

"It's not much time, we must hurry. Were you able to acquire the items I requested?"

"Yes and my dad's recruiting the young men, but I haven't heard from him yet," said Tyler. "I'll go to the truck and get the rest of the things you asked for. The candles are in that box by the front door. Be right back," and he left.

He returned with two more sacks. Placing them on the table, he removed fifteen boxes of plain table salt, "One box for each youth," he explained "and a few extras. *And* for candles, I picked up these scented pillar candles, four are vanilla, four are pine, four are cinnamon and four are unscented, as instructed. Also, I bought these votive lights; they were fifty in a bag for four dollars, that should be plenty. And also, four inch-sized, scented pillars and six tapers, I didn't see those in scents, and I bought only the white ones. That's enough firepower there to burn down a house."

"They all will be needed," said Ruby. "Did you get the ash?"

"Yes," said Kristyn.

"The soil from a love one's grave..."

"We haven't heard from my parents yet," said Tyler.

"The sacrifice..."

For a moment, there was total silence.

"It should be something that is familiar to the victim."

"It doesn't have to be a pet does it?" asked Kristyn.

"I don't think I have ever used a pet; generally I have used chickens, lambs, cattle or a goat but it should be an animal that the person has at least seen."

"A rooster?" said Kristyn.

"Yes, that would do. We need it first, before we begin the ceremony; there must be a burnt blood sacrifice."

"Where are you going to get a rooster?" asked Tyler.

"There's a rooster and several hens out behind the barn, they have a chicken coop but they are not penned up. I haven't bothered about them much, only fill the feeder once a week; I've even gotten a few eggs from them."

"I'll go see if I can catch a rooster," said Tyler as he headed out the back door.

"Okay, sit down and let's talk," said Ruby.

Kristyn took a chair, propped her elbows on the table and gave Ruby her attention.

"I have already experienced this demon, the darkness. He is strong but his range is limited. The potion that I will concoct will enrage him. There is love and sacrifice within the potion, two sentiments which are opposite his. He is hate and selfishness. There is a long history on this land, long before it was settled and farmed, long before this house was built. It resides within the earth, the dirt itself. While we wait for the others to arrive, tell me what you know. It is nearly twilight, so give me the condensed version."

Kristyn related the information that she, herself, had only recently learnt.

****

Chapter Twenty

The Barn's Secret

Tyler halted as he stepped out of the back door. The heat of the late afternoon hit him full in the face; even though he had been in and out of it all day, it still was a shock. But it was August and August was the hottest month of the summer.

There were two backhoes at work on opposite ends of the barn and stacks of discarded lumber were piling up, as meticulously the barn was dismantled.

"Now, how am I suppose to find a rooster out behind the barn" he asked himself aloud. He silently surveyed the proceedings and located two men who appeared to be in charge. He could tell because they were just standing around doing nothing, and that was the usual behavior for a boss; he should know, he was one. He headed towards them.

The two men, it turned out, were Sergeant Murphy and Officer Langston, they spoke before he reached them.

"Hello there, Mr....." said Officer Langston.

"Doyle," Tyler supplied, "Tyler Doyle."

"Yeah, what can we do for you?" asked Sergeant Murphy.

"I need a rooster," Tyler replied.

"Did you say that you need a rooster?" queried Officer Langston, to which Tyler nodded. "Whatever for?"

"Just say he will be needed in a special recipe."

"Aahh," said Sergeant Murphy. "I didn't know folks still killed their own chickens nowadays. Well, there's a few running loose out here, how'd you aim on catching it?"

"I haven't figured it out yet, this is all new to me."

"Well, after it's caught, we could have the backhoe chop its head off..."

"NO!" exclaimed Tyler, "We need him alive!"

"I don't understand, wouldn't it be easier for us to catch and kill it at the same time?" asked Officer Langston with a puzzled expression.

"Let's just let it be alive, if you please. Now, I'm not too wise on this sorta thing, but I would think we will need a net, something with a pole attached," said Tyler, thinking aloud.

"How about a fishing net," asked Officer Langston.

"That would work."

"I have one in my truck," Officer Langston said then. "I'll fetch it," and he headed towards the front yard.

"You best be quick," Sergeant Murphy said then, "It's getting dark and we are just about to call it quits for the day."

Tyler took a moment to look around and knew time *was* short. Just as Officer Langston returned with the net, he saw his father's car pull into the driveway followed by the church van. "Great, they're here."

He called to his father. Pastor Doyle joined him followed by twelve young teenage boys from the Youth Group and their leader. Tyler knew them for he often served on committees and helped with the different projects the Youth group performed.

"Boys, do you think you can help catch a rooster?" asked Tyler with enthusiasm.

The teenagers ranged in age from thirteen to sixteen, from blondes and brunettes to one redhead. They looked at each other and the redheaded boy, who was fifteen and seemed to be a leader, named Toby, said, "I'm game. When I was a kid, I used to love chasing chickens."

"There's one rooster," explained Tyler, "and we want him caught... alive. Who wants the fishing net?"

Toby held out his hand, "I'll take that," he said with a big grin. "Okay boys, we're on a chicken hunt. Let's go!"

The group took off and Pastor Doyle asked, "For the sacrifice?"

Tyler nodded, "Yeah and time is a wasting. It'll be dark in fifteen minutes or so, I hope the boys make quick work of this."

True to his word, Sergeant Murphy called to the crew that it was quitting time. It didn't take the men long to climb into their work van, leaving the backhoes where they were. There only remained the sheriff's car, with just one deputy and of course, the media, but the backyard was empty.

The teens ran in different directions until they flushed out the chickens that had already gone to roost in the hen house. They singled out the rooster and tore around the yard after him. In any direction the cock headed a teen was there to block him. Toby kept shouting instructions to head the fowl towards him where he could throw the net over him. Then in the distance came the low rumble of thunder. Tyler looked towards the south from which the sound came. Lightning lit up the sky on the horizon, followed five seconds later by another clap of thunder. A summer thunderstorm was moving in. Tyler estimated that it would be upon them in thirty minutes or so. That just might hinder the procession around the house tonight, he thought. Ruby would know how to deal with it, he hoped.

Returning his attention to the hunt, Tyler heard Toby shout out, "We have him cornered. He's in a hole. 'C'mom boys, let's git'im.'" Tyler watched as the group gathered around a section towards the rear of the barn. Then he heard another shout, this time it had the ring of urgency, "Mr. Tyler, you gotta come see this!"

Tyler, his father and the Youth leader, looked at each other, then Toby called again, "Pastor Doyle, Mr. Tyler, Mr. Johnson, hurry up!"

"What on earth," exclaimed the Youth leader, as the three men ran in the direction where all the teens were gathered. When they got there, Toby spoke, "He's gone down underneath that board and when I lifted it up... well, you'll see!"

Tyler did. It was getting quite dark now but in the twilight Tyler saw not a hole but a pit, or more like a room, a basement. Then the sky lit up with a bolt of lightning, followed not two second later by the clap of thunder. Although the lighting wasn't good, Tyler shoved the board aside with the toe of his shoe to reveal steps! "Somebody get me a flashlight," he called. Someone replied that they would, and so Tyler waited.

"What do you see, Son," asked Pastor Doyle.

"I'm not sure, it could be just a root cellar but it hasn't been used for a long time now."

Just then, a youth handed him the flashlight, Tyler focused its beam down the steps and taking the lead, stepped down. The steps were very old because the bricks crumbled a bit on the edges when he applied his weight.

"Be careful," he called to those following him down the steps.

Chapter Twenty-One

The Cellar

Now the three adults stood inside of this cellar. The floor was made of virgin rock; it had been carved out to create this natural floor and walls. Tyler passed the light around; two walls held shelves, confirming his suspicion that it was a root cellar. There were odds and ends on the shelves, all dusty now and covered with cobwebs. There were six ladder-back chairs scattered about, some lying on their sides. They were surprisingly new looking.

In the middle of this cellar was a table, Tyler estimated it to be around a hundred and fifty years old, handmade of oak. It was weathered a dark grey and Tyler saw that the items lying about on it were candles! There must have been a hundred or more, all in different stages of use. He picked one up; it was unscented and did not appear to be new although it was of this period. This placed a thought into Tyler's mind. He would investigate it further before saying anything. There were also small animal bones scattered across the table, as if someone had eaten there.

From the ceiling cobwebs fluttered in the waft that rushed in from the entrance. On one of the walls were tools, instruments and decaying ropes hanging from iron pegs, which had been driven into the rock walls.

Then they heard the cluck of the rooster that was cornered in the cellar. He should be easy pickings now. As their eyes adjusted to the ever-increasing darkness, another surprise awaited them. On the floor in a rounded corner were more bones, a large pile of bones!

Tyler was not all that surprised to see them, what with everything that had been found on the farm, in the attic and in the barn thus far. His suspicions proved correct, this cellar had been used to butcher animals and he suspected humans were tortured here. He walked over to the bone pile, and with the toe of his shoe, pushed them around and several human skulls rolled out.

Audible gasps arose from those inside and those peering in from the door of the cellar.

"Oh my god," exclaimed some of the boys.

Looking back at them, Tyler said, "You boys head on back to the main house. They will know who you are. Wait inside for us. Toby, wait a second, and take the rooster with you." Reluctantly, the boys did as they were told, all but Toby who now entered the cellar. As the other boys left, lightning flashed again with coinciding thunder.

"We don't have much time before the rain starts," said Tyler. "Let's catch this rooster!"

The four of them made short work of capturing the exhausted fowl. Tyler finally dropped the net over the bird, and Mr. Johnson and Toby quickly seized it and secured it inside the net.

"Toby, give this rooster to a woman name 'Ruby.' She'll know what it's for. Now hurry before you get wet."

"Yes sir, Mr. Tyler," said Toby taking the rooster now secured within the net by its feet and tucking it beneath his arm. He went cautiously back up the brick steps and then was gone.

Pastor Doyle spoke, "What do you suppose happened here?"

"Well, the entrance must have been well hidden because the forensic team hasn't found it yet. They were close, tomorrow to be sure they would have." Tyler then walked around the cellar, shining the flashlight and moving items about. "The fact that it was so well hidden indicates that someone wanted it kept out of sight. Or it could've been just nature doing what nature does when left to its own devices."

"What're you looking for son?" asked Pastor Doyle.

"Well, according to Sheriff Brown, the Voodoo sect had a meeting place. He suspected the trespassers as being part of it, a secret meeting place, this could be it."

"I suppose, but it doesn't look used in a long time," agreed Pastor Doyle.

Tyler continued his inspection of the cellar. Among the clutter of tools, which hung on pegs driven into the stone, certain items stood out as not being a normal tool for use in a root cellar. There were several large butchers' knives, boning knives, and meat cleavers, which you would expect to see in a place used for butchering animals.

Tyler took his hand and rubbed at the wall where it had a rough look, this revealed etchings, strange symbols that were a permanent part of the stone now. "I don't know what to make of these, though," said Tyler. "I wonder if they have any Voodoo religious significance."

Tyler focused the light at the ceiling, "Just what I expected," he said. In the wooden crossbeams used to support the roof, or the floor of the barn, were large rusted metal hooks, about ten or so. "Meat hooks."

"Do you mean that this was used to cut up animals?" asked Mr. Johnson.

"Well most certainly, back in that day, farm families did their own meat preparations, from raising the animals, to slaughter and butchering them. This cellar was hewed from rock and was probably kept cold with ice. Meat and vegetables probably lasted awhile in here. It was customary to have root cellars. There was probably a smokehouse too at one time and after the meat had cured, it would have been stored down here. A sufficient refrigerator I would say."

"Yeah, I think that the early settlers and farmers had all kinds of tricks to preserve food without having the modern equipment that we have today," said Mr. Johnson.

Going over to the shelves, they rambled through a hodgepodge of trash, from dust, web-covered empty boxes, to broken glass. They came across old masonry jars and bottles of varying sizes, and rusted tin cans. Then Tyler found a wooden box; it was old and had a crude lock hanging from the latch. It was larger than a shoebox, being about fifteen inches square. There were symbols carved into the wood. Things had been strange around here, and the lock gave him reason to wonder. He still possessed the attic key and used it now. He inserted the key and sure enough, the tumblers clicked, and the padlock came loose into Tyler's hand. "Now, this is odd indeed," he said.

"I know! Why do you have a key that fits that lock?" asked Pastor Doyle.

"It's the attic key," explained Tyler, "and it has opened several doors and padlocks since it was found hidden in the master bedroom. It hung on a tack on the back of the desk. Nathan found it. *And now*, here it is opening this lock. This goes back a long ways and makes me wonder if maybe there were two keys. How else would they be able to unlock it?"

He returned the key to his pocket. "Here, shine the flashlight on the box," he told Mr. Johnson as he handed it to him. Tyler brushed the dust from the box and raised the lid; a strong stench emerged, as did moths! They flew out and into their faces, dozens of them.

"How did they get in there?" asked Pastor Doyle as he shielded his face from the frantic insects. "And that smell!"

"Must have been cocoons placed in there some-how, might have been intentional. How'd they survived is what puzzles me."

He pushed the lid on back until it rested on the rear hinges. Inside was a collection of various items. There were several small rag dolls without faces and with human hair sewn on the heads.

"Voodoo dolls," concluded Tyler, laying them to one side. Next was a cloth sack filled with stones, small, smooth and of different colors. Then two chicken feet tied together, which appeared to have a tarry substance on them, "Blood, most likely," said Tyler, laying them to one side.

He unfolded a cloth which proved to be a hand-drawn map. "I can't tell much about this," Tyler said, holding it up and examining it. "It's not for navigation that's for sure, but I think it shows locations of something. It isn't clear what. Maybe the forensic team can analyze it." He refolded it and laid it to the side. There was a small rounded mirror with no frame, and several small candles, a lock of human hair tied with string, and a pouch with a drawstring closure. Tyler untied it and turned it out onto his hand. Small grains poured out, shiny and sparkly, "Gold dust," observed Tyler and closed the pouch up again. Next was a dagger, with a gold hilt with strange symbols and a large ruby set in the handle. It was about eight inches total length. Next were feathers tied with string. Then there was a very small white box; Tyler removed the top and inside were teeth, human teeth. "Well, this is surprising," he said replacing the top. Picking up another similar box, he pulled off the lid and inside were fingernails. "What...?" declared Tyler, removing a nail and looking at it.

"What is it, Son?" asked Pastor Doyle.

"It's a human fingernail!" exclaimed Tyler.

"Clippings?"

"No, it is the complete nail. Judging from the number in here, there must be several sets of finger-nails."

"Show me," said Mr. Johnson. Tyler did.

"Yep, that's what they are alright. I wonder if they were removed post mortem."

"We have no way of knowing," said Tyler.

"These fingernails could be from torture victims," observed Pastor Doyle.

"Most likely that is the case," agreed Tyler. "There are two more larger boxes like that one," he said picking up another one. Upon opening this one, he found human ears. "Now, this is just too much," said Tyler. He removed one ear, it was hard and leathery and brownish in color. He returned it after allowing his father and Mr. Johnson a good look.

"I wonder what's in this other box," he pondered. "Eyeballs?" He wasn't far off, after removing the top, he saw what looked like small oblong disks, he picked one up, on one edge was hair, "Oh no!" he exclaimed.

"What is it, son?"

"It's eyelids," answered Tyler.

"My word! What have we come upon?" gasped Mr. Johnson.

"Wait, there's one more sack," said Tyler lifting out a canvas bag about eight inches tall. He untied the leather strip and shone the flashlight inside. "What on earth...?"

"What is it son?"

"I don't rightly know," replied Tyler. "It looks like small rubber balls," he said as he reached inside and removed one. He held it up for observation; just then a flash of lightning and a loud thunderclap informed them that the storm had arrived in full force, as wind rushed in along with debris and rain.

"We need to get back to the house but I think we can wait until the rain lets up a bit," said Tyler forgetting for the moment the item he held. Then as he subconsciously fingered the item, he looked again at it. He saw that it wasn't completely round but had a ridge and a bump; he turned it over and it was rough and ragged with two small holes running parallel to each other, then it hit him as to what it was, "It's a human nose!" he exclaimed.

"You serious?" asked Mr. Johnson.

"Yeah, but why not, we have eyes, ears and fingernails, I'm surprised there aren't lips here too." He replaced the nose and began putting everything back into the box. "I am taking this with me to keep it safe, until I can give it to Sergeant Murphy."

"Where are you going to put it?" asked Pastor Doyle. "You can't take it into the house."

"I know. Until I can get to my truck, I'll hide it on the back porch, nobody will find it on a night like tonight. Besides, we will be very busy in just a little bit.

Tyler walked over to the entrance. Although it was still raining, he knew he could not put off going to the house. They would just have to get wet. "Well, are you ready for a mad dash to the back porch?"

"Ready as I'll ever be," said Pastor Doyle.

"Same here," agreed Mr. Johnson.

With Tyler leading and with the box secured under his right arm, he headed out. Soon the three of them were running across the back yard through the mud generated by the demolition, with shards of rain pelting them as they ran. Tyler was first and held open the screened door for the other two.

Within a second of being on the back porch, he heard Kristyn call to him. He quickly shoved the box underneath the table and answered, "Yeah, it's us! The rain caught us and we are a bit wet. Can we get a towel?"

"My goodness you did get wet didn't you," Mrs. Doyle stood in the open back door to the kitchen. "I'll be right back," and she retreated into the kitchen. Kristyn, who was just behind Mrs. Doyle, came on to the porch. The rain sounded like rocks hitting the roof and a look on the ground showed small hailstones mixed in with the rain. The lightning strikes were more frequent and sounded like canons firing.

"It seems to be a fit night for how I am feeling," Kristyn said. Tyler caught the sadness and the slight quiver in her voice.

"It does," he replied.

Mrs. Doyle arrived with the towels and the men dried off as best they could. Their shirts were soaked and their pants' legs and shoes muddy, but there wasn't a thing to be done about it now. Tyler pulled off his T-shirt, which was the only shirt he had on and hung it over the back of the chair. The other two men did the same. Hopefully their shirts would dry quickly.

"I'm sorry but I don't have a dryer," apologized Kristyn. "It's on my list to get one."

"Don't worry, it's August," said Pastor Doyle.

"Well, come on in, Ruby has been busy and I think needs our help," said Mrs. Doyle.

"Wait a minute," said Mr. Johnson. He left and returned with clean dry t-shirts. "I had these in the van. They are the shirts we are using to promote the Walk for Christ march next week. I chose the largest ones; at least they will be dry."

The men said 'thanks' and gratefully slipped on the white t-shirts, which had a picture of the Cross with the words 'Walk for Christ' inscribed down and across it.

Chapter Twenty-Two

Execution of the Ritual

They found Ruby in the living room sitting on the Queen Anne sofa. Her face was shrouded by the sheer white veil. Sitting on the coffee table in front of her was a large red stone placed on a small pedestal. The stone seemed to burn like the embers of a dying fire. There were two books opened on either side of the Firestone and completely circling the coffee table's edge were the different scented votive candles. There were four green pine-scented, four red cinnamon-scented, four yellow vanilla-scented and four white, unscented. In small golden urns were the ash and the soil. There was another larger empty crystal bowl. But most surprising of all was the rooster, which she held securely in her arms. He was still alive and calm.

Standing in rows of four along the four walls of the room were the twelve youths dressed in the white robes. They each held a slender pillar candle that had been encircled with a stiff paper shield, so that the hot wax would not drip on to their hands. For now, they were unlit. Toby, the leader, held a large black Bible.

Upon seeing the rest of them enter the living room, Ruby spoke, "I think we can begin. Will you please take your places?"

Mrs. Doyle and Kristyn guided the men to locations in the room predetermined by Ruby to be the most effective for the ritual. Mrs. Doyle stood with her husband on one side the living room's door and Kristyn seemed a natural pairing with Tyler on the other side. Mr. Johnson was a surprise guest but they utilized him by having him stand next to Franklin, who stood behind the sofa at Ruby's back.

"We first must have a prayer. I ask the man of God if he will lead us," began Ruby. She quietly held the rooster, stroking his silken feathers to keep the bird quiet.

Pastor Doyle stepped forward, "Let's bow our heads in prayer. "Our Heavenly Father, we give homage to Your Holy Name and homage to the Son who lives and sits on Your right hand.

"We ask Your blessings and protection upon this small assembly as we confront Your enemy. May the power of the Evil One have no sway on the warriors of Your Army. We go forth into battle carrying with us the armor of the Heavens. In Christ's name, we do pray, Amen!"

"Amen!" echoed the assembly.

From a distance part of the house a low rumble mixed in with the thunder and was unheard by the assembly.

Ruby then tucked the rooster beneath her arm with his tail feathers in front. Ruby quickly pulled out three of the tail feathers causing the fowl to squawk each time. These she laid on the table in front of the Firestone.

"We will now have the sacrifice," announced Ruby. On the table lay a white folded cloth; she folded the sides back and picked up a small dagger.

Tyler would have sworn that it was identical to the dagger they had just found in the box from the cellar! Was it a customary sacrificial knife? He wondered. Then it occurred to him that Ruby meant to perform the sacrifice right here in the living room.

But before he could protest, Ruby rose from her seat, and Franklin as predetermined, followed her, carrying the crystal bowl to the fireplace where he placed the bowl upon the hearth and they both knelt down beside it. Then Tyler realized that there was a fire burning in the fireplace.

"Do you need help?" he asked.

Ruby did not answer, she only held up her free hand in the sign to stop. Tyler realized she planned to sacrifice the rooster alone. The dagger lay on the hearth beside of the bowl. Ruby took the rooster by its neck and its feet and repeating the chant from the Book of Solomon, which Pastor Doyle recognized as Latin, she chanted. At first, it was a whisper, then the tempo increased in decibels. Then the chant stopped abruptly. Ruby moved quickly, releasing the rooster's neck and holding only his feet, she laid the rooster's upper torso upon the hearth where the fowl obligingly stretched out his neck. Then, taking the dagger; she deftly sliced through the neck, severing the head from the body.

The headless body began jerking; blood gushed from the wound, which Ruby caught in the crystal bowl. The body continued to jerk and convulse, as it reacted to the suddenness of not receiving a signal from the brain. After several minutes of draining into the bowl, the flow ceased; the body was empty of its lifeblood! Ruby then tossed the lifeless body into the flames, where the feathers hissed as they caught fire and the convulsing worsened as if the headless corpse felt the pain from the heat. Dark grey smoke billowed up the chimney and the stench of burning feathers infiltrated the room; it was strong to the point of being nauseating.

Ruby took the head and wrapped it in a white silk cloth. She stood, as Franklin retrieved the bowl of blood and returned to the sofa where Franklin rejoined

Mr. Johnson. The sacrifice was over; now came the mixing of the potion.

The spectators each had this feeling of detachment from the proceedings; they saw but were unaffected, no disgust or sympathy, only as witnesses.

"We will continue," said Ruby. She picked up the urn containing the ash and said, "From the hearth of a loving home, we ask for the power of this love, to be our guardian from the forces of darkness." She slowly poured the ash into the blood, where it lay on top of it without mixing in.

Picking up the urn of earth, she repeated the request, "From the grave of a loved one, we invoke his spirit for our fortification." She poured the soil into the bowl, then she unwrapped the rooster's head and dropped it into the bowl atop of the soil and ash.

"A final tribute from the sacrificed victim, to merge the ash, the consecrated earth and the blood," and she buried the head in the bowl.

The mixture began to churn on its own, mixing as though being stirred by unseen hands. Steam rose from the bowl when the cold ash and soil mixed with the hot blood.

"It is good," she said, as she surveyed her handiwork. "Will the man of God speak a prayer?"

Once again, Pastor Doyle said the prayer. "We come before the most holy One on high to send forth the Holy Spirit and thwart the evil which resides in this home. Give success to our quest to release the child Nathan from his bondage. We do ask in the name of Your only Son, Jesus Christ, Amen"

The room's partisans echoed with "Amen!"

At that precise moment, the storm outside increased in intensity, with a flash of lightning and a clap of thunder that shook the house and, from upstairs, a moan was heard. Then all was still as the lights in the house went out.

They weren't in total darkness because of the candles that burned on the coffee table and the fire in the fireplace.

"A power failure," stated Mr. Johnson, an obvious observation.

"It is from where the evil draws its strength. It has drunk its fill and has caused this power failure. But it can no longer utilize that as a power source. It will seek energy elsewhere," said Ruby. "The electric storm outside can be used by the entity to draw energy. That is why the spirits are more active during electrical storms."

She rose from her position, taking with her one candle and motioned to Franklin who knew the next procedure. He picked up the crystal bowl, which held the potion and followed Ruby. She went to the youths and stopped at Toby, "Extend your candle," she ordered. He did. Ruby lit the candle with the one she carried. She then turned to Franklin who presented the bowl; Ruby began the chant and dipped her right thumb into the blood mixture and made the sign of a cross in the middle of Toby's forehead. She repeated the step with each youth. At the conclusion; she looked at them for a moment and ordered, "Pull up your hoods."

They did and now the sole flame of the candles they held illuminated their faces. The flickering flames distorted their features so that they looked malformed with yellowish skin and eyes reflecting red.

"You are to march around the house outside for a count of twelve. As you march, you will one at a time pour out your box of salt. Your leader, this young man here," and she touched Toby's arm, "has learned the song and will sing. At the conclusion of your march, position yourselves on the four corners of the house. Each corner should have four young men with only one type of scent. Remain at your post regardless of whatever you hear or see. Your position is of utmost importance in restricting the entity from leaving the premises. Now, proceed."

"But it is storming outside," protested Mrs. Doyle. "You can't send these young men out in this. They will get soaked and the lightning is dangerous."

"They are well protected, Madam," said Ruby. "The robes have a water repellent finish, which does not attract lightning. They must do this despite the weather. I have already spoken with them and each decided to fulfill his obligation."

She then walked out of the living room and with a motion of her hand, indicated that the youths should follow. She opened the front door, and although the storm raged, lead by Toby, they marched outside. They proceeded in a clockwise direction around the house. Toby began the song while tilting his box of salt; soon he disappeared around the corner of the house.

But they had forgotten the media! Although most of them had left, there were two satellite trucks still parked down the path about fifty feet from Kristyn's driveway. Upon seeing the youths emerge from the house, dressed like Klansmen, a couple of reporters and a cameraman hurried to the front door. It was raining hard and the lightning and thunder frequent but it did not dissuade them. The cameraman began filming. One reporter approached the house.

"Hello there," he shouted.

Ruby ignored him and turned back inside, shutting the front door, only to hear a rude banging seconds later. Tyler opened the door and, as he expected, there stood the reporter with the cameraman, "Good evening sir," the reporter began.

"Turn off the camera," ordered Tyler.

"I'm sorry but we cannot do that. This is a public story and we have the right to broadcast the news."

"Maybe so, but you are trespassing, return to your truck, there is nothing here for you," and Tyler went to shut the door but found he could not. The reporter had stuck his foot into the frame and now the door was wedged open.

"Remove it or lose it," ordered Tyler in a no-nonsense tone.

"I will when you give me a statement. Why is the Klan here?"

"Okay, I've asked, now I am removing you," said Tyler stepping out on to the porch.

The reporter was forced to back up, "Sir, this can be considered an assault," he stammered and all the while, the cameraman continued with the filming.

"Yes, it can," and without warning, Tyler landed a solid right hook to the man's jaw. This sent him stumbling down the steps out into the rain and landing on his backside in the mud! Just then Toby and the youths appeared from around the house.

"I think you have been assaulted," said Tyler, "Why don't you report it?"

Still the cameraman filmed, first on his colleague lying in the mud, next on the furious face of Tyler and then focusing on the group emerging from around the house.

Looking the cameraman straight in the camera's lens, Tyler said, "Do you want to join him?"

Uttering not a word, he lowered the camera and looked at the reporter. "You coming, Wade?" he snapped. "Or are you just going to lie there?" The cameraman walked off without so much as offering Wade a hand up. The reporter watched as Toby and the boys marched passed him. He flipped over onto his knees and tried to get traction in the slippery mud, found it was near impossible and fell facedown into it. Tyler waited without offering aid; soon the reporter's attempts were successful and, covered in mud and soaking wet, he retreated to the truck. "You'll hear from the police tomorrow," he threatened.

"You're going to hear from them right now," replied Tyler, "if you return to this porch. There's a car parked over there."

Without further words, Wade made it to the truck where there was a heated exchanged between him and the cameraman. Tyler watched a few seconds, then saw the satellite trucks both turn on their headlights and leave. Tyler shut the door just as Toby was making the third trip around the house.

"What's next?" he asked, looking at Ruby.

But before she could reply there came another knock at the front door, "I swear those reporters can't take a hint," he stated, as he jerked open the front door only to find the deputy from the patrol car. "I might have known they would be curious as well," said Tyler softly.

"Mr. Doyle, what's going on? My attempt to speak with these young men marching around the house, singing and pouring out salt, only got me a blank stare and they just kept marching past me. What gives?"

Well, Tyler knew he couldn't strong arm the law so he offered as simple explanation as he could. "It is a religious ceremony; you know, to ward off evil spirits."

"Oh, I guess I can understand. But with the weather like it is, looks to me as if this could have waited. But these summer storms usually don't last long, so I'll go back to the cruiser, just give me a shout should you need anything."

"That we'll do, and thank you deputy."

The deputy nodded and retreated back around the house just as the marchers rounded the house for a fourth time.

Tyler returned to the living room where everyone still waited. Kristyn came to him, seeking his protection and companionship. He looked down at her and they exchanged private thoughts. He smiled and winked and she returned his smile. Without words he was telling her that it was going to work out; Nathan would soon be with her. He casually placed his arm about her shoulder as his father came up to him.

"Had a bit of trouble, did you, Son?"

"A bit. I shouldn't have lost my temper and slugged him, but he was just too pushy. His foot in the door was the last straw. But I don't think he will try that again," said Tyler feeling he needed to explained his actions.

"Ruby is waiting to continue," Kristyn reminded him, not wanting to dwell on others right now.

Without another word, Tyler escorted Kristyn back into the living room where the others still waited. Ruby had now removed her veil although it was draped across her shoulders. "It is time for the next phase of the rescue and exorcism. Participants will need a candle and the mark on their foreheads. Who is taking part?"

Tyler, Kristyn, Franklin and Pastor Doyle raised their hands. Ruby looked them over and said, "I will take only the men."

Kristyn took a step towards Ruby, "But I am his mother, I must be there!"

Tyler was confused also, as to why Ruby did not want to include her.

"Why not?" he asked.

"I sense that this entity has power over her already. She is vulnerable and might well thwart our efforts at risk to herself. She is much too close to the victim; she cannot participate. That is final!"

Kristyn looked up at Tyler with a plea in her eyes but he said, "Ruby knows what is best and we should follow her instructions to the letter, we have thus far. You wait down here with Mom. I am sure you will know when Nathan is freed. Mom, take her. And keep her mind positive; only positive thoughts will dissuade this thing, demon, whatever it is."

Standing in the foyer, Ruby, with her veil in place over her head, took the potion and with it marked their foreheads with a large cross, after which she lit their candles, all the while reciting the prayer. At the conclusion, Ruby lifted her veil and laid it back over her head but did not cover her face. She secured it with two hairpins, and then gave instructions:

"Man of God, I want you to go into the attic first. Say a prayer of protection. Then take this potion and paint a partial circle on the floor in front of the mirror. Begin the line on the left by painting a cross on the frame then seal the circle with another cross on the right side of the frame. Then, Tyler and Franklin will take the candles and place them directly on the mark that you have painted. Do not light them; that will be done after we enter the attic. Call me when completed. Then after we are all in the attic, seal the threshold the same way."

Tyler handed his father the attic key, "The doors are locked," was all he said.

"Are we ready?" asked Ruby.

"Yes," was the unanimous response.

"Good. Will the Man of God proceed?"

Pastor Doyle waited briefly as Ruby lit his pine-scented candle and handed him the potion. He headed up the staircase. He halted briefly at the landing and noticed that it was very cold here. But as he began to walk down the hallway towards the attic, the darkness and the cold both departed from before him, as if running away. The attic door was locked; he unlocked it and pushed it open just in time to see the dark mass slide beneath the attic door at the top of the stairs.

Inhaling deeply, he drew upon his faith and gathered his strength from a resource that he had never had to tap before. He bowed his head and uttered a silent prayer. He felt his resolve to complete this task grow strong, and he proceeded up the stairs. It was quite warm now whereas before it was cold. He unlocked this door and pushed it open. Cold air was like a slap in the face as he entered and gloom filled the attic.

The attic looked different from the last time he was here. It was almost empty, the mirror and a side table were all that remained. The mirror stood in the middle of the attic, resting against its support. Approaching it, he took the three feathers, which were secured with string; he dipped them into the blood potion and began painting the circle.

Pastor Doyle tried not to look around the attic as he did this. Nathan's reflection was as it had always been since his imprisonment. He wondered if there would be enough to complete both tasks, as a chicken was not a large bird, but he managed to complete the semi-circle.

Pastor Doyle immediately summoned the others. First, Tyler and Franklin placed the red, cinnamon-scented candles around the mirror, then Pastor Doyle sealed the threshold after everyone was inside.

"Close and lock the door," said Ruby. "Then place the pine-scented candles there and light them. Take the rest of the candles and encircle the room, alternating the scents. Space them evenly and go ahead and light them."

After a few minutes, these tasks were complete. Ruby retrieved the bowl from Pastor Doyle, saying, "I will now distribute the rest about the attic." Taking the feathers and beginning to chant the special prayer in Latin, she used a jerking motion of her wrist to scatter small specks of the potion all about the attic. With the crystal bowl empty, she set it to one side. Now Ruby sat down, Indian style, inside of the circle surrounding the mirror and said, "The rest of you stand outside the circle behind me, take each other's hands, close your eyes and do not open them until I say."

The men did so. Ruby took the Firestone, and holding it in her cupped palms, began to chant the prayer. It didn't take long for the warmth in the attic to be replaced by cold, bone chilling cold. Even as the attic became colder, the Firestone grew brighter! It appeared to have flames leaping from it even as Ruby held it. The attic's interior grew as dark as the cold and were it not for the candles flickering around the attic, it would be in total darkness.

In the attic's interior nothing changed, but the reflection within the mirror and behind Nathan did, a shadowy figure formed, the Shadowman! Yet, his appearance was unseen as everyone still had their eyes shut.

But now, opposite the Shadowman, was another hovering object, it was the Orb! It beamed a bright white and as Ruby continued her prayer, the orb separated into three spheres, co-joined spheres! After a moment, the Orbs approached them, moving forwards, towards the attic's interior! They abruptly stopped, as if an invisible shield prevented any further advancement! The Firestone grew redder, and the flames leapt from it; Ruby felt the warmth increase within it. She knew something was happening but it had not reached the point she needed; she continued the prayer and kept her eyes closed.

Ruby's prayer had entrapped both the Shadowman and the Orb in the spirit realm. Ruby knew that she must keep the two realms separated, keep the spirits in the spirit realm but rescue Nathan and bring him out into the physical realm. The mirror must then be broken, entrapping the spirits. Now the Firestone grew very hot, so hot that Ruby was forced to put it down! She opened her eyes.

Seeing that her objective was accomplished, Ruby ceased the prayer, "You may open your eyes," she said, "but continue to hold hands."

The interior of the attic was no longer gloomy; the soft flickering glow of so many candles chased the shadows about the room. One could not be certain if they were just shadows or something more.

Tyler focused on the mirror and for the first time he saw both the Shadowman and the Orb! Nathan remained with his ankles crossed and his head upon his raised knees. Tyler's heart broke and then beat faster at seeing this child in such a dilemma! Kristyn had been like a zombie ever since his taking three days ago. Had it only been three days? It seemed like a lifetime! So much had happened. And so much more would happen.

"I prayed to God," said Pastor Doyle, "I know He will release this child but we must keep our faith. We must be strong. He has sent us an ally, and we must support her, she will need re-inforcement. We are dealing with the forces of darkness!"

"Thank you, Pastor," said Ruby, "The more positive our thoughts the more the entity will weaken. With help from the spirits, the portal is closed, but we must open it for a moment when Nathan is released but only at the precise time, the time when only he can pass through. Immediately afterwards, the mirror must be broken. That act will close this portal. It will send Nathan out while keeping the spirits in."

****

Mr. Johnson, Kristyn and Mrs. Doyle watched as Tyler, Franklin and Ruby went up the stairs. Tyler looked back down at them after arriving on the landing. His eyes sought Kristyn's face. She saw the worried look there and knew that hers reflected the same emotion. He smiled and she returned it. There was nothing more to say as she watched him disappear. There was only the wait now.

Mrs. Doyle took Kristyn by her upper left arm and said, "Let's wait in the kitchen. I'll fix us a sandwich."

Yes, it was dinnertime and although she wasn't feeling any hunger, she knew she should eat so that she could stay focused. Kristyn allowed herself to be guided back towards the kitchen. The thunderstorm had lessened a bit. Although thunder and lightning were still prominent they were becoming distant as the storm retreated. At least the hard rain was now a light shower.

Mr. Johnson spoke, "Kristyn, you just relax, Mrs. Doyle and I will take care of things," and they proceeded to prepare a light supper.

Kristyn wandered out on to the back porch. The youths were making yet another round of the house. How many trips had it been? This ritual made little sense to her, but then nothing made sense to her anymore. Only a few short weeks ago, her life held no mystique, only the day-to-day struggle of earning her livelihood and raising her five-year-old son. She never would have thought that inheriting her childhood home, a home she loved and which held only fond memories, would bring such tragedy into her life, and in such a short time.

Soft warmth about her ankles and mewing alerted her to Casper's presence. She thought at how grateful she was that he was not the sacrifice. Although, had it been necessary to save Nathan, she would have given him over. After Nathan's release, he would have his beloved kitten.

She stooped to pick up the kitten and, as she wrapped her hand about Casper's middle, something caught her eye. Releasing him, she pulled the heavy wooden box out from under the table. She heaved it on to the tabletop.

"What on earth is this?" she said.

Kristyn lifted the lid and began searching through the contents. Viewing the macabre items in the different boxes and pouches brought dismay, disgust and fear. After a minute or so, she could look no longer, and said, "Someone brought this from the barn. I wonder."

Kristyn was not too much into the paranormal and knew little of it that is until lately, when she had become very well educated in some areas. And this one area was Voodoo! It had been discussed in some detail and what she had heard she had retained. Inside of this wooden box was paraphernalia of Voodoo. What had Tyler discovered? Her curiosity was up and she could not wait until they were through in the attic. Besides, by then her mind would be on the return of Nathan and this wooden box and what was in the barn would be forgotten.

As she contemplated this, she looked out across the backyard. Something had caught her eye. She peered intently through the falling rain; there again! A lightning flash, lighting up the entire area where the barn once stood. Now a noise and the outline of a figure: was that a child and was it crying or was it the whine of a cat? When the thunder ceased and things were silent momentarily, she heard it again, the cry of a baby. She remembered the story of the Dudu-Mtu, and thought could it possibly be it? The legend often stated that it could be heard crying in the distance. She decided to investigate out in the back yard, but she wouldn't go far. She must be near the house when Nathan was found. But her curiosity was up, and she stepped out into the misting rain, absent-mindedly still carrying the box. She gazed towards the barn. There! It was the darkened outline of a man, but now it was gone.

"My eyes are playing tricks on me," she whispered. She began walking towards the remains of the barn, without realizing she was doing so. Making her way across the muddy backyard, she watched as Toby and the youths disappeared around the front of the house. She was grateful that the rain was barely a mist now; she paused a moment and looked towards the attic's windows. There was a soft amber glow coming from them; she wondered what was happening. She returned her attention to her trek across the yard.

Of course, the barn was no longer; it was now just a pile of lumber and dust. She focused her flashlight ahead of her and walked the perimeter of the barn. Arriving at the point where she thought she had seen the figure she waited, she listened. Yes! The cry again. It was near the ground, at her feet. She searched and found the entrance to the cellar. The sound was coming from it. Maybe a lost cat was down there. No time to worry about a cat and she turned to go back to the house, but again the cry, this time more pitiful, more childlike. Kristyn decided, what would it hurt to look? And she did. There came a faint glow from the opening. This drew her in completely. She shifted her flashlight and proceeded down the steps. What would she find? Probably an old tomcat but she felt she would not rest until she knew for certain.

The bricks were wet and slippery and she felt herself almost lose her balance. This kept her attention on her path and not her surroundings. By the time Kristyn knew something was amiss, she had only a glimpse of a room full of black men, wearing only loincloths, with painted faces and odd headdresses, then searing pain on her face as something struck her hard. She felt the blood gush from her nose and the sensation of falling, as darkness closed in on her.

Chapter Twenty-Three

Nathan's Rescue

Progress in the attic was approaching critical conditions.

"I beseech you, release the child, Nathan," commanded Ruby.

Within the confines of the mirror, the Shadowman lowered himself onto the floor of the attic; he placed his shadowy arms about Nathan. In an unearthly voice, he replied, "Never! This young life has restored me. You must open the portal in order to retrieve him. When you do, I will enter also, and regain my power among the living."

Before Ruby could respond, the Orbs began changing, and soon there appeared three beautiful apparitions of the triplets, although it was apparent that they were attached to each other. Their hair shimmered like white dew; their bodies had a slight bluish tint, their eyes burned like green-fire. They were dressed in a sheer delicate fabric, which waved as though blown by a gentle breeze. They spoke as one, speaking simultaneously. "We are the Dudu-Mtu, the ones of the legend. We cannot rest. We were sacrificed and our chi held in a bronze urn that is buried in the earth at the old cemetery. Please recover it, open the urn, this will release us to move on."

The Shadowman continued his hold on Nathan, "Ha, they will never be released. They are here to serve me, just as this child is here to serve me. My compatriots in the mortal realm summoned me from the depths of Hell and it was with my help that they became powerful. But I demanded much in return for my aid. A sacrifice I demanded, young and energetic! Each time I was renewed and my power and influence within the mortal realm grew stronger. But it has been years now since the last and I need fresh blood. This child has not been sacrificed though I have his essence, but I need a life. Those who called upon me know to get a human sacrifice before I will grant them the earthly pleasure and power they seek. You have closed the portal, you must open it again!"

"I command you in the name of Jesus Christ, to release the child or face perdition," Ruby spoke in a harsh tone, and now she stood. "By what name are you known?' asked Ruby of the entity. She wanted to know with whom she battled and also suspected that the devil was a prideful being and would brag about himself, a weakness she could use against him. Ruby was well schooled in the various fallen angels; knowledge much needed in her vocation. She knew their strengths, their weaknesses, and each one differed.

"Aaaa, I am well known by your forefathers," spoke the entity, "I am Azazel, Chief of my line. I battled with Abram before he became Abraham. I took the form of a vulture and devoured his offering to the Eternal. Yes, I am well known. I am a god to some, and devil to others. I am worshipped as a god. They offer human sacrifice to me. In return, I grant power and wealth to my disciples. But only for short periods, then the sacrifice must be repeated. I am long overdue for my renewal."

'*Azazel!*" thought Ruby. *'I have not encountered him before. He usually resides in the deserts of the middle-east and does not venture into the new world.'*

Pastor Doyle knew of this demon although he had never been face to face with a demon, ever. Open evil did not reside within his environment; he strived to avoid the dark side. He had studied demonology when in seminary but the Baptists looked upon them as non-functioning beings with no power, as long as you kept your faith and followed Christ.

What Pastor Doyle did not know was that demons have more power than common men know. Only a few who practiced offbeat religions knew how to summon them. These directives were in the Book of Solomon and used for good by some and for evil by others!

Ruby held the Firestone up over her head, where now it burned blue with blue flames leaping towards the ceiling "I summoned the one from whose grave came this earth! Arise from your slumber. Revenge is yours."

Ruby began the prayer again and although it was difficult, the three men held fast in their places. The Dudu-Mtu joined her in the prayer; this irritated the Shadowman, which was obvious from the shades of black and grey into which he turned.

Then within the mirror, another appeared. This was a male apparition! He was dressed in an army uniform, an American soldier! Tyler knew at once that it was Nathan's Father, Corporal Nathan Lance Spencer. This apparition did not have the look of a ghost, no, he looked very mortal. He appeared behind the Shadowman, who at first was unaware of him. For a short moment, Corporal Spencer looked around him. It was as though he had just awakened from a deep slumber and he was taking in his surroundings. He was not held between realms as the other spirits were. No, he had entered the light and slept within its protectiveness, awaiting the Day of Judgment. His last thoughts were of his wife and his newborn son whom he had never seen.

Ruby spoke, "We have summoned you from your rest to save your son from the Master of Darkness."

Corporal Spencer looked out into the attic. He saw the Spiritualist and the three men behind her. He also saw the conjoined triplets and the last significant thing that drew his eye was the Shadowman! Within the shadowy embrace of this entity was a child. Was this Nathan, his son? The thought registered and he reacted with his military training. The Shadowman did not appear as a solid figure to those in the attic but only as the shadow of a being. Corporal Spencer did not react with the shadow that was seen, but with the devil, which cast the shadow. To the ones in the attic it appeared as though Corporal Spencer wrestled with himself; this he did not, but with a principality from the depths.

Corporal Spencer realized an energy surge within his body, more than a mortal body possessed. He also recognized a rage rising in him and he attacked the devil, which he saw, but the mortals did not. To Corporal Spencer it appeared as a demonic entity, with the torso of a naked man from the waist up, and as a goat from the waist down; slashing a long serpentine tail and with cloven hooves for feet. His head had the face of a man with a mustache and goatee, yet ram's horns grew from either side of his forehead. His skin was a deep burgundy, and flames leaped from the devil's nostrils. Upon his back were twelve miniature wings, leathery and unfurled, which were not reflected in the shadow he cast.

The ability to summon a sleeping spirit required strong faith, an unrelenting devotion, and the secrets of Solomon. This was a gift passed down to the Priestesses of the Solomon's lineage through his son by the Queen of Sheba of Ethiopia. Ruby had performed her craft often and she was comfortable in her own strength and abilities. Although this was her first case of such severity, Ruby still felt confident in its outcome. She knew that she must keep positive thoughts or the devil would sense her doubt and use this to his advantage. She had instilled this thinking into the others before beginning the eradication of the demon and the rescue of Nathan. They must enter this battle with the foreknowledge of winning!

Now, as the events within the spirit realm, as seen through the mirror, unfolded like the scenes of a horror movie, its audience could only watch as the spirits themselves engaged in a confrontation. Nathan was unaware at the moment of the events occurring around him and maintained his position with no signs of awareness.

The Dudu-Mtu triplets who were a sacrificed victim to this demon, settled themselves behind Corporal Spencer, and now the opponents faced each other. Azazel laughed, "I will have you again as a sacrifice, you have no power to resist me."

Ruby came to her feet; she motioned to the men to join her within the circle where she joined hands with them, completing a circle within the circle of potion and candles.

"Repeat after me," she said. "Even though you won't understand what you are saying, it will have a negative influence on Azazel."

In an unknown language, not even Latin, Ruby chanted. With a series of clicks and long and short pauses, much like a spoken Morse code, she led the action. She waited seconds for the men to repeat what she spoke. As the pattern was a short one, the men soon learned it and joined with Ruby in reciting it.

It was obvious that this irritated Azazel, for he looked in their direction and bellowed long and hard.

Fire streaked from his nostrils and drool dripped from his mouth. This had the desired effect in distracting the demon, which gave Corporal Spencer an opportunity to force his advantage. You would wonder what advantage a normal spirit would have against this demon. Love and sacrifice was the advantage! Azazel released Nathan from his shadowy embrace, which is all the mortals on the physical side of the mirror saw. Corporal Spencer walked over to Nathan, stooped down beside his son and cuddled him close. To everyone's surprise, Nathan reacted! Corporal Spencer spoke softly to him, but what was said was unheard by the mortals, but the action was clear. Nathan smiled at his father and wrapped his arms about his neck.

The Dudu-Mtu seized their chance and the three spirits attacked Azazel; they flowed through his fiery shell and laid hands directly on the demon. This was shown in the shadow that was seen by the mortals. Now Azazel was distracted on two sides. The Dudu-Mtu triplets surrounded the demon with their co-joined bodies. The demon, taken by surprise, focused his attention upon the triplets as they circled him, effectively prohibiting him from fighting with Corporal Spencer.

"Take the child away," they said to Corporal Spencer.

Corporal Spencer saw that now was his chance to rescue Nathan. He stood, lifting the child at the same time. He approached the small assembly on the physical side of the mirror. Nathan kept his arms tight about his father's neck. Now they stood directly in front of the assembly. He unwrapped Nathan's arms from his neck and Nathan cried.

"Quickly, before Azazel regains control, take him," said Corporal Spencer, his voice resonated with a surreal quality.

Tyler saw that Corporal Spencer's eyes were on him and understood. Tyler broke the circle but Franklin and Pastor Doyle took each other's hands and closed it again. Tyler did not know what to expect. How was he going to reach Nathan through the solid glass of the mirror? But, taking renewed faith that he would be guided, he came within physical contact with the mirror. Then miraculously, Corporal Spencer's arms holding Nathan, pushed through this barrier, creating undulations on the mirror's surface, much like the ripples on a smooth pool of clear water. Now Nathan was through the mirror and out of the spirit realm and once again within the physical realm.

"Take him!"

Tyler received the child, all the while looking Corporal Spencer in the eye.

"Care for him as your own, and his mother." He withdrew his arms back into the mirror.

Tyler dwelled on the statement a moment and knew that Corporal Spencer was giving Tyler his blessing in replacing him in his family.

"Break the mirror," ordered Ruby.

Franklin reacted, as previously instructed by Ruby. He withdrew a brick he carried in the leg pocket of his coverall's jeans and hurled it at the mirror! The mirror shattered! It dispersed into a shower of light, sparkling and shimmering, as the thousands of pieces rained down on to the attic floor. The shards striking the floor resounded as chimes in a light breeze. Yet, another sound, an unearthly one emitted from the other side as the portal closed and that came from the demon when he realized that his trophy was taken. A threat came through, "I am not finished!"

Silence, no sound, no movement, only the soft warm glow of the many candles that flickered about the attic. A strange sense of calm overcame the residents, then, a soft cry came from Nathan. Tyler shifted the child onto his hip and said, "Nate? Look at me."

Nathan lifted his small tear-streaked face and gazed at Tyler; his bottom lip quivered, "I want my Daddy!"

Not "I want my Mommy," but "Daddy." Had the short contact with his father created a bound already? Perhaps a bond between parent and child was deeper than the surface knowledge of each other. The parent-child bond ran deeper, right to the very soul.

Tyler did not know how to respond, so he replied, "Mommy waits for you downstairs. Are you ready to go and see her?"

Nathan sniffed and nodded.

"Is all complete here," Tyler asked.

"Here? Yes," replied Ruby.

Pastor Doyle spoke, "Let's take Nathan to Kristyn. There's nothing more to do here." He walked to the door, blew out the candles and moved them to the side and unlocked the attic door with the key he still carried. He pushed open the door and lead the way down to the hall. Here it was dark. They had forgotten that the lights were out and they had neglected to carry with them a flashlight. Nathan now wrapped his arms tight about Tyler's neck; much in the same fashion he had with his father. Tyler held the child closer, "It's okay now Nate. Soon you will be with your mother."

They made it safely downstairs. Pastor Doyle and Franklin followed the glow coming from the living room; here they found Mrs. Doyle, alone. She had dozed off and was sitting with her head resting on the arm rest of the sofa. They did not see Kristyn or Mr. Johnson. Not wanting to wake his mother just yet, Tyler headed towards the kitchen where a hurricane lamp burned. There sat Mr. Johnson, who was drinking coffee and reading the church bulletin. He looked up when they entered the kitchen.

"You have the child! Oh, that is splendid. It is over then. I will call the Youths inside. They have waited patiently as instructed." Mr. Johnson rose and made for the back door.

Not seeing Kristyn, Tyler called her. When there was no answer, he looked at Mr. Johnson, "Wait a sec, where's Kristyn?"

"Kristyn?" said Mr. Johnson with a blank look, as though this was the first time he had thought of her. "I guess she's in the living room with Mrs. Doyle."

"No, she isn't. Franklin, take Nathan, she must be on the back porch. I'll look."

Not finding her out there and with no response when he called her, Tyler searched the rest of the house looking for her. He woke his mother who had the same reaction as Mr. Johnson. "She was in the kitchen," was her reply.

Mr. Johnson came back inside and said, "I'm taking the boys home. They haven't seen Kristyn and neither has the deputy. I can't see any sign of her outside, no foot prints, nothing."

"She's not in the house either," said Tyler. She wouldn't have taken off, left; she would be here waiting for Nathan."

"What do you make of this, Son?" asked Pastor Doyle.

"Kristyn is missing. And not by her own will," said Ruby, before Tyler could answer.

Chapter Twenty-Four

Another Disappearance

Four in the morning; by now Mr. Johnson had left with the Youth Group. Tyler had summoned the sheriff and the house was once again active, with the Sheriff's department treating the house like a crime scene. They were acting quickly because it was obvious that Kristyn would not have left on her own, not while her son was still missing.

The one media truck that stuck it out through the night's storm was no longer alone as more media once again lined the dirt path leading to Kristyn's home. How they had learned so quickly that something else was amiss at the old farmhouse is anyone's guess, but here they were, attracted to news like flies to honey. Again, the front lawn was a meeting place for cameramen and reporters, all trying to talk with the Sheriff and being told to stay behind the yellow tape, which now circled the house.

Nathan slept in the den and for now did not know that his mother was missing. The child was exhausted and a medic had taken time for a brief examination of him, and said physically he was fine but that he needed sleep.

Franklin had taken Miss Ruby home, she had not come prepared to stay more than a day but, since her expertise was much needed at this time, she was asked to return after a few hours sleep. She promised that she would.

Tyler found that sleep eluded him, although it had been nearly twenty-four hours since he last slept. Now he wandered out onto the back porch, where the first rays of the rising sun found their way to the back of the house, which still sat in deep shadows. He took a seat in one of the chairs and placed his head in the palms of his hands with his elbows resting on each knee. He wanted to cry, an unmanly thing, so he kept his tears inside and shut his eyes as he prayed. It was a prayer of desperation, of helplessness, of fear.

What had become of her? Tyler knew he had fallen deeply in love with Kristyn. Although the length of their relationship was only a little over a month, it felt as though he had always known her, had always loved her, had always been a part of her life. Could fate be so cruel? Having just found the one he could trust his heart with, was he destined to lose her this quickly? The pain that flowed through him was far worse than any physical pain he had ever felt in his life. Not even when his fiancée had cheated on him and their engagement broken, had he felt this sort of pain. In that episode in his life he had felt only anger. The anger had not lasted, for it was not in his psyche to dwell on what could not be changed but to learn from it, not to repeat it and to move on in his life. Life was far too short, as the old saying goes, to dwell on the past. Never consider, "What if..."

He meditated in earnest prayer, always seeking guidance from God and finding peace in the prayer. Now, there was no peace, only a war that raged within him; a war with conflicting emotions; hate, resentment, fear and love. As he prayed, he became aware of a pressure against his ankles. It was Casper. "Haven't you been fed today, buddy?" Tyler asked the kitten.

As Kristyn had done only hours before, he reached to pick up the kitten, when his mind exploded with a terrifying thought. The wooden box, it was gone!

Tyler knew immediately what had happened. Kristyn had found the box and she knew of the cellar, she had gone there!

The deputies were making a thorough search of the grounds but so far, they had not found a thing. Tyler had not informed the Sheriff of the cellar, it had completely slipped his mind. However, who was to blame him for that? He had not connected the dots but now he had.

****

"The box held some gruesome artifacts," Tyler told Sheriff Brown. "I am no expert but with what I saw in there, looks like it might be connected with human torture and maybe even sacrifice."

They sat at the kitchen table where Tyler drank his fourth cup of coffee since the events in the attic had ended. He needed to stay alert and caffeine was his only friend just now. Sheriff Brown listened intently but did not take notes as he had on previous occasions. He looked at his deputy, "Bert, you know what to do."

Bert nodded, "I'm on it," and headed out the back door.

Looking pointedly at Tyler, Sheriff Brown said, "So, you retrieved the boy from the other-side, I understand."

Tyler nodded, wondering what the Sheriff was getting at.

"I'm not sure if I put too much into this paranormal stuff. Are you sure he wasn't just hiding out in the attic?"

The exact details of the release of Nathan had not been told, knowing that the majority of people did not or would not believe. He would not have, had he not seen with his own eyes. "I guess that's possible," agreed Tyler. What was the point in arguing with the Sheriff?

"Walk with me," said the Sheriff.

Tyler knew their destination, the barn and then the cellar. The rainwater from the storm hung heavily from the plants and the grounds. The soil surrounding the demolished barn was a muddy moat. Their feet made sucking sounds as the pair made their way through the mud, their tracks quickly filling in with the soggy mire. Tyler reasoned that there should be signs if Kristyn had come this way but the mud erased any footprints quickly.

"Where exactly is this cellar? The forensic team doesn't seem to know."

"It's hidden; it's behind and beneath the barn. We found it accidentally. Come, I'll show you."

Tyler took the lead. The entrance, now uncovered from the debris, which once hid it, was spotted easily. Now that it was daytime, it did not look as sinister as it had the evening before, especially with the added lightning and thunder of the storm. Without hesitation, Tyler quickly went down the still damp steps. He wasn't sure what he would find but he hoped Kristyn was there and perhaps had fallen asleep as his mother had. It was too much to hope and the idea he realized, was quite ridiculous. She would not have fallen asleep in the cellar. No, she was not there but there was evidence that someone had been.

Tyler swept the cellar with his eyes and knew it had changed. The most obvious was that the chairs were no longer overturned and now were stacked one upon the other against the wall. The table was cleared of trash and bones, which were nowhere to be seen. It was as though the table had been cleaned and the trash thrown away. Even the shelves had had a cleaning, dust and cobwebs gone.

Except for a pile of wet rags, which were nonchalantly tossed in the corner where the pile of bones had once been, everything was gone! Otherwise, the cellar looked as if professionals had cleaned it. Tyler could not believe what he saw. Had it been a dream? Perhaps it wasn't as bad as he first thought. Then he remembered the wooden box, that had been real and its contents unmistakably macabre. Why had Kristyn taken the box; had she brought it back here to the cellar, and if so, why?

Sheriff Brown cleared his throat and then looked at Tyler, "What are we looking for here?"

Tyler rubbed his hand through his dark hair, which was unkempt already and just stared wide-eyed about him. "When I tell you what we found down here last evening and the mess it was in, you will realize that someone has been here since. They have removed everything and swept the place clean."

Tyler turned to the far left corner and pointed, "There was a pile of bones, human bones in that corner....now, just some rags." Tyler went into detail at what he had seen the previous evening and then what was in the wooden box.

"I'll get the forensic team here down at once, they'll find something, I assure you," said the sheriff. "But if several individuals did come here last night, how is it that my deputy did not see them? He was parked in the drive in plain view of the barn."

Tyler shook his head, indicating he had no clue. "Voodoo?" he said raising one brow questioningly.

Sheriff Brown stared in disbelief and replied, "Don't tell me you really believed that hog-wash?"

"At this point, I'll believe almost anything."

Without further discussions, they left the cellar. The two men trekked back to the house. It was nearing eight in the morning and already the teams were unloading their gear. Tyler went inside as Sheriff Brown went to give them instructions.

Tyler checked on Nathan who still slept. He sat down on the sofa bed next to him, and for a long moment he watched the child's even breathing as he slept soundly. Tyler dreaded having to tell him that his mother was missing after the ordeal he had already experienced. Considering long and hard on just what he would say, Tyler decided not to be completely truthful with him. He would say that Kristyn had to go to the store and would be back soon. Just how long he could get by with that white lie, he didn't know.

****

Nathan finally roused from his slumber a little after noon. He asked for Kristyn and seemed satisfied with Tyler's explanation. For some odd reason, Tyler felt the responsibility of a parent. Nathan had no one but his mother, and Tyler wanted to fill the void in his young life.

"I know someone who wants to see you," said Tyler to Nathan.

"Casper?" he asked wide-eyed.

"For sure," said Tyler. "Let's go get him some food and I bet he would love some milk."

Nathan, holding Tyler's hand, led him to the back-porch, where he did the job of caring for his pet, while Tyler contemplated how best to approach him on his experience.

"Hey Nate," and Nathan looked up from the floor. "Want to talk about what happened yesterday?"

After a few questions, Tyler knew that Nathan had no memory of the events of the last two days. His last memory was of standing in the hall at the attic door. He did not remember entering or the events following but he did remember his father, "I dreamed about my Daddy," he said.

"Oh, I bet that was a good dream," said Tyler.

Nathan nodded and replied, "Yep, first time I ever did see him. He told me that he would come and visit me again. But it will be only in a dream," now Nathan eyes filled with tears and his bottom lip quivered, "I want my Mama."

Tyler sat Nathan upon his knee and held him close. His small body was warm and he snuggled close and wrapped one arm around Tyler's neck, all the while holding his kitten.

****

Franklin and Ruby returned mid-afternoon. They now sat around the kitchen table and their discussion was bleak indeed.

"It's the Deviltry," said Ruby.

"What is that?" asked Pastor Doyle, holding a cold glass of iced-tea but not drinking it.

"Tis the name by which the locals know this outlaw Voodoo sect," she explained. "They have their own title for themselves but it is not known and the only way anyone would know it would be if they were a secret member. A few children have gone missing around these parts over the years and the old timers are still laying these disappearances at the Dudu-Mtu. Old legends die hard in the back woods.

"Which is why the urn containing the remains of the triplets needs to be unearthed from the cemetery, they must get their freedom to cross over."

"I think we have more pressing things right now," inserted Tyler, with a harshness he hasn't intended.

"I do understand," replied Ruby with a stern expression, "but the two go together, even though we do not see the exact connection. The spirits were restraining the demon but they cannot maintain that control and unless they are freed, the demon will only grow strong again and we do not know the recrimination."

Tyler buried his head in his hands again, what were they to do? How were they to approach recovering Kristyn?

The others that were sitting around the table saw this act of despair and could offer no comfort, for there was none. It was nearing three in the afternoon when Tyler felt this overwhelming weariness and he made an apology, "I'm going to stretch out in the den; I can't stay awake any longer. Wake me if anything happens."

Tyler was encouraged to rest, without rest he would be of no use to anyone much less Kristyn.

****

While Tyler slept, Sheriff Brown came to the house. Mrs. Doyle and Ruby were the only ones there. Franklin and Pastor Doyle had decided it was up to them to retrieve the urn from the cemetery. For now things were quiet. Nathan played with Casper on the floor of the living room. The door to the den was shut to give Tyler as much silence and darkness as possible.

The grave expression on the Sheriff's face brought concern to both women. It could only be bad news.

"Can I speak to you in private," he began, glancing at Nathan on the floor.

"Yes," replied Mrs. Doyle, "The kitchen. Nathan," she addressed the child, "I'm fixing you a sandwich, be good and stay there with Casper."

Nathan nodded.

"Where's the others?"

"Tyler's sleeping and my husband's gone to the church. What is it? I know it isn't good from looking at you."

"I had wanted to tell you all, but I can't wait, must get back to the department. Anyway, the 'rags' that were found in the cellar, turned out to be women's clothing. It is a complete outfit, from undergarments to sandals. We think that they might be Mrs Spencer's but we need them to be identified to be sure."

"I can do that," said Mrs. Doyle. "I was probably the last one to see her."

"What was she wearing?"

Mrs. Doyle gave a thorough description of Kristyn's clothing.

"Well, it matches," sighed Sheriff Brown. "We found a small amount of blood on the t-shirt, not enough to worry about but we will test it to be sure that it is hers. The fastest test we can do is a blood test for type, we will begin DNA testing but that can take three weeks or more even with a rush order.

"I'll get her medical history when I go back, and from there.... we will follow the usual procedure for locating missing persons. The forensics will reveal some information and a part of it is already analyzed. I'll get back with you in a few hours."

Chapter Twenty-Five

Retrieval of the Urn

Pastor Doyle and Franklin made their way down the narrow dirt path that led to the caretaker's small cottage, which set on the edge of the cemetery. The path was uneven and lined with dogwood trees. Their dark green foliage gave a bit of shade from the hot August sun. A hot breeze stirred the grasses and leaves; the caw of ravens resounded with a quaint eeriness.

Before heading towards the caretaker's cottage, Pastor Doyle had made the necessary arrangements and obtained the permit for exhuming the grave. All that was needed now was the exact location of the plot.

Old Bill, who cared for the cemetery, was getting on in years but still maintained the cemetery with care. The cottage was small, perfect for one or two and had been the home of the caretaker since the turn of the last century. It was a five-room structure, constructed of masonry blocks of charcoal gray. Green ivory scaled the walls on either side of the front door. There was a small porch, just wide enough for a swing and a rocker.

The door was constructed of rough lumber, unfinished and heavy. Franklin knocked hard three times, for Old Bill was a bit hard of hearing. Bill opened the door. He was an African-American and a mite older than Franklin, with a thick head of white woolly hair but otherwise was clean-shaven. He wore a clean uniform of dark green and had on sandals.

"Well, howdy there Pastor and you Franklin, I ain't seen yer in a spell. I got a call from the secretary. She done and told me what y'all'a wanting. But commo in," and he stepped to one side to allow their entrance into his modest home.

Old Bill had the cottage cool, his shades were pulled almost all the way down to block out the hot summer sun and its heat. His sitting room had a sofa and a couple of comfortable armchairs plus a few side tables and one black metal file cabinet sitting beneath a window.

"Y'all's has a seat," and he indicated the sofa.

After a few comments on the weather and the latest gossip about who had died recently, Pastor Doyle spoke as if this topic had already begun.

"Bill, can you help us locate this burial plot?" and he handed Old Bill a document, a very old and yellowed document.

Old Bill took his reading spectacles from his shirt pocket and stuck them on the bridge of his nose for they had no earpieces. "Gotta have my specs," he explained.

He studied the document briefly looking for the one thing he really needed, the plot number. Removing his glasses and looking at Pastor Doyle, he handed him the document, "Yeah, that's in the oldest sector of the graveyard. It'll be way at the back. I's doubts you'll find it on yer own, I'll have my new 'sistant show it to yer. He's out an' about the grounds on the golf-cart."

"Didn't know you had gotten an assistant," said Pastor Doyle.

"Yeah, Josias. He's the young fellow I'm training to take over. I'm planning on retiring next year. He's single, so we thought it best if he stayed here with me.

After all, this will be his home when I leave. I've fixed up the other bedroom fer'im"

"Josias?" Pastor Doyle raised his brows questioningly. "I haven't heard of him. He must not be from around here."

"Yeah, that's right, he's from Haiti. I'll give him a call on his cell phone. I don't own one meself, don't trust'em much." Old Bill lifted the receiver of an old black rotary dial phone. It was a real antique but worked. The dial clicked as he sprung it with one finger. After a brief conversation, of which Pastor Doyle could only hear mumbles, Old Bill said, "He's on his way."

The three men waited in the small porch; soon a golf-cart was seen coming up the path. When Pastor Doyle first saw Josias, he was shocked. As the young muscular black man stepped down from the cart, Pastor Doyle's eyes swept slowly over him.

Josias was around thirty years old, stood five foot eight, with glistening black skin. His black hair was twisted into thick dreadlocks that touched his shoulders. His eyes were small, close-set and almost black with the whites even appearing brown. His nose was wide, lips were full and when he smiled, he flashed startling white teeth!

A white T-shirt emphasized the blackness of his complexion and tight, hip-hugging jeans revealed thick muscular legs, white sneakers but no socks completed his overbearing appearance.

He dismounted the cart and approached the men waiting for him. "Good day to you, my man," he had a strong Haitian accent. "And what can I do for you this day?"

Pastor Doyle shook himself mentally, and replied, "Can you take us to plot number zero zero thirty nine?"

"Sure thing, my man, sit here and here," he pointed to the cart seats.

Old Bill spoke, "Call me, Josias, if you need to. I'll be inside."

Deftly Josias steered the cart down the narrow footpath back towards the older section of the cemetery. As they traveled pass the divisions, they could read the timeline in the style and age of the headstones. The more dilapidated the tombstones were, the older that section of the graveyard.

Drawing nearer to the oldest section of the boneyard, the forest suddenly loomed ahead, dark and thick; it was beginning to encroach onto the cemetery grounds. This section was overgrown, with tall thick wiregrasses covering most of the graves. It was plain that Old Bill or perhaps it was Josias, had neglected this division. A tall wrought iron rusting fence surrounded this small area of the cemetery, or portions of it did, for large gaps appeared here and there, which allowed for animals and the forest to intrude! Here the caw of crows echoed through the trees and small flocks were seen perched in the pines and flying just above the treetops.

Josias stopped the cart, "Here we go, my man. This be what you want. The graves are not numbered, so we count'em and compare'em to this map. See, this grave here is one. Here it is here," and he pointed, "on the map. So, we count."

Josias began walking down the uneven rows; this section had no pre-determined layout, as the deceased were buried in whatever free place was available at the time. As there were only a few graves, which had the dates etched clearly, it was plainly seen that there was no order.

He stopped, "This be the one, my man."

After Josias marked the grave with a small white surveyor's flag, they returned to the cottage. From there Pastor Doyle called Tyler.

****

"Okay, Dad. I'll meet you," said Tyler. His mother had awakened Tyler when she heard his cell phone ring. He awoke from a disturbing dream of Kristyn trapped in a whirlpool of dark green water. No matter how he tried to reach her, something kept hold of his legs, trapping him in place as her terrifying screams for help resounded through the air.

He checked on Nathan and asked his mother if she wanted to take Nathan to her house. Tyler felt uncertain about leaving them alone here. Mrs. Doyle agreed it would be best. So after gathering a few things for Nathan and Casper, they left just minutes ahead of Tyler who was turning off lights and locking doors.

The forensic team had completed their investigation of the cellar and had left a little before Mrs. Doyle had. Now the farm was empty, not even a sheriff's car remained; even the media had lost patience and gone home. All that remained was the yellow crime-scene tape, which had broken in some places and now fluttered in the slight breezes of approaching darkness.

****

As Tyler drove to the church, he called Franklin. "Where are you?"

"I'm at home. Miss Ruby has gone to see Miss Lilly. Says she needs to talk with her about all of this. Miss Ruby thinks the older lady might shed some light on a few things. Why, do you need her, or me?"

"I'm on my way to the cemetery, wanna ride along? I need some company."

"Why, shor-a-nuff," Franklin replied. "Be waiting on yer."

After picking up Franklin, the two discussed what had transpired and what they thought the outcome might be.

"I's telling ya, Miss Kristyn gettin' gone like that has something to do with what going on out yonder in that cellar," declared Franklin.

"I gotta agree with you on that," replied Tyler. "But I can't make the connection. I am wondering however, just how exhuming the triplets' grave is going to help get Kristyn back. Nathan was crying for her this afternoon when she hadn't returned from the market, which is the story I told him. Mama has taken him to our house. I didn't want to leave them alone in Kristyn's house, not with all that is happening right now. She will just keep him there for now."

"Good idea," agreed Franklin.

They drove on in silence, both men lost in their thoughts. Minutes later, they arrived at the caretaker's cottage. Also waiting was a two-man crew with a backhoe. Everyone else was standing in a small group, talking.

Tyler and Franklin joined them, "Isn't it a bit late in the day to exhume a grave?" asked Tyler. "It's going to be eight thirty in a few minutes, which leaves us only about half an hour of twilight."

"We don't have the leisure of waiting," his father replied. "We are only looking for an urn. We need every minute allowed us and it isn't a casket, only an urn, so it won't be a major job. Let's get on with it."

Tyler considered what his father said and knew he was correct. Every second counted, and time was moving too fast. They needed help from the spirit realm and the release of the *Dudu-Mtu* spirit was a major source of aid. The urn did not hold the mortal remains or ashes of the triplets. Only the part that gave them their life and uniqueness, was locked away, like a genie in the proverbial bottle, imprisoned there by an evil Jinn.

****

Had it not been for the half moon, which shone brightly, and the headlights on the backhoe, the crew would have been operating in darkness. The evening still held the heat of the day and thick fog formed and swirled around their legs, from the moisture in the earth. The night sounds began erupting; crickets chirped and frogs croaked from an unseen pond. Fireflies flickered here and there, and a solitary owl watched from the lower branches of an oak, giving an occasional hoot.

The air was heavy and stifling but they ignored this discomfort and set about unearthing the *Dudu-Mtu's* grave. With a sharp slice, the shovel bit into the soft moist ground and dug out huge volumes of dirt.

It did not take long for the grave to be emptied. Soon a thud was heard as the shovel struck a more solid object. The crew completed unearthing the object with shovels. Between them, they hauled up a child-sized wooden casket. It was obvious that the casket was in an advanced state of decay and a few strikes with a shovel sent splinters flying. At the same moment, a white mist escaped and evaporated with a hiss. This did not go by without note but since it happened so swiftly, nothing was said concerning what it might be. Water vapor perhaps, thought Tyler, that when hitting the warm night air boiled and evaporated.

There, on the blackened dirt, lay a bronze urn. A workman handed it to Pastor Doyle, "Is this what you're looking for?" he asked.

Pastor Doyle studied it for a moment, he turned it over in his hand, brushing away webs and wooden debris, "Yep, this is it."

The urn was discolored and had a screw on lid. "We'll take this back to the church," he said. "Thank you gentlemen for working after dark like this," he said, looking at the two.

"Sure thing, Pastor Doyle," replied one. "Just curious as to why this here urn is so important? Why did it have to be dug up tonight?"

"I don't really know why, only that it is important that we do what we need to do ... and soon. Outside of that, I can't say any more," Pastor Doyle hoped that his vague explanation would be enough to satisfy the curiosity of the workmen.

"Whatever you say Pastor, well we're out of here. My wife's holding supper for me. I hadn't had the chance to go home when your call came. I know I'm hungry enough to eat a horse."

With that, the men steered the backhoe back towards Old Bill's cottage. Pastor Doyle, Tyler and Franklin used the golf cart and followed them. "We'll open this at the church," said Pastor Doyle indicating the urn. "I'll leave it locked in my office for tonight and tomorrow we will do what we can."

"I think that will do," agreed Tyler. "I want to check on Nathan."

Tyler was driving and the three men became quiet, each lost in his own thoughts as to what might happen next.

Tyler's mind dwelled hard on what was happening to Kristyn at this very moment. If only he was with her, in spirit, if not in body.

Chapter Twenty-Six

Opening the Urn

They returned to the church later the next day. The sheriff had kept Tyler busy with questions about firstly, Nathan's disappearance, and now Kristyn's. Both he and his father were asked to look at photos of some suspects in the hope that they might have been seen by them. But Tyler could not recognize any. Sunday was upon them and they knew they couldn't conduct a ritual at that time, so their first opportunity was Tuesday.

It was past noon when the three returned to the church. Pastor Doyle retrieved the urn from his office. They made their way to the back of the church. This was the oldest section of the building, built as part of the original structure but now only used by the deacons for their bi-monthly meetings. Franklin did not attend this church although he had visited. He wasn't much of a church attendee but had his private sessions with God, worshipping Him with simple prayer and simple requests for forgiveness and blessings. He read his Bible but kept a low profile when it came to how he saw things and his beliefs were not always the same as the view held by main-stream Christianity.

Tyler entered first, after his father had unlocked the door. He switched on the light to reveal a long narrow room with scarce furnishings. There were four tall windows on the back wall, with white blinds closing out the light. There was no carpet except for a rug beneath a long table which had six chairs on each side. The table was a smooth almost black mahogany, polished to a glistening sheen. There was a lone sideboard, which held a pitcher and glasses, with a gold-framed mirror hanging above it.

"Let's sit down," said Pastor Doyle as he placed the urn on to the table. They all sat at one end of the table. "How do we go about this?" asked Tyler.

"I's not real sure," said Franklin. "Shouldn't Miss Ruby be here?"

"Have you seen her over the last few days?" Tyler asked.

"I has."

"Did you mention the urn's retrieval?"

"I did. She only said that care must be taken and that Miss Ruby would check the book."

"I guess she should be here," said Tyler.

At that moment, the door was pushed open and there stood not only Miss Ruby but Miss Lilly as well. "How did you know?" asked Pastor Doyle.

Ruby did not reply at first, as she guided her elderly grandmother into the room without an invitation, she already knew she didn't need one.

Both Tyler and Franklin rose from their seats to aid the lady to a comfortable seat at the table. Miss Lilly was a frail looking woman with medium brown skin tones and white hair, which she wore in a bun at the nape of her neck. She had on a floor length frock of muted shades of indigo and low-heeled black shoes. About her thin shoulders was a peach colored knitted shawl. Upon the bridge of her nose was perched a pair of half moon glasses. With light brown eyes, she peered at them before she answered for Ruby, "She didn't, but I did."

"Yes, that is so," said Ruby speaking for the first time. "With what Franklin told us and things I knew already, she just clued in to what was. We were going through the book looking for an incantation when she said we needed to come here. I didn't ask how or why, I just brought her."

"I have the sight," said Miss Lilly as way of explanation. "You haven't much time. Too many days has passed already. You can wait no longer. Your lady friend is in much danger but the ones who have her will do her no harm," Miss Lilly paused, "...for now. They will wait for the full moon, which is in less than two weeks. Miss Lilly now turned her attention to her granddaughter, "Ruby, you may begin."

Ruby sat a black duffle bag on the table next to the urn, which she avoided touching; she removed from it the Book of Solomon, placing it down carefully. Next, she removed three pillar candles, a red, green and white one, the Bible and the red Firestone. Silently she arranged them, lit the candles, sat the Firestone on its pedestal, then said, "Please turn out the lights."

Tyler did so, plunging the room into semi-darkness except where the three candles burned and cast tall dancing shadows against the walls.

Miss Lilly then spoke, "What we are about to do will be frightening. It requires faith and fortitude. If you think that you will react in any way at all, you need to leave."

She waited. No one left.

"It is good. Please divide yourselves evenly on either side of the table and hold hands."

Ruby had positioned herself at the end of the table, her Grandmother and Tyler to her right, Pastor Doyle and Franklin on Ruby's left. Everyone but Ruby held hands.

"What we have here, in this urn," Ruby said carefully picking it up for the first time, "is the essence of the deceased person, or in this case, persons. We already know that the mortal remains of these individuals were buried in the backyard at the barn. At the time of the sacrifice, the spirit remained on the premises. The demon, with foresight, and with the help of his followers, took another part of the person, its *chi* or life force, which has no awareness, and locked it up. In this way, the person would never be able to enter the light; never have peace, nor rest. We will be releasing this to reunite with the spirits. Once this is done, the spirits will be able to resist the demon and escape the power this demon has over them."

"Chi," said Tyler. "Isn't that Asian, Chinese? That's another religion, one we do not give credit to."

"Indeed it is," replied Miss Lilly. "But what Christians do not realize, is that all religions have a connection. Over the centuries this has been corrupted and separated, but on the Day of Judgment it will be cleansed of the deception and truth will be seen. This book," and she touched the Book of Solomon, "reveals to us this working and much, that I dare say, you Pastor Doyle would call pagan," then Miss Lilly looked at her granddaughter, "Carry on Ruby."

Ruby acknowledged her grandmother's order and taking the Bible, she opened it to the book of Leviticus and here she read, "They shall no longer sacrifice their sacrifices to the goat demons with which they play the harlot. This shall be a permanent statute to them throughout their generations."

When concluded, she turned to the book of Deuteronomy and read, "You shall not behave thus toward the LORD your God, for every abominable act which the LORD hates they have done for their gods; for they even burn their sons and daughters in the fire to their gods."

"This is what the Deviltry believes and has merged into their corrupted version of Voodoo, what is not in true Voodoo. But my grandmother and I have found the incantation in the Book of Solomon that will release the Chi."

Opening the Book of Solomon, Ruby said, "Since most of you here are unfamiliar with this book, I will read an introduction of the first paragraph, then I will reveal the incantation needed."

Ruby pulled one candle closer to the book so to highlight it for easier reading. Then she read:

'Every one knoweth in the present day that from time immemorial Solomon possessed knowledge inspired by the wise teachings of an angel, to which he appeared so submissive and obedient, that in addition to the gift of wisdom, which he demanded, he obtained with profusion all the other virtues; which happened in order that knowledge worthy of eternal preservation might not be buried with his body.

Being, so to speak, near his end, he left to his son Roboam a Testament which should contain all (the Wisdom) he had possessed prior to his death. The Rabbins, who were careful to cultivate (the same knowledge) after him, called this Testament The Clavicle, or Key of Solomon, which they caused to be engraved on pieces of the bark of trees, while the Pentacles were inscribed in Hebrew letters on plates of copper, so that they might be carefully preserved in the Temple which that wise king had caused to be built.'

Having completed this task, Ruby said. "I will now bring up the incantation for the release of the Chi.

"First we must draw a circle," Ruby then took chalk and drew on the table a circle, three feet in diameter.

"Next a circle within this circle," which she did.

"Now an X, pointing toward the four corners of the earth." Ruby removed a compass, lined up exactly and drew the X from whence the four winds would blow.

"Now, in the space between the two circles we will draw hexagonal pentacles."

She drew four, at each corner of the compass, six-sided circles and within each circle, she drew a five pointed star.

"Now on each pentacle, I will write one of the four names of God."

Between the east and the south she wrote, 'IHVH, Tetragrammaton.'

Between the South and the West she wrote, 'the Essential Tetragrammatic Name AHIH, Eheieh.'

Between the West and the North, she wrote the Name of Power, 'ALIVN, Elion.'

And between the North and the East she wrote the Great Name, 'ALH, Eloah.'

"Now a box within a box must enclose the circles, and the angels of protection will be committed to our aid."

Now Ruby took the Urn and placed it in the center of this diagram. Then in Latin she recited a prayer.

Afterwards, she looked at Pastor Doyle, "You may now remove the lid."

Pastor Doyle stood and looked around the room. He wasn't at all sure about this ritual, which sounded much like witchcraft to him but he knew that Ruby had used the names of God and provoked the protection of the angels, and without lifting the Urn from the table, he unscrewed the lid. He laid the top down next to the Urn. He sat down and waited.

At first, all was quiet. Then on the table, a whirl-wind appeared at each corner of the earth. These miniature twisters headed towards the Urn and one by one, from north to west entered the Urn. The Urn glowed until it became almost white and the heat emitting from it was felt by those surrounding it. Then a hissing sound began and steam rose from the mouth of the Urn. The mist grew larger, without shape or form and hung in the air.

Ruby spoke in Latin and the vapor floated towards the mirror. The mirror fogged up and then cleared, as the mist penetrated it. Now the mist could be seen again but within the mirror and not as a reflection. It was over in less time than it took to draw the circles. Silence returned. No one spoke, and then Ruby said, "It is finished. You may turn on the lights."

Tyler went to do so.

Before the question could be asked, Miss Lilly explained, "Mirrors are often portals to the Other side. Only with certain people and under certain situations can a mirror be used. The Chi is one of those instances and it took the quickest path it could find."

"What now?" Tyler asked.

Miss Lilly replied, "The Chi is free but it is incomplete without the spirit. The Chi will find the spirit of the Dudu-Mtu and unite with it. Then, the Dudu-Mtu can enter the light when the light returns for her. But for now, the Dudu-Mtu is our most powerful ally in the spirit realm. Your task must be completed before the full moon and before the Dudu-Mtu crosses the boundary between the spirit realm and the upper plain. There is no return from the upper plain until Judgment and the Dudu-Mtu will then enter the sleep of the dead, unaware of the passage of time."

"Where do we begin our search for Kristyn," asked Tyler who chose not to linger on that explanation, as it had no bearing on the immediate problem, which was rescuing Kristyn. What he felt now was frustration. "The authorities have begun their investigation and as we know, they take the most logical approach and are starting from the place of abduction, the cellar," Tyler continued, although he knew he was only speaking of what they knew. "You say we are to take a different direction?"

"Yes," replied Ruby. "The direction in which we search cannot be found in the physical realm. I will inform you later of that. Be sure to contact us, if you find more tangible news."

It was nearly dark when they finished in the church. Tyler and Pastor Doyle went home. They did not go by Kristyn's house.

Chapter Twenty-Seven

Kristyn's Predicament

A hum broke through the darkness, a darkness accentuated by a spinning spiral and bold pulsating colors. Then pain erupted in her head, a pain so severe that Kristyn opened her eyes, only to be met with more darkness; at least the hypnotic spinning spiral was gone but not the hum. For a long time she lay still, trying to recall what had transpired, where she was and for how long she had been here.

She raised her hand to touch her face, but something was wrong! Her hand did not respond to her brain's instructions. Again, she tried, no response, the other hand also remained motionless. Kristyn then realized that she could not mentally feel her body or her extremities. She was paralyzed!

Now as awareness became more acute, Kristyn could tell that it wasn't quite as dark and that something was covering her face. A canvas sack covered her head; its weave was porous enough for her to breathe and for scattered bits of light to penetrate but through this gloom, no concrete shapes or forms were discernible.

The pain in her head became a throbbing beat; she then connected the beat with that of a drum. Its rhythm was a three, three, three monotonous beat accompanied by the low whine of a motor.

Nathan! The memory of her son exploded in her thoughts like fireworks on the Fourth of July. He was lost, captured in the netherworld, held there by unnatural forces.

"Oh God! I need you," this short prayer was heard only in her mind, as Kristyn attempted to make sounds and couldn't. It would seem that her only functioning senses were sight and hearing.

What'd happened in the attic, she wondered. Had Nathan been saved? Had Tyler and the others missed her and knew she was gone? Kristyn had no way of knowing what had taken place.

Then another picture jumped to the forefront of her mind, the photographic image of muscular young black men, naked to the waist, a detail she barely had had time to consider before her lights went out.

Sometime later, Kristyn had no idea when, the semi-darkness suddenly became very bright. She heard shuffles of sounds like someone or something was moving about her. A shadow paused over her, a dark shapeless form, and then abruptly, this form jerked her roughly to a sitting position, and lifted her. She wanted to resist, but no part of her body responded to her mental demands to fight. Her eyes hurt from the sudden brightness and she kept closing them as she tried to see who had manhandled her. Kristyn felt herself being carried in someone's arms. Through the thin weave of the sack, she was surprised to see, overhead, rough wooden beams with fluttering webs dangling from them.

Then she was carefully maneuvered into a small enclosure, sat in an upright position, and her head supported against someone's shoulder.

Strangely, the men with her did not speak, not to her or to each other. She wasn't given much time to think about this turn of events, when she sensed that the vehicle she was now in was moving. The drive was rough as if traveling along old dirt paths. She sensed rather than felt the bumps as she felt nausea from the sway of the vehicle.

Kristyn knew that there was more than one person although she had not seen them clearly. The vehicle stopped. Once again she was lifted into someone's arms and taken outside; she could tell that it was dark, it must be just after sunset, she thought.

She heard the chirps of crickets and felt the warmth of the night after the cool air of the vehicle. Everything was quiet as they carried her into yet another dwelling. In this building, she could not make out any recognizable objects, for in here it was darker than the previous place. She sensed support of her limp body against the soft firmness of a man's chest. She knew that she was carried upwards, from her equilibrium, another functioning sense, it would seem. Now, she was leveled but not for long, again an ascent into even more darkness, but this time the smell was familiar.

****

Chapter Twenty-Eight

The Attic

Tyler paced the floor of his parents' den. Still Kristyn was missing, in a few days, the moon would be full and the prediction by Miss Lilly loomed like a brick wall ahead of them. Nathan had become a sad little boy who only found pleasure when he held his kitten, Casper. He asked dozens of times a day for his mother and each time the feeble lie that he was told only brought fresh rounds of tears. There was no consoling him at these times, as his small body would shake with great sobs.

With each day, rage grew within Tyler. A rage he had never experienced before, not even when he had discovered the unfaithfulness of his fiancée. In his mind's eye, he saw what he would do to the ones who had brought this pain into his life and into the lives of the ones he loved. He stayed in contact with the police, who would have leads that only lead to a dead-end!

How could someone vanish so completely, right before the eyes of so many who were there that night? The deputy, who watched from his cruiser, only saw the boys marching around the house. He admitted that this kept his attention more so than watching the barn. Also, the night was stormy and foggy which made visibility low. The church's Youths had been interviewed and each one said the same thing; that with the hoods over their heads, their field of vision was limited, what with the rain and the darkness.

Even the media that had parked along the path, admitted to only watching the march of the youths and none had seen anything unusual near the barn. Days were passing; days that brought them closer to an appointment which he did not want to keep. He had not returned to the farmhouse.

****

During this search for Kristyn, Tyler had not gone to Sunday or Wednesday's church services, although his parents had kept their usual schedule. How could he keep up a front when he felt so betrayed by God? Oh, he knew that he should keep the faith but sometimes it was necessary to act on your own and not wait for a higher power to intercede. He recalled the saying, 'God helped those that helped themselves.' This quote from Benjamin Franklin made a good deal of sense.

The world was full of evil, and although good men fought to keep the dark side at bay, sometimes it was apparent that it was more twilight than night or day. There was no fine line anymore, but one smudged line in the dirt.

On the morning of the full moon, which happened to be the equinox and the first full moon to occur on the first day of autumn, a true Harvest moon, the phone call he was subconsciously waiting for came through. However, it was from an unexpected source, it came from Old Bill, the Caretaker. Pastor Doyle took the call. He summoned his wife and son into the den.

"What's going on, Dad?" asked Tyler, as he balanced Nathan on his knee. "What have you heard or learned?"

"To make it short," began Pastor Doyle, "Old Bill has reason to suspect that his new assistant might know about Kristyn. Now hold on," cautioned Pastor Doyle, when Tyler jumped up, almost dumping Nathan onto the floor. "We can't act yet. Old Bill hasn't confronted Josias yet, said he thought he should call me first. Old Bill went into Josias room, said he was looking for something he had stored in Josias closet before Josias moved in. He discovered a makeshift voodoo altar inside of the man's closet. What'd made Bill suspicious was a photograph he found on the altar, that of a young blond woman and a small boy. He thinks it is Kristyn and Nathan. You and I are heading over there right now. Bill said Josias is out and if we want to see it to come straight away."

They had forgotten Nathan who now piped up with, "You're gonna go get my Mama?"

The three adults looked at each other; they had forgotten him, not quite knowing how to answer. Mrs. Doyle came and took Nathan from Tyler, "Let's go get some milk and cookies, want to?"

To everyone's surprise Nathan answered violently, "No! Don't want no cookies. I want my Mama!" As he spoke tears escaped his eyes but the child tried so hard not to cry. "I'm gonna go with you," he declared.

Tyler took Nathan back into his arms and held him close, which only encouraged Nathan's tears. "Nathan, you know that I will do everything possible to bring your Mama home but you must be strong and pray very hard for her safe return. We can't take you with us but I promise I'll call if we learn anything at all, okay?"

Tyler looked at the small boy's tear streaked face; he brushed away a tear rolling down one cheek. "You know, your mama would want you to be brave. She needs for you to be brave. I can't help her if I am worried about you. Understand?"

Nathan nodded. Mrs. Doyle took him again and set him onto the floor. "Milk and cookies," she said, "and we will give Casper some milk too."

Reluctantly Nathan allowed Mrs. Doyle to lead him towards the kitchen. No sooner had he vacated the den, than Tyler and Pastor Doyle did the same.

"Let's take my truck," called Tyler running toward it. They made the trip to the church in break-neck time, with Tyler driving like a demon, breaking the speed limit and with rolling stops at stop signs.

Pastor Doyle kept cautioning him, "We will lose valuable time, Son, if the Hi-Way Patrol pulls you over."

Pastor Doyle's warning fell on deaf ears, Tyler remained silent, concentrating on the road, keeping a sharp eye in the rear-view mirror, and silently praying that he would make it there without incident. They arrived at the church in three quarters of the usual travel time. Tyler headed his pick-up towards the back of the church and drove up to the entrance of the cemetery and stopped. Vehicles could not enter here but this was the closest entrance to the cottage. They half ran and half walked up the path. Old Bill awaited them, sitting on the swing on the front poach.

They arrived breathless and before they could speak, Old Bill said, "He's still out. Come with me."

It was now nearing noon, the air was heavy and hot, even on this mid-September day. Beads of sweat ran down both men's faces; they wiped the beads of perspiration from their foreheads as they followed Old Bill towards Josias' bedroom. After the bright sunlight, their eyes took a few minutes to adjust and by that time, they were looking in the closet.

It took a long moment to take in the scene before him, but Tyler saw what amounted to a typical altar for performing Voodoo ceremonial rites. A strong scent of incense rushed out to meet them. It was an unrecognizable scent, but obviously came from the ornate incense burner, which occupied the center lower section of the altar. Tyler's eyes swept the scene, which was lit by a flashlight held by Old Bill. The closet was not a walk in type so this display was small and left no room for hanging garments. There were bottles and pots with glitter and sequins glued onto them. There was an abundance of candles that set upon a blue velvet cloth. Tyler's eyes froze when they spotted a picture sitting atop of the altar. It was the picture of Kristyn with Nathan clinging close to her side, that he had seen when first coming to her house. It was in a frame in the living room. When had it gone missing? Had no one missed it? Especially Kristyn herself?

He couldn't tell where the picture was taken but Nathan looked to be at least a year younger than he was now, perhaps three and half years old. He removed the picture and stared at it for a long moment. Hundreds of questions rushed through his mind. Whoever these kidnappers were, they had had access to the farmhouse even while Kristyn and Nathan occupied it!

"Why...?" He asked with his voice trailing to a whisper and a look of puzzlement. "He must be involved with her disappearance. Dad, call the police. Have them meet us at the church. Let's leave this as it is, for now, in case he returns here." Tyler replaced the picture and closed the closet door.

Pastor Doyle quickly called the authorities and spoke directly with the sergeant in charge of the investigation.

"Come quickly, but do not use lights or sirens. It might scare him away. We are at the back of the church, near the cemetery's entrance."

Tyler's thoughts focused on the coming events. If they caught this man, it would be best to take him by surprise. Tyler hoped that he would be quick in revealing the whereabouts of Kristyn. If Miss Lilly's predictions were correct, the sacrifice would happen tonight. Could it be this easy after three plus weeks and nothing? Tyler must have faith that it would be and that the deathly prediction by Miss Lilly could be thwarted.

Chapter Twenty-Nine

Realization

The movement finally stopped and Kristyn remained motionless; what choice did she have? She was unable to move. Only her heart raced as her fear grew heavy. She shifted her eyes trying to make out what was what. Then suddenly the canvas sack was removed from her head. She now saw her subjugator. He was a black man. He leaned over her and grinned, revealing stark white even teeth. His skin was so dark that he disappeared in the gloom leaving only his deep brown eyes surrounded by the whites, and white teeth, appearing to hover in mid-air; no face, just eyes and teeth!

These eyes drew nearer as this man lifted and moved her. The man spoke but she did not understand him, for it was a foreign tongue to her. Then another man appeared and aided the other in her transference from the stretcher. So, there were two men, perhaps more, she had no way of knowing.

Then the room grew slowly brighter and Kristyn smelt the unmistakable scent of matches burning and sensed that candles were lit. After a bit, these men once again attended her. They removed all her clothing; she assumed she still wore the clothes she had on the day of her abduction, but she could not be sure.

She was unsure of even how long she had been in captivity. Her innards felt empty but yet she felt no hunger. She didn't feel hot or cold. She felt no need for the usual functions of the human body. It was as if she was in suspended animation. Was such a condition possible? Her sense of time was surreal.

The man lifted her into a sitting position, her head bobbed forward; she could not hold it erect. He continued with his administrations until she was completely nude. She felt her embarrassment rise as strange eyes peered at her nakedness, but there was no intimate touching of her body, only the impersonal disrobing as though this was a medical facility and they were medical personnel.

She now lay nude without the ability to hide her shame. They then re-dressed her in a white garment as unceremoniously as she had been disrobed. What the garment was exactly she could not tell, but guessed it was a gown. Silently the two men continued with their preparations, again she could not tell what they did exactly, but as the candles burned and the room became brighter, Kristyn was able to see more of her captors.

Both men seemed young, no more than thirty and the older one seemed to be in charge as it was he that kept giving whispered orders as if he did not want her or perhaps others to hear.

He was less than six feet tall, almost short in fact, Kristyn thought, maybe five seven or eight. He was shorter than his cohort. Both men were shirtless but had on either blue jeans or khaki cargo shorts. The flickering flames from the candles cast a yellowish sheen to their muscular bodies.

One man's hair was short and he had a mustache and a small goatee but the one in charge looked diabolical, for he wore his black hair twisted into long thick dreadlocks that he pulled back from his face in a bulky ponytail that touched his shoulders. Otherwise, both men sported the features of the Negro race, wide nose and full lips and almond shaped eyes.

As Kristyn took in as much of her surroundings as she could, she had a strange deja vu feeling about the place. She had been here before. Recognition flashed through her senses, she was in her own attic!

****

Chapter Thirty

Aid from an Angel

Tyler and his father waited for the police to arrive. While waiting, he called Franklin.

"Hi, where are you?" Tyler asked, when Franklin answered his cell.

"I'm home."

"I'm going to catch you up and then I want you to let Miss Lilly and Ruby know."

Tyler related the surprise findings in Josias' closet and that they were now awaiting the authorities.

"I'm coming down thar," Franklin exclaimed.

"That'll be fine, but call the ladies first, and then a couple of the guys, the single ones, see if they will be on standby tonight. Maybe with it being Tuesday, they'll have no plans. Just give them a heads up for me."

"Will do, Boss."

A half hour later, three patrol cars drove down the path to the back of the church where Pastor Doyle and Tyler waited. He wondered if perhaps Josias had returned to the cottage for lunch, and spoiled the chance of a surprise capture.

They met the sergeant and directed him to the cottage.

"Call the caretaker," the sergeant told Tyler, "to see if the suspect has arrived yet. If not, we will wait inside, but if he has, we'll rush the cottage and arrest him then."

Tyler made the call. "He's not there," Tyler informed the sergeant.

"That's good. We have our chance," the sergeant looked pleased.

Old Bill was seen coming down the path. He was allowed to exit completely before the sergeant addressed him with questions.

Sergeant Murphy let Tyler and his father know. "According to the caretaker, it's unusual for this man not to return for lunch, so he expects him any minute now. I'm sending my men inside to wait for him. Everything needs to seem normal."

Then the sergeant spoke to another officer, "Let's get all these marked cars out of here and bring in a few unmarked ones. And hurry. We don't have an exact time-frame." He hurried off as he gave instructions. An organized rush commenced as the ambush was implemented. So now, they waited.

The hour passed, yet their suspect did not return. Tyler grew anxious as the minutes ticked by without a sign of Josias. With a worried expression, he looked at his father, "Something is wrong! Either he knows about the stake-out or..."

"Or he is making arrangements even now for..." Pastor Doyle halted, not wanting to voice aloud what the both of them were thinking. "He is not returning at all!"

"Yeah, that's obvious! I'm going to talk with Ruby and Miss Lilly. They came with Franklin after he called them and are waiting in the Fellowship Hall. You stay here and keep me posted," said Tyler, getting out of his father's car and hoofing it quickly back to the church.

The three of them, Miss Lilly, Ruby and Franklin waited in the Deacon's Meeting chamber. Upon seeing

Tyler, Franklin stood; expecting news, but the news was not what he wanted.

Answering Franklin's unasked question, Tyler said, "Josias hasn't made an appearance. Something is not right. Miss Lilly have you any thoughts on what is going on?"

Miss Lilly raised her eyes and looked vacantly at the ceiling, then she directed her steely gaze on Tyler. "It is the night of the Harvest moon," she said with the slightest quiver in her voice. "They are making their preparations even now. They will make the sacrifice at the hour of midnight. They have begun early so I suspect a long ceremony will be performed before the sacrifice."

Tyler allowed this new information to register before replying, "It's nearly three, we've gotta hurry. Is there anything else you can tell me? Where will they be holding her?"

Again, Miss Lilly focused on the ceiling and closed her eyes. Ruby took one of the old lady's frail hands in her own and together, the both of them concentrated on the ceiling. Minutes passed; Tyler became anxious, he did not have patience right now, he needed action, he needed to get Kristyn.

Then the women lowered their gaze and Ruby spoke, "We cannot focus our minds, we are blocked. They know of our search and have summoned a fallen angel, a lesser demon to block us. I think we can break through this veil but I must have time and we will need some items." Ruby retrieved her satchel from the floor, where she removed the Book of Solomon and, without further explanation, began thumbing through the pages.

After several searches through the book, Ruby paused on a page, and silently read. She looked at them and said, "We must summon an angel to aid us. I will need a fire or anything that produces heat, a stove or a burner..."

"We can use the church's kitchen," said Tyler.

Without another word, they left the deacon's room and crossed the hall to the large cafeteria-style kitchen. Ruby chose a small burner on the electric six-burner stove. She looked around and found a small saucepot. She placed it on the burner but did not turn it on.

"I need cinnamon," she said.

Tyler quickly found it on the spice rack. "What else?"

"Lavender and wormwood."

"There's lavender growing in the flower bed, will it do?" asked Tyler.

"Yes."

"But wormwood? What is that? Wood with termites?" asked Tyler, for he had only heard of this term from the Book of Revelations, where it was foretold that a star named '*Wormwood*' would fall upon the Earth during the Great Tribulation.

Ruby smiled, and shook her head, "No, it is a bitter herb used for stomach problems and some other complaints, but it is sometimes grown for just its beauty. It grows wild sometimes. I know what the plant looks like. I will go with you to get the lavender and see if there is any growing about."

Leaving Miss Lilly and Franklin, Tyler and Ruby went to the church's flower garden. "Okay, here's the lavender," said Tyler as he stooped to break off several of the stems with the purple flowers that traversed the stem.

Ruby wandered about and stopped, "Yes, here is some." She was looking at a tall silvery-green plant with small drooping yellow flowers. Quickly she harvested the plant and the two of them hurried back to the kitchen.

Ruby chopped the herbs into a manageable size and placed them into the pot with a small amount of olive oil to act as a binder. The ingredients soon produced a pungent smoke that rose from the pot. It was both pleasant and putrid and Tyler felt his eyes water when he passe through it.

Ruby removed the saucepot from the heat and poured its contents into a stoneware bowl. They returned to the Deacon's Meeting Chamber. Sitting the bowl on to the table surface, she removed from her satchel a crystal bell with a silver handle, about the size of a water glass. She then said, "Hold hands and form a circle around the potion."

There were only the four of them, but it would have to do.

"Close your eyes," she instructed.

When satisfied that these instructions were followed, Ruby recited a prayer but she spoke in English rather than Latin.

"Blood of my blood, you spirits of love. Come from below and from above; Entities loving who wish me well. Come to this circle when I sound the bell!"

Then a clear crisp ringing as the bell was shaken, then a chilling silence as they awaited the arrival of their invited guest.

Nothing happened. "The spirits are meeting with resistance from the spirit realm," said Miss Lilly. "Ruby, try again."

"Let's all repeat the prayer and continue until we have a visit."

Together they all did as asked.

"Blood of my blood, you spirits of love. Come from below and from above; Entities loving who wish me well. Come to this circle when I sound the bell!"

Three times they repeated this charm and three times the crystal bell rang, without an appearance of an angel. Tyler was getting frustrated and was about to break the circle when a rush of air arising from the bowl blasted them to the point of throwing them off balance. Miss Lilly was forced to sit down. The room grew dark, as a black mist rose from the potion. It smelled of the herbs in the potion and swirled all around them until they could see nothing, not even each other.

"Hold fast to each other's hands," cautioned Ruby.

They did and Tyler felt pressure coming from the mist. It was as though he was wrapped in a thick shroud and it was suffocating. He knew this was not the angel they sought but a sinister entity, trying to block their request for help from the benevolent spirits. Going against the advice of Ruby, Tyler broke the circle, wrenching his hands free of those on either side of him.

"Ruby, this is evil, break the circle, and do not contain it!" How Tyler knew to do this, he did not know. Looking into the blackness, he shouted, "In the name of the Son of Jehovah, Jesus Christ, leave here or suffer the consequences!" Tyler knew that the angelic host must obey a command given in the name of Jesus, be it demonic or angelic!

An unearthly screech, piercing and deafening, filled the deacon's chamber, and the occupants were forced to cover their ears in protection for their eardrums. But, this entity did not exit by way of the door, windows, or even the one mirror in the room, no, it retreated back into the bowl! Since this place was a place of worship, the demon could not tolerate the benevolent atmosphere, for it brought it great pain. So it went back to the depths of Hell from where it arose!

The black mist dissolved, the room once again was bright. "They are using strong charms to fight against us," said Miss Lilly, with a tremble to her voice. "They too are using the spirits to aid them. This Azazel demon uses his powers to intercede for his followers, for he needs this sacrifice badly. Try the incantation again, Ruby."

Ruby sighed deeply and again they joined hands. "Recite with me," she instructed.

"Blood of my blood, you spirits of love. Come from below and from above; Entities loving who wish me well. Come to this circle when I sound the bell!"

The bell sounded, then was silent. The air in the room was still, each one held their breath. The hour was approaching five. Had it really been over an hour since the first incantation? The seconds ticked by. Just when Ruby was about to repeat the request, a white smoke billowed from the bowl. It was as thick as the black smoke before it. It smelled of lavender and cinnamon. It felt like silk next to their skin.

They watched as an angel appeared. However, this angel was not the beautiful young girl usually depicted in Renaissance paintings of old, no, this was a masculine angel. His skin was the color of bronze. His hair hung down his back in a single golden braid. He unfurled six silvery-white wings from his back, two revealing his face, and two more showing his legs. A white, knee-length tunic with a leather belt from which hung a sword, and knee-high strapped sandals completed his formidable attire. He was clean-shaven with radiating azure eyes. An emerald green halo crowned his head. In his right hand was a gold rod with living entwining serpents at its end.

His wings flailed slowly as he hovered just above the table top and then he spoke. "Your purpose in summoning Raphael?"

Franklin felt fear upon seeing this messenger of God, fell upon his knees, and laid his forehead on the wooden floor. He was visibly shaken as his body was racked with trembles. Tyler watched but he himself was also in awe and could only stare.

"Upon your feet, man. Only the Eternal is worthy of worship."

Franklin rose.

Now, the room was bathed in a rose-colored mist and the scent of roses permeated the air, although roses had not been used in the incantation. As roses represented love, the occupants felt this love invade their souls and thus felt the armor of the angel.

Again Raphael asked, "Why am I summoned?"

Miss Lilly spoke, "There is a demon, Azazel…"

Upon hearing the demon's name, Raphael interrupted, "My foe. What evil is he engaged in?"

"He holds power over a certain band of humans and has done so for centuries now. But until now, his name was unknown. He demands human sacrifice and, tonight, one is scheduled to be performed. We need aid in locating this band and saving Kristyn, the one to be sacrificed."

"I will search out this fallen one. He has moved his place since last I engaged him. That was Asia-Minor, many eons ago. Give me time. I will search him out in his new domain and return with the information for you."

At that statement, Raphael dissolved back into the bowl.

"We must wait here for his return," said Ruby.

"How long…?" asked Tyler.

Ruby only shook her head. And so, time that was short already became like a snail as darkness fell and the harvest moon rode low on the horizon. Tyler stepped out into the night and surveyed the heavens as the stars began popping out into the velvet sky. The moon was a shocking yellow and unbelievably huge. A few wispy clouds drifted across its face. The sounds of the night penetrated his thoughts; crickets sang their evening song and frogs croaked in reply. The night birds called, the whippoorwill's distinguishing cry went unanswered and the lonely hoot of the owl concluded the serenade. The sweet sounds of the night and the beauty of twilight, how belying it was, for it cared not that evil was afoot.

Sweat broke out on Tyler's forehead, for this September eve was warm; it hid the approach of fall, which had not yet taken root. The Indian summer hung on, but the harvest moon spelled its demise.

How long must they wait? Would this Seraph even return? A commotion from within the deacon's chamber jerked his mind back to the present and Tyler quickly re-entered, just in time to see Raphael appearing.

The archangel did not wait for a question, he stated, "The one you seek resides at her original place." He then vanished.

"'Her original place'?" repeated Tyler. "What is that supposed to mean? This angel gives us riddles instead of answers!"

"We must think through his words," said Ruby. "Where did Kristyn come from?"

Tyler began an uneasy pacing and ran his hand through his hair, trying to recall what he knew of Kristyn's past. "She moved here in July. Before that, she lived in Rock Haven. But before that she lived at her grandparent's house. Her original home.... place. She's at the house!"

Everyone was stunned at the thought of this prospect. The Victorian home had been abandoned several weeks ago, no one had been back, why would they return, no one was there. It would be conceivable that the perpetrators might know this and were using the home place again, as they had in the past. No one would know.

"Franklin, call Sergeant Murphy while I get my father."

Chapter Thirty-One

Ritual Begins

Kristyn knew that events were about to change and in her deepest intuitive she suspected that she was in grave danger. The facts, as she understood them from the history of the manor and of the graves found in her barn, clearly indicated that she was about to become a ritual sacrifice! She lay upon a crudely constructed table, the only item that had not been removed from the attic. Her face was no longer covered; the attic was brightly lit with hundreds of candles, which meant that she saw most of what was taking place around her. She heard movement and watched as the attic filled with young black men! They wore no shirts; their faces were painted with different symbols, some with white, some with yellow and some with red paint.

The man that had been with her all day, the one with the long dreadlocks, now donned a headdress constructed of feathers and the stark white bony skull of a ram, which sat atop of his head. The horns of the ram were huge and added ferociousness to his appearance. The group did not speak, with the only sound being the low rumble of walking and moving about the attic.

The silence was broken by the thump, thump of a drum as the group gathered in a semi-circle around her, while their leader stood on the opposite side of the table. Their bodies glistened with scented oil, a strong but pleasant scent that Kristyn did not recognize.

The one who seemed to be in charge, who wore the headdress, spoke but it was an unknown language to her. He motioned strongly with his hands, raising them high and then sweeping them across her prostrate body. He never touched her but continued with the sweeping from her head to her feet several times. He then halted, he focused his attention on her face and she cringed from his searing gaze.

"I know you can hear," he said to her. "You are being honored. Tonight, at mid-night we will offer your life to our lord. You are a zombie. A serum was transfused into you weeks ago. This is why you have no concept of time, why you do not experience hunger or pain or pleasure. I have awakened you only partially. This is necessary for our ceremony. Your mind must be alert and responsive to do honor to our lord. It will not be long now."

He then stepped into the center of the attic where, with white chalk, he drew a circle onto the wooden planks. Within the circle he drew a pentagram, which is the five-pointed star with connecting lines. At each one of the five points, he wrote a name in foreign script. It was the name of the demon, which he wanted to summon. He stood in the center of the circle and of the star, and removed from a small pouch hanging from his waist, chicken bones. He tossed these into the air where they fell haphazardly to the floor and then sizzled as though in a frypan.

He then instigated a chant, this time in English, he spoke the verse and the half-dozen or so men with him repeated it.

"Azazel, hear my cry. I summon you from the other side. Come to me and cross the great divide."

This chant had a monotone feel to it, hypnotizing in its affect upon Kristyn. She felt her body lift up and she rose slowly into the air, hovering there.

'How?' she asked herself. 'This is not possible,' but yet it was.

Each man marched around her as they slid their hands across her body; most were impersonal contact, which she saw rather than felt. All the while, they chanted. Abruptly they ceased. She lowered again to the tabletop and once more rested upon it.

"I heard you call," boomed a raspy voice. "I claim my accolade. It is long overdue and I am weak from lack of substance. Satisfy me!"

The leader spoke, "For which we are truly sorry. It has been most difficult to find a suitable candidate, one worthy of your most glorious banquet."

Kristyn tried to see from where the voice came, but it seemed to come from everywhere and she could not see this being.

****

Tyler was anxious; it was late in the evening when they figured out where Kristyn might be. But they just couldn't rush to the house, they needed help from the police. It seemed forever before his father answered his cell.

"Hello, Tyler," Pastor Doyle spoke first, when the caller ID showed Tyler on the cell-phone. "I'm sorry son, but Josias has not returned. We're still watching for him,"

"It doesn't matter, Dad," Tyler almost shouted.

"What do you mean?' began Pastor Doyle. But Tyler's heightened tone stopped him.

"She's at *her* house," Tyler almost shouted. He was breathless, for he was running for his truck with Franklin at his side, trying to keep pace with the younger man. They climbed into Tyler's truck simultaneously.

"I need for you to bring Ruby and Miss Lilly to the house and wait along side of the main road. Do not approach the house without instructions from me or the police," said Tyler as he steered the truck out onto the freeway, squealing tires as he went.

He disconnected from his father without a good bye, or waiting to explain further. He looked at Franklin and Franklin answered without being asked, "Yeah sir, I got'im. He wanted to talk but I let'im know, we got no time for chat, just get his men to da house. He's on it."

As Franklin finished speaking, Tyler heard sirens behind him as several unmarked sheriffs' cars joined him on the highway. There was no need for stealth now but he hoped they would tone it down once they were close to Kristyn's house, for a warning to the cult might inspire them to sacrifice Kristyn before the hour of mid-night. It mattered not to them, only that it be completed. There was no way of knowing.

One patrol car sped past Tyler and took the lead with sirens and lights blaring. Tyler knew this was the safest for now, as his truck had none of this emergency apparatus. They sailed along through the twilight; the moon illuminating the terrain almost as if it was day. As they sped along, horrible thoughts marched through Tyler's mind. Horrific scenes that made him cringe and wish he could materialize where Kristyn was.

Then the car ahead turned off its siren and lights and Tyler recognized that they were on the road that led to the path to Kristyn's house. The car pulled off the road as did Tyler and the two cars behind him. The sheriff emerged from the first car and walked back to meet Tyler who was getting out of his truck. Franklin joined them, as did the other deputies.

The sheriff surveyed the area up where the house stood. It could not be seen from this distance.

"Everything looks quiet up the path. We are just too far away to tell much but I can't risk getting closer with the vehicles," said Sheriff Brown.

"I know," Tyler replied.

"Tell me," said Sheriff Brown, "how do you know she is being held there? We haven't gotten any reliable information on that."

Tyler hesitated, he knew his answer would not be well received and before he could answer, Franklin supplied the sheriff with a reasonable explanation that had nothing to do with the paranormal. "We just figures it out, is all. What's with everything that happ'ned, it happ'ned at da house or da barn or da attic. Where's else would they have they cer'mony?"

"Makes sense," agreed the sheriff.

Franklin winked at Tyler, who mouthed the word, *'thanks.'*

"Tonight is the night of the ritual and the offering, so it just had to be held at the house. There is no way of knowing, but evidently, this cult has been using the farmhouse ever since Kristyn's grandparents vacated it. And, I suspect, that the basement beneath the barn has been used for their meetings for a very long time, probably without the grandparents' knowledge."

"We need to get closer," said the sheriff. "I'll get the ball a'rolling. I'll instruct my men to head slowly down the path. Try not to give a warning to the cult."

The sheriff then gave instructions and the deputies, with drawn guns, proceeded down the path keeping close to the shoulder, where the shadows created by the trees and bushes hid them. They didn't use a source of light, for the moon gave enough.

Tyler wanted to join them but needed to see his father before he did. Finally, the pastor's car pulled up and parked behind the row of deputies' cars. Both Tyler and Franklin went to meet him.

Pastor Doyle and Ruby were in the front with Miss Lilly alone in the back. Pastor Doyle climbed out as Tyler and Franklin walked toward him.

"You didn't say much, Son, what's going on? Why are we at Kristyn's house? There's no one there."

"We think Kristyn is held there," answered Tyler. "We received reliable information, didn't Ruby tell you?"

With that question, they both looked at Ruby, who shook her head, "I didn't."

"No, actually she didn't say anything."

"Well, at the church," began Tyler, then went into a short explanation of what had occurred and the information received.

Pastor Doyle's eyes grew wide in surprise. Even though he was a man of the clergy; he had never had a spiritual visitation. "Wish I'd been there," was all he said and then, "So, what's now?"

"Ruby?" Father and son looked towards the Spiritualist.

She got out of the car and was met in the front of it, "Grandma and I must get as close as possible. We need a solitary place to called Raphael again."

"Will you need the same items?" asked Tyler.

"Yes, but not to worry, I brought them with me from church. They're in the trunk. A fire is all that I need now. But a location?"

"Can it be outside? With an open fire, like a campfire?"

"That would work. I just need to know where exactly she is."

"I think she might be in the basement beneath the barn. That's where they captured her and where their other ceremonies were held. I'll let you know as soon as I know."

****

While Tyler and the law enforcement officers searched for Kristyn in the wrong places, the activity in the attic heated up. Kristyn tried to see the entity and finally she did. It was the Shadowman! He loomed large and occupied most of the west wall. But this shadow did not stay plastered flat against the wall, it erupted from the planks like a plant pushing up from the dirt to become a free standing shadow, in the shape of a man. But as Kristyn watched, this shadow changed, it sprouted bat-like wings which had a translucent quality and the head grew rams' horns. Then the demon materialized in a shower of sparks.

Kristyn felt fear as she never had before in her life, not even at the death of her husband or the loss of her son, Nathan.

Nathan! She hadn't thought of him in several hours now. Her own dire predicament had exclusively occupied her mind. She felt somehow that Tyler had been successful in rescuing her son. By believing he was safe, she could focus on escaping her captors. Although she also knew that she was totally helpless and at their mercy and that there would be no mercy. Although paralyzed, her mind was sharp and she concentrated on the attic and the activities beginning.

With the materialization of the demon, the men fell to the attic floor with their foreheads pressed against its wooden surface, in both fear and worship.

"Upon your feet!" ordered Azazel.

The band stood but kept their faces diverted from the blinding fire and smoke that surrounded the demon. There was a strong scent of sulphur and smoke that caused Kristyn's eyes to water and her nose to burn. The demon stood as tall as the ceiling and gave the impression that he was as big as he needed to be.

He could be even bigger or smaller as the situation called for.

Then Josias separated from the group, he approached a few feet toward the demon and spoke, "Oh Master," and he bowed, then straightened, "you honor us with your presence. We beg forgiveness in not attending to your needs before now. The residents of this small place have made it difficult over the last few years to carry out your instructions. But see, here, we have your sacrifice. A perfect specimen she is."

Then as though he needed to prove the worth of the sacrifice, Josias ripped open the grown which Kristyn wore, her nakedness once again revealed before them. But she did not feel shame but rage, and even more fear. She could do nothing but accept her fate.

"See, nice firm flesh, young and ready for your pleasure. Shall I continue with the offering?" He then pulled from his belt a dagger, one exactly like the one that Ruby had used to sacrifice the rooster, he raised it over his head with his eye focused on Kristyn's naked breast, where her heart beat wildly.

Was this how she was going to meet her demise? What about the ritual that went with a sacrifice? It would be over quickly. Then she resigned herself to this end, and thought, "it is good, I do not want to linger and wait. Make it quick."

"Halt, not yet," screamed the demon. "She is much too beautiful to die. I will copulate with her instead and then take her back with me to the Underworld. She will be mother to a league of Nephilim."

Azazel then shrank in size and his bat like wings folded back and vanished. There stood a handsome human male, with none of the characteristics of the demon. Angels or demons have always had the ability to change their guise, as suited their needs. Azazel needed right now not to appear threatening to the young woman who lay all but nude before him, powerless to resist his advances but as a man, ready to fulfill his unholy lust for the flesh of a human female.

"Release her from her stupor," he ordered.

Josias stepped forward, "Your Lordship, then she will be able to fight and might escape."

Azazel's face became distorted as he turned on this human who dared question his orders. Josias knew he had crossed a boundary and quickly hastened to carry out the command. His thoughts were confused. In all the years that he had conducted the ritual sacrifice, Azazel had never rejected it and was always eager to consume the flesh of the newly offered victim. But this had been the first truly beautiful female he had ever been offered, the rest had been men of varying ages. This woman had awakened a different kind of lust in the demon. A lust which had befallen the angels from the beginning of time. What was the demon's plan? To have intercourse with her, here and now? Josias was unsure if he could be part of, or watch, such an unholy union. But he also knew he could not alter things and so must do as ordered. He lifted Kristyn's left arm and jabbed the hypodermic into her tender flesh, injecting the antidote.

Chapter Thirty-Two

Azazel Attacks

"Blood of my blood, you spirits of love,
Come from below and from above;
Entities loving who wish me well,
Come to this circle when I sound the bell."

Ruby summoned Raphael for the second time that day. A fire had been built and it was just she and Miss Lilly. Tyler had left with the others to search for Kristyn. They had just now reached the end of the path and the house was in view. The house looked dark and empty and they proceeded towards the back to the barn.

Raphael appeared, "You have need of me?"

"It's the demon, Azazel, your perpetual enemy. Seek him out and release the girl, Kristyn!"

Raphael's eyes flashed at the mention of Azazel's name. He did not answer but rose into the night, using two of his six wings for flight.

****

Kristyn felt immediately the affect of the antidote; a stinging burning pain in her arms and legs as sensation returned. She also experienced the intake of air into her lungs that she had not felt before, and after all of that, she knew a deep gnawing hunger! She tried to sit up and found just how weak she was. Even so, Josias pushed her back down on to the table which now felt hard beneath her. She weakly pulled her open gown closed and balled herself up into the fetus position to hide her shame and to protect herself.

Trying hard to control her emotions, she began to whimper, like a kitten. Then tremors took over her entire being and she shook like a leaf in a strong wind. These reactions came about because of the drugged state she had been in for four weeks.

The entourage stared at her in surprise and they became fearful. They had never revived a victim before, and these violent reactions actually frightened them and they backed away from Kristyn.

But not Azazel. He approached the quivering mass of humanity. Kristyn did not see him; for her eyes were tightly closed as she tried to shut out the room and its occupants. Azazel took hold of one arm and forced her to open up her position to him. She had no choice, she was too weak. The demon positioned her beneath him as he prepared to mount her. Kristyn struggled but to no avail, she could not resist him. She opened her eyes and stared the demon full in the face. He was not the hideous creature she expected and she was shocked to see Tyler's face form from the blur before her. What was going on? Was this Tyler? And was he about to make love to her? No, no, Tyler would not take her in such a fashion; again she struggled and the face changed to that of the demon, with red skin, burning yellow eyes and ram horns protruding from his forehead and smoke smoldering from his nostrils.

Above them, a light materialized into three orbs, and then the three merged into one large orb. It hovered near the ceiling as if sizing up the situation below. Only a moment did it take before the Orb descended over Kristyn and quickly entered into the helpless woman by way of her breath.

Immediately, immense power erupted from Kristyn and she felt the strength of many people imbued within her. She sat up, grabbed the demon by his horns and mightily hurled him across the room, slamming him into the wall, with a loud thud and a screeching sound.

Kristyn heard a voice but it came from her own mouth, "We have joined with you. We are the Dudu-Mtu. We are freed but before we cross into the light we must send Azazel back to the depths from which he came!"

****

Tyler and Franklin and two deputies wandered about the demolished barn looking for signs, when they did not find Kristyn in the basement.

"It's makes no sense, Boss," said Franklin. I's cain't 'magine where's else she'd be."

"Neither can I," replied Tyler, dragging his hand through his unruly hair and, as he did, a flash of light drew his attention. He looked around and then up, towards the house and up at the attic. There the attic's windows were lit up and he exclaimed, "She's in the attic!" at the same time pointing in that direction.

"I'll call the others," said a deputy. "In the house, in the attic," he shouted into the walkie-talkie; he then rushed after the others but not catching up with them, as they entered the back door.

Tyler thought, "Would they make it in time?" It was nearly the midnight hour. He and Franklin and the two deputies bounded up the hallway stairs, rushed down the hall, to the attic door. Locked! Tyler still carried the key and as quickly as possible, unlocked the hallway door to the attic's stairs.

Downstairs, the sheriff and more deputies quietly entered through the front door, just in time to hear the thump from upstairs. They headed after Tyler.

****

Kristyn, still aware of this immense strength, sat up, and got off of the table. The men backed away from her, and stood as close to the opposite wall from her and the demon, as they could. Her torn gown barely covered her; her tangled blond hair attested that it had not received attention in a while. Her bare limbs were smooth and white and glistened like dew on the rose. But her eyes, yes, her eyes, they flashed green as she surveyed the members of the cult. Her searing gaze melted their resolve and they cringed together like baby sparrows in the nest.

Kristyn did not know what she was going to do, but just then the attic's door flew open and Tyler rushed in, followed by Franklin and two deputies.

****

Seeing Kristyn standing, Tyler halted briefly. He was taken aback by her appearance, especially her near nakedness. Her blond mop of hair was in such disarray that it covered most of her face as she pushed it aside, but the look in her eye was intimidating. She then saw him and did not hesitate, but ran to him, and impulse made him catch her and hold her tight. Was she really safe? She felt so small and thin in his arms. When he touched her bare skin, he immediately removed his button front shirt and helped her into it. He buttoned it up where it offered modest coverage, ending at mid-thigh.

Just then, Kristyn's face became pale, her eyes closed and her head bobbed backwards as she collapsed. Tyler caught her and confusion racked his mind. Then there was an audible sigh, when her breath left her as a fine white mist escaped, forming the Orb. But as the Orb retreated from them, Tyler guessed what had happened and looking at the Orb, said, "Thank you."

The Orb flashed brightly in answer and moved toward the demon, which remained against the wall. Still supporting Kristyn's now limp body, Tyler surveyed the attic. His quick assessment brought fury. Franklin stood close and sensed this change in Tyler. He gently took Kristyn from him, and, as Tyler relinquished her to Franklin's protection; he eyed the one man in the room that he recognized from the photograph, Josias! The shirtless black man was attempting to leave the attic, but his compatriots also fought for the exit. Moving swiftly, Tyler hurled himself towards the mass and singled out their leader. He seized Josias by both upper arms and spun him around to face him. Josias, realizing he was now the focus of this madman's retaliation began swinging his fists at Tyler, but his aim was off and only swept air. Dodging the blows, Tyler did not miss and landed one on Josias' torso. The man doubled over with an audible grunt as he lost his breath and pain shot though his body. He attempted a hard kick and caught Tyler's leg throwing him off balance. As Tyler went down, so did Josias. Together they hit the attic floor with a thud. Tyler's rage burned hot and he took advantage of Josias lying on his back and began pummeling the man's face and upper torso regions with his bare fists. He struck Josias until his knuckles bled. His blows were fast and solid and Tyler saw blood gush from Josias' nose; he felt his knuckles strike teeth as they were knocked out of the man's mouth and went flying to the floor, together with sweat and blood.

Tyler had the momentum and had no intention of stopping, but someone grabbed him around the waist, "Mr. Doyle, that's enough. You're going to kill him." It was the sheriff, and Tyler quickly came back to his senses and allowed himself to be separated from Josias. Breathing hard Tyler stepped back as Josias lay motionless at his feet. Tyler looked at Sheriff Brown, "I'm done," he said as he wiped the back of his hand across his bloodied mouth.

The sheriff and four more deputies aimed their guns at the men now huddled together against the far wall. The fight in them had now gone, yes, brave they were against a defenseless woman but not so much against armed men. The nine men were quickly and quietly taken into custody.

For whatever reason, the deputies or the sheriff did not or could not see the demon or the Orb, but acted as if the young men were the only villains there. Moments after they escorted their prisoners out, a loud clap of thunder shook the house as Raphael made his appearance. He broke into the attic by flying through a window. The window being too small, he also took with it a section of the wall, leaving a huge gap. Splinters of wood and shards of glass showered the attic.

Azazel, on seeing this messenger from God, felt his rage increase and moved towards the angel as he grew in size. Raphael stood firm on the floor. His guise was startling; his six silvery wings beat steadily in an irritated fashion. His bronze skin glistened like polished metal. His stance was with legs straight and spread. Azazel matched the angel's facade and drew himself up straight and tall. His black bat-like wings continuously unfurled matching the irritation of Raphael.

****

Pastor Doyle met the sheriff with their prisoners just as they exited the house and as he was about to enter. Briefly they spoke.

"Where is Tyler," asked Pastor Doyle.

"They're all in the attic," replied the sheriff. "We've got everyone involved."

"Was Kristyn...?"

"She's fine but weak. Your son and his man are up there with her. He should be coming down anytime."

The sheriff then left the Pastor standing at the steps watching after them. Pastor Doyle thought for a moment on what might have occurred up in the attic. The sheriff seemed confident that this was over, for he now led his deputies with their prisoners away from Kristyn's house. This took just a matter of minutes and Pastor Doyle wondered why was it taking Tyler so long to come down. He had best go to see if Tyler needed him. But before he could enter, another clap of thunder with a flash of lightning, lit up the cloudless sky. The moon still beamed full and bright down upon the earth. There were no more signs of an approaching storm. Heat lightning, it must be, thought Pastor Doyle.

As Pastor Doyle looked up into the night sky, a mass appeared which covered the moon, accompanied by a loud crashing sound and lightning bolts darting away from the mass. What on earth was that? Whatever it was, was shuffling and shifting, changing shape and producing odd sounds that wafted down to him. With the brightness of the harvest moon behind the mass, it gave the appearance of an irregular eclipse. Silvery rays spread out on all sides of the ever-changing mass. But any recognizable object failed to appear.

Pastor Doyle's heart raced as terror struck within it. Whatever this was, it was evil. Pastor Doyle dropped to his knees and began a prayer.

"Oh, our Eternal Father, I beseech You in the name of Your Son, Jesus Christ, to intervene on our behalf against the forces of evil. Amen!"

"Not to worry, Dad," Tyler's voice from behind him, startled the pastor. He turned to see Franklin and Tyler emerge from the door with a weak Kristyn, barely standing, between them. The pastor immediately saw that Kristyn was in a bad way. She wore Tyler's plaid shirt and it appeared that was all she had on. Her face was pale and showed signs of harsh treatment. Her hair was a tangled mass, and she moaned weakly as Tyler helped her to one of the porch chairs. What had the poor girl been through? Whatever it was, it had taken a heavy toll on her.

"God already has," Tyler continued. "That's Raphael fighting the Demon, Azazel. I did not know that they were arch-enemies."

They looked skyward, and flashes of light blazed out of the battle, as blows were struck and returned. With every flash, various images were seen and Raphael's silhouette was pronounced, with his six wings holding him steady in mid-air. The demon's bat wings beat furiously as the two danced a deadly tango. Around and around, they danced as lightning bolts flew and thunder rolled.

The small human audience included Ruby and Miss Lilly who had come nearer to the house, for they had seen, at a distance, Raphael enter the attic. When he drew Azazel out, Tyler wanted to get Kristyn to the hospital for he knew she was very sick, but his attempt to leave was halted by Kristyn's refusal.

"No, I must see," she protested, shaking her head and looking intently to the heavens.

So, Tyler stood by her chair and they watched the aerial battle. As it continued, the sky became even blacker and purple clouds swirled about; now even the moon was totally blocked out.

"They are evenly matched," shouted Tyler. "It cannot end. Does not good overcome evil?"

"Sometime son, it does not," noted Pastor Doyle. "The battle between the good and the wicked will continue until the end of time. The best we can hope for is a draw, one keeping the other at bay and always ready to battle."

The purple rolling clouds began spinning, like a mighty wind and as they did, a vortex opened up, grew larger, and larger still, and a strong suction commenced to pull on the combatants. Heedless of developing danger, the two fought on, although it seemed that Azazel would have retreated when he saw the vortex, as if knowing the consequences should he lose. Did he know that if Raphael managed to drag him into it that he would be locked away until eternity? Indeed, he did know and Raphael knew and forced his assault more vigorously.

The wind distorted the clouds until they formed a whirlwind, swirling and twisting violently, producing the unmistakable sound of an oncoming locomotive. The vacuum was fervent and starting pulling on everything, drawing it towards the aperture at its center. The humans on the ground felt its tug and Tyler shouted, "Grab something. Hold on tight."

They seized the porch posts, wrapping their arms around them as debris and leaves in the yard began flying around and upwards toward the fissure. The roar of the wind changed into a high pitched whistle, and it was at this point that they saw the pair whisked away, spinning as they went, higher into the sky, till they were barely seen by those on the ground. Then they vanished! The opening quickly closed. The wind died down as the dust and leaves settled back on to the earth. Then all was quiet. No sounds, not a cricket nor a frog broke the silence. The moon once again shone down upon the earth, from a clear cloudless sky. All was as it should be. Had he not been a witness to this event, Tyler would have sworn it had never happened.

Then the stillness was once again broken as a blinding light descended from the broken attic window. As it lowered to their level, it was recognizable as the Orb. The Orb separated into three. Then from the heavens a bright ray of light reached down to the earth.

The three smaller orbs brightened and then, one by one, each materialized into a beautiful young girl. Each was identical to the other. Their hair was a dark blond! Their eyes a sage green! They stood firmly upon the ground, not as spirits but as mortal women. They were barefoot and had on a loose fitting toga-style frock. It was what they had worn at their death. They were not joined and each had four limbs, completely separated, as they had not been in life.

"You are the Dudu-Mtu," said Tyler.

"Yes," they replied in unison.

Then one spoke, "I am Abby."

Then the middle one spoke, "I am Bella."

The third one said, "And I am Callie."

"Thank you for liberating us." They spoke as one. "We can now cross into the light."

"We thank you from the bottom of our hearts for saving Nathan, and tonight for saving Kristyn," said Tyler.

"We are glad we were able to stop Azazel. It has been difficult staying away from him. As one of the many who were sacrificed to this demon, we resisted the light when it came for us. We wanted to stop him and knew that it would happen one day. His other victims have all crossed over now and we will join them. Then we shall sleep until the end of days."

The three sisters wrapped their arms about each other, their physical bodies dissolved and they were once again spirits. Together, they walked into the waiting beam. The beam closed around them and then in a blink, shot into the heavens, where it vanished.

Looking down at Kristyn, whom he held tightly in his arms, Tyler said, "Let's get you to the hospital."

As though the thought had just occurred to her, Kristyn's eyes asked the question that she was too weak to do, and Tyler answered, "Nathan is safe. He is at Dad's house with Mom. So, you concentrate on getting better. Now, to the hospital."

Chapter Thirty-Three

Reunion

Kristyn slowly opened her eyes; the room was in twilight and a steady hum filled the otherwise quiet room. Her head hurt and she could not remember what day it was or even where she was. After a moment, she looked around; she saw beige colored walls with a light avocado trim, a solid wood panel door was across the room from the foot of her bed and a long window with blinds drawn was on her right. Here was an I.V. station with tubing connected to her right wrist.

"I'm in a hospital," she concluded. When she attempted to sit up, the room spun and a gentle pressure on her left arm encouraged her to lie back down. She looked to her left, and there was Tyler. He had been sitting in the chair next to her bed but now stood, leaning over her.

"Welcome back to the world of the living," he said, with a slight smile. "You are going to be fine," he explained further. "Do you remember what happened?"

Kristyn replied with a slight nod, "Some, but most of it is a blur, like a bad dream. I tried to wake and couldn't. The nightmare went on and on. What happened? What is today? Where am I?"

"Where you are is Forest Road Memorial. Today is Thursday, the twenty-forth of September. And as to what happened..."

Tyler briefly explained the events of the last four weeks.

"The last things I remember were the final few days of August. And the cellar beneath the barn, nothing much after that until...." Kristyn sat up again, "the attic!"

"Yes, the attic!" said Tyler with a slight aversion in the tone of his voice. What had transpired there would haunt him forever. He trembled when he realized how close he had come to losing Kristyn.

"Nathan!" Kristyn almost shouted.

"He is fine and with my mother. We were able to rescue him the same night as your abduction. Miss Lilly thinks it was part of a master plan by the demon; he used the humans to carry out this plan and they were none the wiser of it. While we were distracted with the rescue of Nathan, the real target was you."

"Miss Lilly?" Kristyn asked, with a puzzled expression.

"She's Ruby's grandmother, she joined Ruby after your abduction. She is a wise woman. We could not have done what we did, had it not been for the both of them."

"When can I see my son?" Kristyn changed the subject.

"I would say in a few minutes. Mom and Dad are on their way here."

"What time is it?'

"A few minutes after three."

"And it's September?"

Tyler nodded.

"I've lost a month!"

"Yeah, you have."

"Why am I so hungry!" Kristyn exclaimed.

"You should be, you haven't eaten in a month. You'll be getting solid food today I guess. You were in a poor state when we found you. They had turned you into a zombie, kept you in suspended animation for four weeks. Why you didn't die....."

"Zombie?!" Kristyn's eyes opened wider. "I thought that was a myth..."

"No, very real."

Then there was a tapping at the door. "Who is it?" called Tyler.

"It's me, Boss," it was Franklin.

"Come in," invited Tyler.

The old black man pushed open the door and entered. He was dressed much the same way as when Kristyn had first met him. "Hello Franklin," said Kristyn softly. She was glad to see him.

"You're shore is a sight fer sore eyes," Franklin responded. "Miss Ruby's in the hall and wants to speak with ya, that is ifum, yer're up to it."

Tyler went to the door, opened it wider and called, "Come in, Ruby."

Ruby stepped through the door and quickly approached Kristyn's bed. "It is grand to see you, Miss. I had to see for myself that you are alive and well."

Kristyn laughed softly and said, "Alive, yes, but how well, do not know that yet."

"You're going to be as right as rain in no time," beamed Franklin.

Again Kristyn smiled and held up her arms to Franklin and he obliged by giving her a gentle hug. "I am glad to know you, Franklin," she whispered into his ear. Franklin grinned as he backed away.

Tyler sat down on the edge of her bed; Kristyn took solace in his nearness, even though she did not verbally acknowledge it, she knew that he felt it.

Kristyn looked questioningly at Ruby and said, "Can you tell me, explain what... I don't even know what it is I want to know."

"You were the target of the demon from the beginning," said Ruby. "He only used Nathan as a distraction. The cult was cunning, even though they did not realize it at the time. The leader followed Azazel's commands blindly. The demon communicated through visions when Josias indulged in his drug habit. While in this drugged-induced trance, Azazel instructed him."

"How?' began Kristyn.

"My grandmother summoned Raphael, the arch-angel and mortal enemy of this demon. He has taken Azazel into the Void and left him there."

"Void? I've never heard of this before."

"This truth is known only to my faith. Since angels and demons are immortal, the best that can be done is to restrain them and the Void is oblivion, a place of restraint for the fallen ones. Its location is secret but we all suspect it is at the center of the Milky Way, the gigantic black hole which is located there."

Silence fell over the room as this tidbit of information sank in. Just then the door to the corridor opened slightly, and Mrs. Doyle peeped through the crack, as if checking to be certain it was all right to enter. Tyler went to the door and opened it further, "She's awake, come on in."

But before Mrs. Doyle could enter, a small figure darted past her and ran to Kristyn. Even though she was still weak, and she was very sore, Kristyn grabbed her son in a bear hug. She began crying, as she kissed his forehead. "Oh Nate, I was so worried about you."

"I'm okay Mom. Why are you crying? Guess what?" he said, not waiting for her to say why she cried.

Kristyn smiled at how quickly he bounced from one topic to another. "What?" she asked.

"I saw my Daddy"

"You did?" Kristyn then looked at Tyler and then at Ruby.

"It seems that your late husband had a hand in the rescue of Nathan. That is the only part he remembers, though," said Ruby.

"I'll explain all of what happened tomorrow, right now, we want you to rest," said Tyler as he gently placed his right arm around her shoulders, and pulled her close.

"How do you feel, my dear?" asked Mrs. Doyle, as she walked nearer the bed.

"So much better," replied Kristyn. "A bit tired and weak still. I feel like I've been away for a long time. I remember dreams that seemed so real. But right now, I am so hungry. When are they going to bring me something?"

Tyler chuckled, "That's the second time she's said that."

Pastor Doyle said, "Tell you what, Kristyn. I'll check with a nurse and if allowed, we'll bring you a plate from the cafeteria. Any requests?"

"Whatever you have, will be fine," she smiled.

Ruby spoke, "I think I will leave you now, Kristyn," she came forward and took Kristyn's hand. "You are going to be just fine, just hang in there and give it time." She leaned forward and pressed a kiss on Kristyn forehead.

"You will visit me again, won't you?"

Without replying, Ruby nodded. Ruby looked at Franklin and asked, "Franklin, are you ready?"

So the four of them left, leaving Tyler, Nathan and Kristyn alone. The room was again quiet, with only the hum of the machinery filling the silence. Kristyn still held Nathan, a little too tightly it seemed, for he said, "Mama, I cain't breathe."

Loosening her hold on her son but not releasing him completely, Kristyn smiled and said, "Sorry Nate. I've just missed you so much."

"And we have missed you," said Tyler. "I think they will be releasing you soon, do you know what you want to do?"

There was a long pause before Kristyn replied, "I don't want to go back to the house just now. Maybe later. I know I need to make a decision..."

"Well, an attic window and a section of the roof are blown out, so the house isn't livable right now. I had my men to lay a tarpaulin on it for now, can't do much more than that until the sheriff releases the property. They're doing more investigating. And the news media are back, I imagine it will be all over the papers and TV."

He cupped her chin and turned her to face him. "You and Nathan can come to Mom's and Dad's for awhile. Until you decide."

Kristyn's heartbeat speeded up, and she nervously licked her lips. His nearness seemed to have taken her voice and she was unable to speak, or breathe. She was too aware of his masculinity, his musk and strength. A strength she so needed for she did not feel confident in her own. The best she could do was nod.

"Would you even want to continue to live there?" he asked.

Kristyn's thoughts were mixed, "It was my childhood home," she finally replied. "And I would love for Nathan to have the kind of rearing I had. I still think of it as home."

Tyler smiled and nodded, "I know. Well, don't decide yet. There is time."

"Yes," she agreed.

"You know, I have come to realize something," he said, as he searched the depths of her green eyes.

"What's that?" she whispered.

"That I am very much in love with you."

"Oh."

"I do not want you or Nathan out of my life. Whatever decision you make, I want to be included."

"I see."

"Do you think you can tolerate the son of a preacher man for the rest of your life?"

"If he's the same preacher man's son I am looking at right now, yes."

Tyler smiled. "Will you and Nathan become my wife and son?"

A single tear escaped Kristyn's eye; had she found love again? Not a love to replace her lost one but a love to add to it. For one could not replace the other. Nathan was wedged between them still as she laid her head on Tyler's shoulder. "Yes, we would be proud," she whispered.

Nathan squirmed loose and turned and looked at them both, "Oh boy, I did get my wish."

Tyler and Kristyn looked down at Nathan, then at each other, and together said, "So did we!"

The End!

About the Author

I was born July 14, 1947 as the third child of eight children, second daughter to Woodrow and Anna Parisher in the small town of Maury, North Carolina. I was named, Marian Alice.

I met Autrey Nichols in December of 1962. We married May 16, 1964. We have/had three sons: Tommy, Ronnie and Kaylon. I adopted my grand-daughter, Lauren, when she was four.

I lost my eldest son, Tommy in a motorcycle accident in August of 1985.

I worked part time during my children's youth. I began my writing career late in life, after my children were grown and just before I adopted Lauren around the year of 1999.

I lived with my family in a mid-sized city, Rocky Mount, NC. I have four grand children and one step grandchild.

Thus far, I have written five books: *The Curse, House of Riddles, Second Event Chronicles, Millennial Chronicles* and now, *Within the Attic.*

I run a web site, which I use mainly to promote my books. Please visit to stay updated.

Characters Environments, LLT

http://characters-environments.com

You may e-mail me; marian_nichols@msn.com

Thank you for your purchase and it is my hope that you received enjoyment from reading it.

God Bless,

Marian Parisher-Nichols